Witchbloods

Georgia Tell

Because magic is real.

Table of Contents

Chapter 1 - Sylvia

Sylvia Hargrove always felt uneasy around children that talked with the buzzing enthusiasm of an unexploded bomb.

Magnolia — an undetonated nuclear weapon with dirty blonde pigtails — raised her hand.

"Yes?" Sylvia asked. She felt herself tense almost unconsciously, as if preparing herself for the blast.

"What are you going to do for Halloween, Ms. Hargrove?" the girl asked, speaking very quickly. It was always how she spoke.

Sylvia eyed the clock and erased the part on the board where she had written in careful big block letters: "No Homework. Happy Halloween!"

"I'm going to be a witch. What about you, Miss Magnolia?" she asked, enjoying the irony of her answer entirely too much.

Magnolia's eyes brightened. "I'm thinking

about being a ghost," she said. Her energy was only rivaled by rabbits. "My mom says it's an easy costume." The girl launched into a monologue about something else her mom had said, which started her on another point and another. It was a siege.

Sylvia watched the girl speak, nodding at the appropriate parts. Rabbits were cute, she decided, barely listening. They bounced with enthusiasm, shaking to contain their zest for life. She liked them. And she liked her young student, despite that unsettling, boundless energy.

As the class made its way to the front of the school to meet their parents for pick-up, the sixth-graders chattered about their weekend plans: a party, candy, baking, nothing, candy, pumpkins, candy, candy, candy, family, candy... all manner of plans. Sylvia plotted her evening and waited with the yard duties until each of her students was picked up.

In her classroom, Halloween decorations still adorned the walls and her desk. Orange and black streamers were twisted and taped near the ceiling in a haphazard way. Cat cutouts were taped to the windows, and after a month in the sun, their once black color had faded to brownish-maroon. A single strand of ghost-shaped lights adorned the room's sideboard. Stuck with double-sided tape on each of the kids' desk was a graveyard cutout and the carefully cursive letters of their names. Sylvia adored Halloween. She packed up all these decorations into a box neatly labeled "October." She was most sad about putting her "Witch's Brew" mug wrapped in craft paper on the top of all of it. She headed outside.

The sky was a mix of white, fluffy clouds and cheery blue. Not very witchy in the popular sense of the word, but her skin prickled with excitement nonetheless. She felt an autumn wind in the air, and her fingers tingled with magic. This time of year was when her magic was the most replenished and powerful. The increase magic made her feel alive and present, even at the old age of 114 — middle-aged by witch standards. Luckily, her non-magical colleagues at the school thought she was 62. Being a witch had its benefits.

She placed the "October" box in the trunk and drove home.

Over the past twenty years, she had gotten her home in Burbank just as she wanted it to be. She had painted the stucco green and the trim white. Her spacious porch had a rocking chair, and green ivy wrapped around the white handrails. Sylvia's mother, a perfunctory and stern woman, always nodded her approval as she stepped over the non-creaky boards of the porch when she visited Sylvia on her birthday every year.

Instead of heading straight inside, she browsed through her garage for the next month's decorations, her "November" box. She exchanged it with her "October" box.

The feeling of being watched raised the

hairs on the back of her neck, and she turned.

Across the street, her neighbor David Rather stared at her with narrowed eyes. He sported dark brown — almost black — hair, brown eyes, and plain but not unhandsome features. She couldn't imagine what he did for a living because he was always wearing jeans and a slightly too big t-shirt — usually green. He had lived across the street for eight years, and he always surveyed her with sharp eyes, like a crotchety old man keeping the neighborhood kids off his lawn. He disapproved of her, and she couldn't figure out why. Despite this, she put on a grin and waved. No reason to be a bad neighbor.

He looked away after making eye contact for too long and continued trimming his tree, snipping the clippers with unwarranted vigor.

"David!" Sylvia called over to him and walked to the curb on her side of the street. "You excited for kids trick or treating tomorrow?"

He stopped, taking a moment before turning. His face was sour. "No."

Sylvia didn't get him. She felt like she would never "get" him, but she sighed and went inside.

In her living room, she had her bookshelves. The room was just like how she liked it. The left two shelves housed her fiction. She had *The Picture of Dorian Grey* by Oscar Wilde, the *Harry Potter* series by J.K. Rowling, and *Six Tales of Witchy Shenanigans* by Gloria Isolde, one of her favorites from childhood. The right two shelves held her many spell books, written histories, textbooks, encyclopedias, and dictionaries. Just looking at the orderliness of it all relaxed her.

Her doorbell chimed a high-pitched version of Greensleeves.

The hollering that followed was even more high-pitched. Mrs. Potalecky was a force of nature — one of many that Sylvia knew. Plump and pushy, Mrs. Potalecky was a long-time patron of hers. The woman hung one of Sylvia's whiff charms in every room of her house and gave them out as gifts to her loved ones. She was not a witch or magical in anyway. What she did possess, however, was an uncanny ability to take in every bit of information that came her way and believe it. "Yoohoo!"

Though Sylvia was sure she had locked her front door when she'd come into the house, Mrs. Potalecky was now inside. A mere locked door was nothing for this woman of indomitable will.

"I hope you have something good for me!" Mrs. Potalecky said as she swooped past Sylvia to stand in the living room, looking expectant. Her big chest heaved, making the bottom hem of her loose bohemian dress bounce up and down.

"Actually, I didn't expect you to be here today," Sylvia said, trying to keep the annoyance from her face. Once her day with her students was over, she didn't have the energy to deal with anything extra unexpected.

"I'd love to look over your stock, to see if

anything interests me."

"You know I don't keep stock, the charms go too quickly."

"But your ad says otherwise," Mrs. Potalecky said, eyes alight.

"My ad? I haven't changed that in years, and you know it." Her regular ad in the local paper was automatically billed from her credit card. She didn't even think about it.

Mrs. Potalecky glided past her into the kitchen. "I'll make you a meal if you make me a really strong whiff. My nephew is sending out his college apps and believe me, he needs all the luck he can get."

Sylvia's mouth hardened, but she knew she wouldn't say no. Curse her never-ending selflessness. "What're you going to make for me?"

Mrs. Potalecky smiled wide. "That's the spirit, honey."

"I'm older than you," Sylvia said, chafing at the use of the word "honey." It wouldn't normally upset her, but Mrs. Potalecky vexed her, yet again.

The woman examined the kitchen, perusing all the As-Seen-On-TV gadgets that Sylvia had in her organized drawers. Her fingers landed on a device sitting on the counter that Chrysa — Sylvia's best friend — had given her as a present two years earlier. "Breakfast-O-Magic?" Mrs. Potalecky laughed breathily. "Cute! You witches are all so clever."

"All? You haven't met any other than me,"

Sylvia said, regretting — not for the first time — that she knew the woman. She felt steamrolled around her.

"I'll know more when you introduce me!" Mrs. Potalecky said. "I'll make you ratatouille. My nephew has rats, and I'm quite fond of them."

Sylvia shut her mouth, figuring it was best to just get to work. There was nothing further that she could do. When she was in teacher mode, she could do anything. But Mrs. Potalecky made her feel incapable; it was completely unlike any other relationship that Sylvia had.

She made her way to the bookshelves in the other room and grabbed her most used spell book: Griselda's Guide to Domestic Magic by Griselda Grudges. The binding was worn, and every page opened effortlessly. She never needed to weigh down the edges.

Whiff charms were invariably Sylvia's specialty. Useful and subtle, she always imbued a little luck spell to help her patrons out with finding lost items and getting their technology to work. The luck required to get Mrs. Potalecky's under-achieving nephew into college would require quite a high volume of luck.

The bustling in the kitchen distracted Sylvia as she looked through her box of found objects. Found objects were the best types for charms. Their essence was empty of specific purpose, and their wandering nature made them pliable and easy to spell.

The stove ticked, and plastic crinkled in the other room. She ignored the noise and grabbed an object — a used bottle cap she'd found in the teachers' lounge at school — and set it carefully on her working table, a worn wood surface crammed between the bureau and the corner. She knew the collection of spells she used to make whiffs by heart, but she turned Griselda's Guide to the page about luck spells anyway. It was habit. The luck spell was first; the spell's subtlety depended on it. They couldn't have Mrs. Potalecky's nephew suddenly turning water into wine or landing a coveted position at the New York Times without even applying. It just wasn't right.

Sylvia preferred magic that was barely noticeable; it kept her hidden in plain sight. She wondered if some of her patrons doubted her abilities, and she liked the idea. She certainly had a back-up story involving chickens and a surprising amount of luck lined up in case there ever was any sort of witch-hunt, though she was pretty sure there wouldn't be one.

Carved subtly into her tabletop was a perfect circle. She put the bottle cap in the center. It was a misconception that all witches used pentagrams. Witches used equilateral shapes that suited their fancy. Circles had always been Sylvia's shape of choice. It seemed wholesome and good and complete. A witch's shape was basically a visual aid to help contain and concentrate her magic. Some witches didn't use shapes at all because they had other methods for focusing, but Sylvia was a traditionalist.

She concentrated her magic into her right index finger and drew a circle along the inner edge of the one on the table. She focused to keep the magic in the table's circle. Next, she put her index finger on the bottle cap itself. In her mind, she repeated the phrase Lady Luck, get small difficulties unstuck! three times. Three was a very witchy number, and it worked for Sylvia, so she didn't question it.

When she felt the bottle cap accept the bit of magic she had done, she unfocused and smiled at her handiwork. She could see the faint teal aura around the beaten up bottle cap. Teal was the color of her magic. The aura was almost always faint. Her body didn't produce a lot of magic; it was why she aged faster than other witches. Since daily workings almost always used up more of her magic than she made, she aged every day. The unfairness used to make her cry, but she'd accepted it.

The bottle cap absorbed this spell like a sponge. She considered adding a skill spell which helped nearby people to increase intelligence for limit task — maybe Mrs. Potalecky's nephew could write better admissions essays. The bottle cap was made of metal, and it was fairly sturdy, despite its beaten up appearance. She figured it might be able to contain one small bit of skill magic.

She held her palm directly above the cap and sang aloud, "Small skill without a drill! Small

skill without a drill! Small skill without a drill!"
She didn't need to do it aloud, but it felt right.
Magic, after all, was more about intuition and
focus than any "proper" way of doing it.

For the scent spell to complete the whiff,
Sylvia took in a deep breath and slowly blew on the
bottle cap, mentally repeating the phrase Scent of
flowers and fresh showers! three times. It was
imperative she keep a steady amount of air
blowing at the object, the even pressure helped
with the spell's longevity.

Her head buzzed with pleasure, that slight
feeling one might have after a glass of wine. It was
marvelous. She never understood why some
witches hoarded their magic and never used it. It
was beautifully relaxing and calming to charm a
few things each night. As natural and pure as
breathing. Sylvia figured that's why she used more
magic than she should.

She examined the bottle cap and found that
it still had room left, but she wasn't going to push
her luck. She smiled clandestinely at the whiff. She
enjoyed puns way too much.

She pranced, quite literally, to the kitchen,
looking more spritely than an excited stud at a
horse show. "I have it!" she said, beaming.
"Perhaps your nephew might now be accepted!"
She breathed in the heady smell of vegetables

Mrs. Potalecky laughed when she saw
Sylvia's exuberant display, and the pan of
vegetables. "Did you sneak some Chardonnay

while I wasn't looking?"

"No! Not while I work," Sylvia said, forcibly bringing her focus back onto being professional. Mrs. Potalecky wasn't her friend. Indulging in the lovely feeling of magic was much too intimate.

She downed the meal, not enjoying her somberness. "This is better than I expected."

"I was the oldest of my siblings. You learn to cook," she said, pride lighting up her face.

As Mrs. Potalecky prattled on about one of her nieces' recital, Sylvia focused on the food, and tried to remain professional when she really felt like singing.

After Mrs. Potalecky left, Sylvia cleaned, wiping the crumbs off the counter and then sweeping them into a dustpan — most witches used brooms for cleaning. Sylvia only knew one witch wild enough to try actually flying on a broom. Chrysa did not recommend.

She made four more whiff charms before her energy was sapped. Even after she was done, the giddiness remained for singing, tidying and reading. She was so giddy that she did not notice when the wind outside picked up and rattled against her windows.

Chapter 2 - Thom

Thom glared at the suffocating rock walls of his parents' home in Tirt. He didn't want to go, but his opinion had washed over his parents like water over glass.

One of their servants hefted Thom's bag over his shoulder and wordlessly left the room.

He considered just not leaving his room, hiding until his parents were forced to leave to make their flight.

The tiny black tunnel that served as ventilation for the room and the rest of the city sparked his attention. It would not be comfortable to crawl through the deafening black of the ducts, scraping up his knees and arms. But if it meant staying close to Zoranna and away from the humans, maybe it was worth it.

The door to his room opened, and Thom sighed wistfully. His half-hatched escape plan was already dashed. It would be much easier for him to escape if he knew how to use magic, but that was still two years away when he was thirteen.

"Are you ready?" his mother asked curtly.

She did not look at him. Her pale blue eyes were trained on a sheaf of papers in her hands.

He just followed her out.

They entered the Mundane Realm led by one of the resident human experts. His glassy eyes reflected back Thom's grumpy reflection.

Crossing the Veil was an odd experience. Every time he did it, Thom rubbed his head against his shoulders to rid himself of the sense of hands all over his body. Walking through to the Mundane Realm wasn't supposed to be easy; he usually had to use all of his strength to push through the thick air that tried its damnedest to push him back.

A car waited for them on the side of the dusty road, which led to a gigantic metal hull hurtling through the air with way too much faith for Thom's comfort. It was a plane. A monstrous human invention.

"Isn't it wonderful?" the expert asked from the row in front of them. His eyebrows were lifted high on his face, similar to the Glamour that court jesters cast when they were performing.

"No," Thom said.

Mother smiled while she pinched his arm. "Honey, what do you mean?"

The tension in her face was familiar, and Thom knew what it meant. He had to salvage his comment so that it didn't seem like the whiny complaint of an average 11 year old. He was better than that. He hated it. He said something passable and turned his attention to the window.

The Mundane Realm was so brown. The land beneath them stretched out in complex patterns of lines and squares. Humans were ants, burrowing into the surface of their world. Thom said as much to his mother.

She snorted in a ladylike way. "Humans are odd creatures. Magic is robust, but still they toil."

Thom knew that humans were generally not aware of magic. But he couldn't conceptualize that. He couldn't use magic yet. He'd start learning when he was thirteen, but at least he knew it was there. How sad it was to not know of its existence.

His thoughts popped into and out of coherence for the rest of the day. He barely paid attention as they drove from the airplane to the house they'd be staying at.

Father walked out of the house towards them. He greeted Mother, but he didn't smile. His face was blank, and his mind was churning. Father always had schemes. They were distracted.

Thom realized he was on his own, and he struggled against the weight of his leather travel bag. Neither of his parents' two guards even bothered to come over and help him. They were useless.

A wave of heat encased his body for a moment before a breeze drew it away. This place was too hot. While there were some trees, they are paled in comparison to the glittering emerald leaves of the forest in Tirt. They were alive, jewels waiting to be climbed.

He surveyed the very square house that he and his parents were to stay at for the next few weeks and knew instantly that he hated it. Everything about it exuded stuffy and adult.

Only adults would chose to build a regular old plain box and admire its artistic qualities.

"It's very pretty," Mother had said when they drove up. "Very different from home."

Thom had to agree with that. It was nothing like home with its deep and dark caverns and glittering gems. He didn't like the caves of Tirt, but at least Zoranna was there. Here, he was alone with just Mother and Father. The corners of his mouth sunk.

He was allowed to pick any room he wanted. Mother had smiled like she was gifting him the Monarch's Jewel. Thom didn't smile; the prospect wasn't exciting.

Mother and the guards left him alone as they hauled in Mother's numerous bags.

He entered the "borrowed" house. He did not feel the least bit bad that Father had magicked the actual residents to take a hazy and hasty vacation.

The cold air assaulted him, completely unnatural from the heat outdoors. His shoes slapped against the white marble as he stomped into the entryway. The noise echoed. He flicked his attention from the large painting of a family in black turtleneck sweaters on the far wall to the oddly ornate pedestals lining the room. Extra chill creeped up his legs from the floor to his arms, cold as the caves.

"This place sucks," he said to no one.

He mounted the railing-free staircase, pulling his bag behind him. The smooth walls and rounded corners made him feel as if he were walking through a cloud. The thought did not cheer him, and he slogged up the stairs.

The room with the window to the backyard was the best room, though not by much. He dropped his bag near the door and went to the window to open it. There was not a latch or lever, unlike the windows in the cabin that Zoranna would sometimes take him to when he couldn't take the dark caves anymore.

Anger boiled under his skin. Stupid fake window. He shoved away from it.

He hated absolutely everything. Mother and Father only ever thought of themselves. Power and greed and all that stuff that meant nothing. They knew nothing of power if they didn't climb trees. He felt powerful perched on the branches of a tall tree, swaying above the ground. His stomach floated, and his breath slinked, mixing with the delightfully gentle wind. That was power. It felt wonderful.

Not this place. It was nothing close to wonderful; it was prison. He threw himself against the bed. The room had white walls, but it was dark. They looked more gray. This room was so cold and empty. Nothing like home.

He wanted to cry, but the tears didn't come.

"Thomas," came his mother's stern voice from the doorway. She must have brought everything in already. Her slight frame in the doorway seemed impossibly thin, like her sharp bones might slice through her skin and cut up the room. He didn't like when she would hug him. It felt dangerous.

"Yes," Thom answered, but he really didn't want to.

"You know this is for the best," she said.

"I want Zoranna," Thom said. His governess would rub her hand on his back and soothe him. Mother just stood there in the doorway, unmovable like a mountain, jagged as rocks.

"She had to stay behind and manage the estate. You know that."

"I do." But he didn't want to know it. He gritted his teeth. He wanted to scream and kick, show them his rage, show them how upset he was. But the last time he'd done that, he earned a red mark on his face from Father's hand. Screaming and kicking did not accomplish anything. He knew that, but he didn't want to know that.

Mother left him.

Thom pulled the stiff and unyielding sheets over himself. He had to calm down, or she would bring Father into it.

He breathed slowly and allowed his mind to wander back to Zoranna. Her tall frame and gentle black eyes that he felt wrapped up in, like the black fur of the panther companion of Sir Panlone who visited them over the summer.

Zoranna had been with their family since way before Thom was born. She took care of him when his parents were at Court functions. She made his favorite meals when he was sad. She hugged him whenever he wanted, pulling him into the folds of her thick home robes. He loved the feel of her soft skin on his arms. The lines in her face seemed as if she was always smiling, and she didn't Glamour them away.

He decided to pen a letter to her. Maybe she would write back to him before the Fairy Court left Los Angeles. These two weeks were going to be unbearable without his governess.

Dearest Zoranna,

I miss you already. Please respond.

I don't want to be here anymore. It's only been a few hours, and I'm miserable.

I know you said to think of this as an adventure, but I just can't. The house my parents have taken is too big and empty without you. I don't understand why I couldn't just stay at home with you.

Love,
Thom

He gave the letter to his Mother solemnly and then marched back to his room to sleep. But the ceiling in the room seemed impossibly far from him, making him feel small and insignificant.

He listened to the low rumble of the air conditioner blast air into the room. They didn't have those at home. Zoranna used magic to keep the temperature of the room steady. The human's way of doing this was disruptive. Cool air pounded on his face in annoying blasts, making his face too cold and his arms too hot.

He decided then that he hated humans with their stupid contraptions. Magic was better. He lay awake for hours by himself. Thankfully Mother schemed with Father downstairs.

Sleep came deep into the night. Blackness accompanied him in his nothing dreams.

The next day, when Mother and a guard ferried him to the Fairy Court, he asked in a rare moment of brave curiosity, "Why don't humans just use magic instead of air conditioners?"

The guard, a lean man with a weird hook nose despite Glamour, snickered.

Thom frowned, and his face reddened. He narrowed his eyes at the back of the guard's seat. So what if he didn't know? It wasn't nice to laugh. That was the last time he'd ask a question. He clenched his fists and turned to Mother.

Her sharp silhouette cut the fast-disappearing pictures on the side of the freeway — a special type of road where cars went fast as his mother had explained. "Humans don't have magic. You know that."

"Why don't they go get it?" The question escaped him despite his resolution.

"They can't."

"But they have witches. They can do the same as us."

"They are not magical," his mother said with a shrug. "I don't know how else to explain it."

Thom crossed his arms over his chest. It didn't make sense. Magic was a simpler solution. Faint and subtle magic was in everything here. All they had to do was harness it. They made cars. He was sure they could make a magic machine.

He sighed and put his head against the side of the car door. At least the cars were cool. Maybe he didn't hate the human contraptions so much. He loved how the car rolled over the concrete roads, sturdier than the boat that he and Zoranna took onto the lake near home, less bumpy than carriages drawn by horses or magic.

He lifted his head to see out the window. The now-blank walls surrounding the freeway zipped past. Humans with bored faces draped just one hand — Mother's guard used two tightly clenched ones — on the wheel for steering. He didn't know how they weren't even a little bit thrilled to go fast. "Can I open the window?"

"No, it's dangerous," Mother said quickly.

Thom slammed himself into the seat. "Going to Court is dangerously boring."

He didn't get a response, and he decided he would be a pain. A goblin boy that Thom met once in the forest when he'd been separated from Zoranna taught him about "being difficult." At the time, Thom had thought the boy was silly. He didn't want to make things difficult for Zoranna.

But now he set his jaw, hoping he'd be enough of a pain they'd send him home.

When they parked, Mother took him upstairs first. Her skin stretched tightly against her bones, and she looked like a ghoul with her wide, odd smile. It didn't make him feel warm. "I want you to see the beautiful building."

They climbed some stairs with red carpet and stood at an overlook. Below was an uninteresting carpeted room and big glass windows and large columns revealing a sparse green space across the road.

Above them though was the glittering glass of great big "chandeliers," as Mother called them. It was like the starry sky without any of the darkness.

He smiled at them, taking pleasure from the beauty.

"How do you like them?"

"I like them. They're pretty," he said, barely paying attention to his mother's words. "How are they made?"

Mother seemed to think for a moment before answering. "They harvest them from the sky."

It was a much more beautiful harvest than the fairies', Thom decided. Humans were good for something. He admired the million little stars and wondered what contraption had been used to harvest them.

When Mother pulled his hand away, Thom resisted. It was a chance to be difficult and he loved the star chandeliers.

"I don't want to go," he said.

Mother didn't argue. She dragged him to a small box room and pressed a button that lit up. The doors automatically closed, and the room groaned. When the doors opened again, they were in a gray tunnel.

It was magic, he thought. They exited the small box room.

He remembered his rebellion and struggled against Mother's unyielding grip.

She sighed. "Henry?"

The guard scooped up Thom, bouncing him up and down as he strode down the tunnel.

His face grew hot, and he stopped wriggling. He'd lost. "I'll be good," he acquiesced.

The guard Henry let him down.

Mother walked faster now. Thom pushed himself to keep up. It wasn't fair that her legs were longer, he thought as his shoes slapped against the stone floor.

The tunnel was cold and very similar to the caves of their home, except for the texture. He could not see the marks of pick axes in the smooth and shiny walls.

When they stopped, Thom read the red painted letters on the double doors. "Storage Room?"

Neither Mother nor Henry answered, instead pulling the doors open.

It was both remarkable and unremarkable. The giant room brimmed full of hundreds of fairies — both common and noble — in an exact replica of Tirt's Court underneath the mountain. Thom had seen it hundreds of times, since his room in the Tirt palace was only two stone hallways away.

"Your boy's in awe," said Uncle, Father's brother. He towered over Mother, sporting the same dark blonde hair as Father and the same amber eyes as Grandmother.

"He hasn't started training yet," Mother said simply.

"Boys need to know their power." Uncle smirked, as if he knew something they didn't know.

"Boys need the maturity to use their power," said Mother, echoing what Zoranna always said when either Mother or Father wanted him to start training. Most other fairy children were starting by now, making his parents squirm with unease. But they listened to his governess and stayed patient.

"Boys will be behind."

Thom crossed his arms over his chest. He hated when they spoke about him as if he weren't there. Uncle never directly addressed him. It frustrated Thom to no end. He was real. He was a fairy. He turned his attention to the Tirt Court replica, busying himself with finding a difference between this and the real thing.

The ceiling was curved, arching down from the pinnacle in the center of the room in intricately cut designs in the stone face. Little bits of gems and crystals embedded in the designs. It was rainbow rain threatening to fall from the ceiling. Thick tapestries hung from nothing high above their heads, depicting various great deeds, old stories and Lodes royalty.

Thom squinted but gave up. Everything was exactly as he knew it. It didn't comfort him.

He ignored the conversations as fairies talked feet above him but listened to the comments of the periphery.

"She thinks she's so much better than us," said a rich common fairy known for his dealings with the goblins.

"Has common blood just like us," sneered another. "Doesn't know her place."

"It's rather silly," said a noble that Thom didn't know by name. "Pitiful actually."

It was all loud enough for Mother to hear. Muscles in her jaw clenched, but she continued talking as if she had heard nothing.

Thom ignored it too, like he usually did.

At home that night, Father wrote in his notebook on the fluffy couch while Mother cut gems.

Mother's magic cut the slowly rotating and floating sapphire, cutting thousands of tiny facets into the stone.

"Can you teach me that one day?" Thom asked, mesmerized by the light bouncing off in so many directions.

"All Lodes children learn that," Father said curtly.

"Of course, I'll teach you," Mother said quickly, throwing a look at Father.

"I don't want to learn just the Lodes traditions," Thom said. He found the animal magic of the Fauna family fascinating too. He imagined himself leaping onto the back of his lifelong companion lion and riding across a field of flames. The lion's mane would undulate in the gentle wind, and the flames would throw shadow onto his face, making him look scary and powerful. No one would take him to places he didn't want to go. His beloved lion would bite them. "I want to have a lion."

"You're Lodes nobility," Father said. "That is not allowed."

"Shouldn't nobility be able to do whatever they want to do?"

Mother put a soft hand on Thom's arm. The sensation surprised him. "That's not how it works. You know that."

Thom understood in a very distant way that he would only learn the magic of his kind. He frowned. "Why?"

"It just is," Father said. Anger threatened in his voice.

Thom put his head down. It was best not to ask any more questions. He stared at the still-spinning sapphire, hoping to turn invisible.

"I do not know why," Mother said. "But even if you trained to learn their animal magic, you wouldn't be able to do it. They are different from us."

"But if I was the child of a Lode and a Fauna, would I be able to do both?" Thom blurted out, forgetting that he was supposed to be quiet.

Mother perked. "That's an interesting question."

"Only one," Father interjected without looking up. "There are often marriages between the noble families, and the child is only able to do the magic of his family. The family that absorbed the noble from the other family."

Mother nodded. "Magic just knows."

"But what if I was a common fairy?"

"You," Father said sharply, "are not a common fairy."

That was the end of the conversation.

Mother suggested that Thom go to bed.

He clenched his fists but did as he was told. As he climbed up the stairs, he peered over the edge. It would be easy to throw himself off the edge without the railings. He wondered what Mother and Father would think if he died. Would they care? He scrunched up his face, knowing the answer but not wanting to admit it to himself. They wouldn't care, as long as he wasn't a common fairy.

His heart hurt. The dark of the room invaded him, pulling him to his bed. Under the covers, he stared wide-eyed at the door, hoping maybe Zoranna would just appear — powerful Folk could do it — and sit next to him, rubbing his back. Maybe they could cuddle and he could bury his face against her back, like she occasionally let him do. He'd be safe and wanted. Loved. Maybe it would happen if he wished hard enough.

He squeezed his eyes shut, pouring every ounce of hope he possessed into his wish.

"Thomas."

His eyes flew open.

Mother stood in the door, like an ice statue during the Thauma's late autumn Festival of Kings. Cold and distant, almost completely transparent.

Disappointed, Thom pulled the covers over his eyes.

"We're going to enroll you in one of the local schools," Mother said, without waiting for further acknowledgement. "You can get a little education on the mundane ways before you start your training next year. It's good to understand the humans." Her voice was perfunctory. He knew she didn't care. She just wanted him out of her hair.

"But how am I going to be any smarter at a

27

human school than I would be back home with Zoranna?!" he asked incredulously. It didn't make any sense. What could humans teach him?

"New experiences are good for you," Mother said. She had no sympathy on her Glamourized face. Among the perfect nose and the sharp brilliant blue eyes, where was there room for sympathy?

He crossed his arms.

"Don't be a brat." She left his room.

It wasn't actually his room — its actual owner was off on some fog-filled vacation. Nothing was right. These were going to be the longest two weeks.

Chapter 3 - Sylvia

On Saturday morning, Sylvia's body felt incredibly heavy; it was times like this she truly felt old. She always overdid her spell casting on Fridays when she knew she had the entire weekend to recover. It was immature. Though Mrs. Potalecky certainly didn't help.

She pulled herself together and dragged her body to the market. It was crowded. Mothers led their children up and down the aisles, putting back items the children grabbed with their candy-sticky fingers. Hipsters travelled in flocks, picking up pre-made platters and cases of various alcoholic drinks. Young professionals perused the aisles with slightly more discerning eyes — they had recipes. Sylvia had already picked up candy to give to any trick-or-treaters a week before. She was here for ingredients for dinner with Chrysa tonight.

Thinking about the charm and the fact that it was Halloween, Sylvia decided to splurge and get USDA Prime instead of Choice.

The day crawled by until Sylvia started

cooking. She whisked about the kitchen, throwing a dash of salt and pepper onto the steaks. Before she knew it, Chrysa rang the bell.

Sylvia barely had the door open and Chrysa pushed her way into the house. A cloud of curly red hair bounced in with her.

"Sylvia, darling! I want to do magic tonight!" Chrysa announced. Her voice was rich and hearty, and it reminded Sylvia of chocolate cake. She wore a high-necked faux fur coat over a tunic dress and tights.

"I'm fresh out, unfortunately," Sylvia said with a shrug of her shoulders.

"Out?" Chrysa said slowly. She breathed in a mock-gasp. "I think you do that a bit too much."

"I can watch you." She didn't respond to the second half. Her friend never let her get away with anything.

"It's not quite the same thing," Chrysa said. She pushed past Sylvia and bustled to the kitchen with a bottle of wine in each hand. She put them down, peeked at what Sylvia had cooking and then elegantly leaned against the counter. She had a flare for drama. "Perhaps we should get into some other shenanigans?" She raised her eyebrows, brimming with enthusiasm.

Sylvia squirmed. Shenanigans meant trouble. She avoided trouble.

An exaggerated sigh escaped her friend's lips. "It's just that right now, there is a great deal of magical energy. Can you feel it?"

"N-" Sylvia started. She was magically blind, and Chrysa always forgot that.

"Oh wait, I forgot. It's there, trust me. And I don't know the reason yet. Magical anomalies pop up all the time, but this feels ominous somehow. And exciting, and there must be something we can do to participate," Chrysa said, just a bit too fast. Her movements were jerky and full of energy. She was just like Magnolia: a bomb waiting to explode. It was miraculous they were still friends after all these years.

"Maybe it's dangerous?" Sylvia interjected.

"My dear friend, danger is nothing when you're 274 years old," Chrysa said. She flashed a smile.

"I'm not as old as you yet," Sylvia reminded her. She knew then that she'd be taken along for Chrysa's ride. Their friendship survived because Chrysa was adventurous and Sylvia liked that. "What did you have in mind?"

Chrysa's face lit up like a child seeing Santa Claus at the mall for the first time. "Whitnall Park! I drove past it on my way here."

"The slanty park?" Sylvia asked. The park, which wasn't far from her house, was squeezed in a diagonal block, instead of square.

"Precisely. I like the vibe of those powerlines," Chrysa said. She pointed her index finger at nothing in particular.

"But those are my powerlines," Sylvia said protectively.

They weren't technically hers. They belonged to the city or the electrical company or someone. But they were her favorite spot to go and be in awe of power. It was peaceful, like a special secret just for her.

But she knew that she would now share the park with her friend; Chrysa had a knack for commandeering everything in her basic vicinity to be part of her. It was partly because of her magnetic personality and partly because of her relentless will.

The two women gabbed over dinner, eating quickly and talking even faster.

"Penelope is back home," Chrysa announced, her face beaming.

"She's cured?" Sylvia asked incredulously. Their friend Penelope, a witch and mother of three teenaged daughters, had breast cancer.

"Full remission!"

Sylvia hadn't been able to watch her friend deteriorate. The already stick-thin Penelope shrank. Her brown skin turned gray. Sylvia stopped visiting her, not being able to bear the death that clung to the woman.

Sylvia tried to smile. It was the best news in the world to hear, but guilt weighed down her stomach like a brick. She had not supported Penelope enough; she was a bad person for that. At least her friend was alive. "Her family must be so happy."

"My salve worked. Maybe I have some

healer ability in me after all," Chrysa said, shimmying her shoulders and not acknowledging Sylvia's lackluster response. Chrysa had made a salve imbued with aggressive magic to root out the cancerous cells and contain them.

"I'm pretty sure the chemo helped," Sylvia said. She wanted to believe that they had helped. Even she had done a trio of complementary charms that she placed in an equilateral triangle around Penelope's bed months before. Was that enough to make up for the fact that she couldn't go see the woman? She would do anything for the Thins. Apparently, "anything" stopped short of watching a woman slowly die.

Regardless of whose efforts were effective, Penelope was still here for her daughters: Maria, Ellie and Loni. She had to find happiness in that. She shouldn't make this about herself.

"Maria is really growing up," Sylvia said quietly, trying to change the subject.

"She certainly looks like a woman," Chrysa confirmed. "That last dance performance we saw from her was beautiful."

"Makes me wonder if she was ever supposed to be a witch," Sylvia said.

"What makes you say that? She's powerful," Chrysa said. "She could very well be a magnificent witch someday. Of course, not as good as me." Maria, named after her infamous grandma Maria Zaragoza, possessed an inordinate amount of ambient magic. Even Sylvia could see her bright

33

blue aura.

"Of course." Sylvia distractedly examined her own meager teal aura. All witches had an aura. Most Folk — magical beings — had them too. In comparison to most witches and other Folk, Sylvia was pitifully weak.

"She solidly belongs among the humans," Sylvia said. The girl just felt different... normal. She didn't want to think that amount of power determined level of witchiness. Then, she would be barely a whisper of a witch.

"I would say you do too," Chrysa said, then pursed her lips.

The comment cut Sylvia. "I know, I know. It's just she feels so... human. There's no eccentricity to her at all." At least Sylvia tried to be a bit eccentric.

"We don't know her that well," Chrysa reminded.

"Okay, Ellie though. She's eccentric. She's witchy. She's different. Even Loni's got something different about her." She was grasping at nothing. She had no point.

"It's odd to see you judging other witches this way," Chrysa said. "Gatekeeping does not suit you."

Sometimes, she had something poignant to say.

Sylvia felt even worse now. Their conversation meandered.

When she swallowed her last bite of

homemade cake, Chrysa clapped her hands together. "Off to the park, now?"

"We're still going?" Sylvia asked, hoping her friend would just drop it.

"Of course!" Chrysa did not notice the heavy hints or maybe she intentionally ignored them — it was part of her charm.

They were definitely going.

Underneath the gentle hum of the gigantic power lines in the park, Sylvia craned her neck upward so she could stare unobstructed. The thin metal structure spindled up to the sky, filling Sylvia with an undeniable sense of being part of something much bigger than herself. It invigorated her. She felt as if she could float up to the top of the structure and become it. The momentary flight of fantasy made her giggle, because she wasn't a little girl anymore. She knew more than she ever had. She understood dark witches, light witches, all sorts of magical creatures, potions, charms, sacred dances and more than she could remember in that particular moment. And yet, she still was awestruck at this marvel of human engineering that seemed to so perfectly encapsulate the melding of human technology and magic. If there was any human analog to magic, electricity would be it. It was wild, uncontrollable, but simultaneously easy to direct and manipulate. The perfect contradiction. Sylvia found much wonder in it. She always made sure to spend a class with her sixth graders talking about electricity.

After more than a minute of staring, Chrysa cleared her throat. She liked all attention on her after all, and Sylvia usually obliged. "I was thinking we could try a summoning."

At first, her friend's words did not properly register, but she hadn't misheard.

A summoning was more than dangerous. Not just for what was summoned — the actual process took a great deal of magic and left a witch incredibly weak. Sylvia realized that was why she was there, to protect her friend in perhaps her weakest state. "I'll be here," Sylvia said. "But I don't think you should be doing this, for the record."

"I expected nothing else from you, my dear," Chrysa said. Her voice was quieter than usual. Both of them knew something could go wrong; even Chrysa's grandiosity toned down.

Sylvia surveyed the park while her best friend prepared herself solemnly. There were too many children in the distance, entering an apartment building. Sylvia wondered if this summoning was just too reckless. The electrical interference of the powerlines afforded a sort of protection from the Magical Realm, but Sylvia certainly didn't know how much. While similar, magic and electricity didn't always interact well. Sylvia understood the clash better than many of her witch counterparts. She managed to carefully maneuver her magic to coexist with electricity, using fundamentals of electricity that she taught her sixth graders — insulators. The Magical Realm did not possess any intentional electrical system, nor did most its residents care to use electricity, as humans did. Magic was equally effective, and only Folk occupied the realms — and the occasional magically-aware human.

A couple of runners jogged awfully close to where Chrysa was silently meditating in the center of the power line base. Sylvia resisted the urge to shoo them; the best way to keep invisible was to not cause a scene.

Chrysa stood and began a dance to ward off evil. Sylvia recognized that one. She rarely had cause to do the dance, and she didn't want to frivolously use her limited magic on an evil-dispersing dance. Chrysa chanted something aloud, but Sylvia was not quite able to hear. She wasn't sure if it was English or another language. Generally, magic did not need specific phrases, movements or shapes to activate or succeed, but these aids helped witches focus their energy precisely and safely.

A warm breeze rolled over to Sylvia, and she realized the chanting was a cleansing spell. Personally, Sylvia would not have wasted her precious magic on a cleansing spell, but she also did not have the excess that Chrysa had. She always thought of Chrysa as the reckless one between the two of them, but Sylvia ultimately took more risks because she had less magic.

Chrysa stood still for a moment before

doing a slow spin, dragging her pointed toe on the half-dead grass. She preferred circles, just like Sylvia.

Again, she chanted, and the air buzzed with more than just electricity. Sylvia was sure there was more power than she even noticed. Sweat formed on Chrysa's brow, indicating to Sylvia that her friend was making more effort than she'd anticipated.

Chrysa's orange aura reached out tendrils towards the sky. Sylvia's heart caught in her throat; her magic was tiny in comparison.

None of the other people in the park even seemed to notice this awe-inspiring scene. Perhaps it only seemed like the wind picking up.

The orange tendril seemed to find a crack in the sky, and Sylvia realized she was holding her breath. She breathed in through her mouth sharply. The tendrils ripped open the crack, and light temporarily blinded Sylvia. A loud thud reached her ears.

She scrambled forward to check on her friend. "Chrysa?" she called shrilly as her eyes cleared.

Chrysa was knocked out. Sylvia hurriedly checked her pulse and breathed a sigh of relief. Chrysa's heart beat steadily — a bit fast though.

No one at the park seemed concerned, and Sylvia gently shook Chrysa while surveying the immediate areas for any magical creatures or Folk. Amidst the white spots in her eyes: nothing. Thank goodness. She couldn't fight a demon without Chrysa.

She blinked to see if that cleared her vision.

Chrysa stirred. "Wwww- zit?" she mumbled, fighting to open her eyes.

"Shhh," Sylvia said. "It's okay." She petted her curly red hair.

Sylvia looked around at the humans in the park. A jogger's ponytail rocked side to side. The man on the exercise equipment scrunched up his face as he pushed against the bar. Everything was business as usual. Sylvia was endlessly confused how humans never noticed the magic. Or if they did, they immediately wrote it off as some fluke. After more than a hundred years in their world, she still felt nothing like them.

Chrysa pushed against the ground to get up and Sylvia pulled her. She gritted her teeth against her friend's weight, which was heavier than she would've imagined. Once on her own feet, Chrysa managed to walk on her own, which was a blessing.

A jittery feeling filled Sylvia. Something felt off as they walked back to her house.

"Something's wrong," Chrysa mumbled. She pushed her fingers against her skin, on her face and her arms. "I'm so numb, can't even talk right."

"Like Lidocaine at the dentist?"

Chrysa nodded, tenderly testing every inch of herself. "I remember this feeling." Her green-brown eyes narrowed, and her jaw set.

Sylvia's stomach clenched as she realized what she saw on her friend's face: fear.

Chapter 4 - Thom

"Why am I not in school?" Thom asked grumpily.

"Human children take Sundays off," Mother said, gripping his hand tightly. "And your grandmother wanted to see you."

Thom stared hard at the ground, willing everyone to know how unhappy he was. He'd probably prefer human school to the Court again. While Mother didn't deserve his sympathy, the berating whispers of the other fairies upset him as if he were Mother. He didn't understand his own feelings sometimes.

When they entered Court, the endless socializing buzzed with full force. The first witches had been harvested — the first of the crop.

"I don't know why they show off so much," remarked a noble whose servants had not been so fruitful. "Everyone knows the first witches are always the weakest."

Thom turned his attention to the rainbow rain glittering in the domed ceiling. The original was the work of common lodes fairies, not the

Lodes noble family. It was beautiful, but of all fairies, his family — the Lodes — and the common lodes were the only ones who preferred caves. He hated it. Their magic came from the rocks, gems, metals and minerals of the Earth. Back in Tirt — the Lodes' capital city — they lived in great underground caverns that twisted and turned into elaborate mazes that only his family and the common lodes seemed to be able to navigate among the rocks intuitively. The Thauma, Flora and Fauna visitors in Tirt were always asking for guides.

Thom was not different from his fairies in that respect. When underground, he always understood where he was. But he yearned for the sky, the trees and air of above ground. Zoranna took him up every chance they had. He ran outside, not tripping over a single rock — he intuitively felt each pile of dirt, each pebble beneath his feet. The awareness was acute. When he was above ground, it lessened and he felt free, splashing in puddles and laughing until it felt as if his lungs might burst with the pressure. He climbed the trees back home and surveyed the land, pretending to be a great adventurer. Wind caressed his skin, billowing his shirt. The sun warmed his face. Blissful freedom. Until he would inevitably have to go back under the ground.

Since the Lodes were the hosts for this Harvest, they had chosen the Court location. That was why it was in the storage room far beneath the star chandeliers.

Grandmother was down here, among the other socializing fairies in the center of the room, but she was apart from them, a diamond among quartz.

Mother gripped his hand tighter and pulled him further into the throng of fairies in their finest.

He heard snippets of conversation as they walked through.

"My fighting fairies have been doing magnificently. We already have two witch souls."

"Common fairies are teaming up. It's rather humorous to try their hands at wealth."

"I wish it were more acceptable for us to go out Harvesting. It's terribly dull down here. Stuffy too." Thom looked up to see who had said that: Duke Puck of the Thauma Family. His dark complexion sparked with energy. Spindly lightning flashed across his short curly hair. Some said the lightning addled his brain. Of all the Thauma weather magic, the lightning was known to be unpredictable.

Thom smiled, both for the Duke's comment and for the fact that the Thauma dealt with the sky. He envied them.

When he was old enough to start his training, he'd discover his aptitude, whether it was for metal, rock, gem or quaking. He did not yet know what it would be, but he knew that his specialty would be nothing close to sky or trees. He wish he had been born to another family.

Mother stopped suddenly, yanking his arm. "My Queen," she said with the appropriate bow of a princess to her queen.

"My grandson," Grandmother said, ignoring Mother altogether. A smile stretched slowly onto her sagging face. Like Zoranna, she did not use Glamour to completely erase all signs of aging. It made her seem more regal, more important somehow.

He met her brown eyes. They seemed to glow orange, like the fire of a forge. "My Queen," he said with a bow, as he had been taught.

"What do you think of the festivities, Thomas?"

"Beautiful," he responded. He looked up to Mother for approval. She gave him a near-imperceptible nod.

Grandmother laughed a little. "What do you really think?"

"I don't like being underground," he said. He didn't dare look up at his mother now. He was sure she wouldn't approve.

"Perhaps magic had humor when she dispatched you into our family."

"A twisted sense of humor." Thom pulled his mouth to the side in a dissatisfied half-smile. Magic had a mind of its own, despite anyone's efforts to control it. It would writhe and wriggle out of the simplest commands if not wielded properly. Like a petulant child with semantic

44

genius, Zoranna often told him. It didn't surprise him that magic would plant a wolf in a meadow of monkshood. He hoped his life wasn't that cruel of a joke.

"Have you yet witnessed a soul harvest?" she asked.

Thom shook his head. He doubted that many fairies had seen a soul harvest. Few were still alive from the last one, and the rest of the time it was illegal.

"Tomorrow we might do one in Court, I will expect you to be here," Grandmother said.

"He's starting school tomorrow," Mother said with a start.

Grandmother narrowed her eyes and said sharply, "Then whenever he is free."

When the interaction was done, Mother wrenched his hand away from the Court. Her face held embarrassment and rage. It made her ugly. Thom didn't attempt to make her feel better like he usually did at home every time after she left Court. If he couldn't be happy, neither could she.

Chapter 5 - Sylvia

Sylvia sat on the edge of the bed and stared.

Chrysa was barely speaking. She seemed shell-shocked.

"What is so scary?" Sylvia asked.

Chrysa admitted, "I was hoping for a cat with wings maybe. A sagacious talking one for a companion. I met a few while I was in the Magical Realm. But then I lost focus. Summoning is much harder than I remember." Her eyes didn't meet Sylvia's.

"What's really wrong?" Sylvia asked. Magic sometimes did weird things when wielded without focus but Chrysa wasn't the type to be fazed by small magical mishaps. Perhaps the accident hurt her brain? Witches sometimes went crazy. The magic addled them. They were the witches of human lore, the ones who didn't care who knew about them. They wished to boil children or raise the dead — a job better left to necromancers. Normal witches steered clear of addled witches.

"I hardly have any magic left," Chrysa said, with a sharp alertness that made Sylvia second guess her insanity idea.

"Probably shouldn't do that again," Sylvia said. Her friend never listened to her advice, but she still said it anyway. The phrase 'Doing the same thing over and over again and expecting different results is the definition of insanity' was apt. Perhaps the magic addled her brain.

"I'll be out of action for a while," Chrysa said. "I think this spell definitely made me age." She swished her hand as if she would be doing some sort of magic but her magic fizzled like sparks on rocks. "No fuel." She swore and pressed her lips together in a grimace. "Could you get me a mirror?" she asked through gritted teeth.

"That weak?" Sylvia asked, finding the hand mirror she kept on her white dresser across the room.

Their eyes met for a long moment. Sylvia's brown eyes and Chrysa's green ones that reminded Sylvia of the Guatemalan forests that she drove past on one of her vacations: dense, deep and camouflaging so much within.

Sylvia didn't know what to say. It all felt completely meaningless in comparison to Chrysa's very rare seriousness. Chrysa was always flippant, gallivanting anywhere in the world she pleased and rarely did a crease ever appear on her forehead. She didn't work. In her youth, Chrysa had sent up numerous accounts at banks and investments in business over the years that grew into her large fortune. Sylvia admired her friend's foresight and followed suit, investing her witching profits so that — if she should ever choose to — she could retire. But she had started much later and had no such nest egg.

But this was out of character for Chrysa.

She didn't say much the entire day as her friend recuperated enough to go home.

When Chrysa collapsed into the driver's seat of her car, she exhaled loudly. "Well, let's hope."

"Hope what?"

Chrysa pulled her driver's door shut and gave Sylvia a half-hearted, close-mouthed smile. It was more a straight line than anything resembling a smile.

With her home empty, Sylvia went to sit on her porch.

David glared at her. He was in his front room, not even bothering to pretend he wasn't looking this time.

Sylvia went back inside and wound down the busy weekend with chores and some reading.

On Monday morning she received a note in her teacher's box at school. She was getting a new student. Most students didn't join mid-year like this, but families moved for many reasons and it was never the child's fault, so she would do everything she could to ease his adjustment to class.

The room was rowdy when the bell rang. Magnolia and her friends were already gossiping.

The boys in the class were less verbose, but Andrew rocked in his chair. He seemed to want to rocket into space. Sylvia always had to bolster herself before interacting with him. That energy was overwhelming.

Her new student was a mousy boy with white blonde hair and ocean blue eyes. He stood uncomfortably in the doorway, squirming against the stiff brand new straps of his blue backpack.

She got him seated and started class with a story and without an introduction of the new boy.

Most of her children threw glances his way, and whispers blossomed throughout the entire room.

She launched into a story like she did every day. "Class, I want to tell you the story of a goat named Derrick."

Some of the girls in the class giggled at the silliness. Sylvia smiled, glad she had chosen the name. Though she received at least two eye rolls — that was to be expected in a sixth grade classroom.

"Derrick loved to eat grass from the mountainside. He climb up the mountain every day to stand there and chew on the grass and admire the view. The higher he went, the cooler it was. In summer, Derrick climbed to towering heights." Sylvia put her hand up to illustrate her point. "One day, Derrick meets a new goat who he's never seen before. And Derrick talks with him and they laugh. Eventually, Derrick says he must go eat. And he climbs the mountain, like he does every day." Sylvia mimes climbing a mountain, though she knows that's not what it looks like when a goat climbs a mountain. "And the next day, he sees the new goat again. They chat. And they jabber." She smiled and asked, "Does anyone know what jabber means?"

One hand shot up and the student gave a reasonably accurate answer.

"Exactly! Perfect," she said with an enthusiastic smile. Over the years, she realized that any answer was a good answer. "Derrick thinks the new goat is very groooovy." More amused eye rolls. She was hitting her maximum embarrassment stride! "But he doesn't invite him to go climbing with him. He climbs by himself, solitary again. The next day they talk, and the new goat asks if he can join Derrick on the mountainside. Derrick makes excuses. He likes his time on the mountain. He can't imagine changing it."

"He's not a very friendly goat," Sophia in the back of the class said loudly.

Sylvia smiled. Someone was getting it. "So when Derrick climbs the mountain this day, he climbs extra high, because he's exhilarated to climb. But!" Sylvia paused for dramatic effect. She loved seeing the look of utter exasperation in the eyes of the few particularly self-aware students who were starting their angsty stages.

"He got stuck!" Sylvia said. "The rocks were unstable and he needed assistance getting down.

But he had no friend to help him. He baAAAaaaaAAAhhhed his lament to the mountain. He had to get down somehow. So he attempted to do it himself, since there was no other option. Unfortunately, the rocks beneath his hooves were unsteady and he slipped." Sylvia did an exaggerated pretend-fall. "He fell down the mountain. Luckily, though, goats are sure-footed." She looked around the room before asking, "Does anyone know what sure-footed means?"

Ashley's hand raised, and Sylvia nodded. She scrunched up her face. "To be sure of your feet? Like not slipping and falling a lot?"

"Exactly!" Sylvia said. "Eventually he regained his balance and stopped falling, because Derrick was a sure-footed goat. But now his ankle hurt. And he walked home limping by himself. The next day his ankle got swollen so he could barely walk. But the new goat came and visited him and spent the whole day with him. And once his ankle healed, he invited the new goat up the mountain everyday with him. And they had so much fun, he never realized it'd be more fun with a friend."

Her students did the obligatory clap. Some of them sought out the eyes of their friends and smiled at each other.

"So class, what was the point of this story?" Sylvia asked.

Three hands raised. Sylvia called on the one in the back of the class. "Friends are good."

"Good, Ashley. Anything else?" Sylvia

asked.

"Just 'cause you like something, doesn't mean it can't be made better?" Ashley added, unsure.

"Yes. And why do you think I told this story today?" Sylvia asked.

One hand shot up.

"Yes, Joey?" Sylvia said.

"'Cause the new kid," he said proudly. He was seated right next to the new kid, a pale and blonde boy who had not said a word up to this point.

"Exactly. Joey got it! I want everyone to make a real effort to include our new friend Thom. Not just in class, but out on the playground too."

She had each of her students go up to the front of class and introduce themselves to Thom.

The small boy barely seemed to care at all. New students usually liked when all the other students introduced themselves first. It put them at ease and established a level playing field.

Sylvia set the class on individual assignments so she could get Thom to smile and open up. She made her rounds, checking on students that she knew might be struggling on this particular assignment. She checked on a few students randomly. Finally she made her way to Thom.

"Hi Thom," she said. She kneeled so her eyes were level with his.

Thom pointed his bright blue eyes at hers.

"Hello."

His directness unnerved her a bit, but she smiled and asked about his family.

"My father is a financial advisor. My mother does not work," he said with a bored voice that made Sylvia think he had memorized this.

"Do you have siblings?" Sylvia asked.

"No," he said.

Sylvia spent the next ten minutes trying to extract any information from him, but it seemed that he only answered direct questions.

Sylvia learned that he had come from Kentucky. He came for his father's job. He liked the color purple. His mom liked to arrange flowers.

The marathon of question-asking exhausted Sylvia, and she wondered if one of her students might have better luck loosening up this little boy. She paired up everyone in class for a scavenger hunt. She assigned Thom to Magnolia. Everyone loved her.

On the board, she wrote what she wanted. She noticed that her more observant students copied the list onto their own sheet of paper to carry around campus with them. The impulsive pairs left before they saw this. Magnolia and Thom wrote the list down in Magnolia's flower notebook, and the two left as most of the students left the room.

Sylvia helped a lingering pair with a hint on where to find acorns, since only one tree on campus dropped them.

With everyone gone, she tidied up and texted Chrysa.

"Ms. Hargrove, you text?" said a squeaky girl's voice. It was Rebecca, one of the impulsive ones.

Sylvia let out a soft laugh and nodded.

"But you're old!" Rebecca said.

"Not that old. I've always been quick to adopt technology. Now, are you and Tiffany done with the scavenger hunt?" Sylvia asked.

Rebecca shook her head. "Just checking one of the things on the list. Also, I saw Magnolia crying. I don't think Thom is very nice."

Sylvia stood abruptly and went outside to find them. When she found the tear-stained Magnolia, she kneeled and did a visual inspection for any marks. The young girl's eyes were accompanied by puffy redness, but her arms and legs were free of scratches. "Magnolia, what happened?"

Magnolia sniffled. "Thom said he wouldn't mind if a black widow bit me. And if a black widow bites you, and you don't get to the hospital in eight seconds, you die. Eight seconds isn't very long, I'd die!" She wasn't crying anymore but gave Sylvia such a sad look.

"Why do you think he said that?" Sylvia asked.

"I don't know," Magnolia said. "He's so mean. He just says he wants to go home."

"Are you okay?"

"Yeah," Magnolia said. "I don't want to do the scavenger hunt with Thom anymore."

Sylvia sent the girl to another group and went in search of her new student.

Thom had climbed one of the pine trees and wedged himself between two big branches so that he didn't need to hold himself up. His hair was mussed and he had scratches on his arms.

"Thom, why don't you come down and tell me why Magnolia is crying?" Sylvia called up to him.

He ignored her and traced the outline of multiple leaves while she watched.

"I will call your parents," she said, hoping this would snap him out of it. It did not. If he wanted to go home, he probably wanted to get in trouble. She wouldn't ring his parents. She wondered if a story might bring him to his sense, but considering his apathy for the first story, that was iffy. She wracked her brain before deciding to just simplify everything. "What do you want?"

That perked the boy's ears, but he didn't turn or let on that he was interested. If Sylvia wasn't used to dealing with a multitude of 11 year olds, she might not have caught it.

She continued. "I'm willing to listen and see if I can help, if you tell me what you want."

"I want to go home," he said quietly.

"Home where?" Sylvia asked.

"In... Kentucky," he said. "I already miss the

trees and my governess. And it's too hot here."

Hot? Sylvia thought. It was cold outside — the low 60s. And a governess? What an old-fashioned concept. She was around when some folks still had governesses, and it was such an antiquated idea, kind of interesting nonetheless, because it meant several things for Thom's family. They were old-fashioned. They had money. It was probably old money. Old money didn't move for a job.

"That decision is up to your parents, but maybe I can help with the trees," Sylvia said.

"How?" he asked.

"There's a park called Griffith Park, and —" she started.

"I'm not allowed in the city by myself. It's dangerous," he said, then he looked like he had done something wrong. He probably wasn't supposed to share that.

"That it is," Sylvia said. "Maybe your parents can take you?"

"They're busy. They don't want to spend their time going to parks with me."

"You're their son. I'm sure they will," Sylvia said.

"No, they won't. And it still won't be as many trees as in Kentucky," he said glumly.

This boy was a pessimist, Sylvia thought. "What else do you like?" They went back and forth for many minutes, and nothing that Sylvia could do was to Thom's taste. He did, however, come down from the tree. She had him talking and that was a start! She soon decided that she needed to make him a charm. But not one of her usual whiffs. Something stronger and with different spells.

That evening, she looked up optimism and popular spells. Optimism was a must, but she debated putting a popularity booster in the charm. This could backfire or be too strong and everyone starts being way too devoted to him. Sometimes she wondered if charismatic leaders had a witch on their payroll to sway public favor in their direction. She'd seen a dull brown aura around Clinton when he won all those years ago.

She dug through her found items bin. A tattered old gray and black scarf. A rock with googly eyes glued on and a smiley face drawn on with black marker. An old matchbox car with a missing wheel and a flaking blue paint job.

She decided on the matchbox car. It was perfectly suited to a young boy. She brought it to her work table, ready to imbue it with optimism, popularity and friendliness. She hoped all three would take. She did the optimism spell first, mentally chanting the line: "Things are on the up and up." Which was entirely true: Sylvia was on the case.

The next spell was popularity. She repeated the chant ten times now to ensure that it would stick for longer than her spells usually did. "Talk to him like your own kin."

The friendly chant was weakest, and she only felt the need to repeat it three times again: "Friendly eyes mean a good time."

The matchbox car struggled to hold all this magic, and Sylvia held it to her chest to compress the magic and keep it inside the charm. Though that might make it unstable, she felt that Thom needed all the magic he could get.

That one charm exhausted her, so she crawled into her bed and took the charm with her.

In the morning, Sylvia barely woke up. Maybe adding some luck would've been more important than the friendliness. She wasn't sure, and she didn't want to wait longer to give her student the charm.

The morning went as it usually did, slow but nice and easy. Her students mostly followed the rules, because she knew how to make sure they weren't incentivized to break rules. And she did love them, each and every one. She loved talking about her students to the other teachers during breaks. They seemed to want to talk about something else usually, though. Sylvia's enthusiasm was often unmatched.

Mid-morning, she set the matchbox car on Thom's desk. "Look what I found," she said, pushing it slightly towards him. He examined it with incurious eyes, and he seemed to want to turn to someone else for approval of this object she brought. But for once, she guessed, the decision was up to him: to take or to reject. He took and immediately pocketed the car. Sylvia kind of wished she had more of these little cars, because she suspected that little Thom was quite taken with his prize.

She smiled at him warmly, then made her rounds for the rest of the morning. She noticed a few students writing and drawing stories, and she bustled over to see if she could help in some way. Two students had stories about dragons. Sylvia couldn't help but smile.

She checked in on Thom's story, it was about climbing trees in the forest after running away from home. She internally debated whether this warranted contacting his parents, but she decided to wait until the next day to see Thom's resolution.

That evening she visited Chrysa's house. Her house was just like her personality, odd and eclectic. The front was painted pink with faded mint trim. The front window was not flat, but rather a corner that jutted out of the wall. Sylvia's friend loved to sit there and enjoy the scenery. Inside, doo-dads and baubles littered the walls and every surface. Chrysa was in her circular bedroom, eating Rocky Road out of the tub. Chrysa's aura did not show up on Sylvia's radar at all, though her magical radar had always been weak. "Just in time, my dear," she said. "I have but one lament."

"Huh?" Sylvia asked.

"I do not regret overextending myself. But I do regret that it also caused my hair to gray. It's a travesty," she said matter-of-factly as she licked the spoon clean. She examined the bowed surface before digging it back into the mountain of Rocky Road.

"You already had gray hair," Sylvia said, trying to keep a smug look from her face. Sylvia had taken years — perhaps decades — to accept her full head of tired gray hairs.

"Now it's a whole streak!" Chrysa bemoaned. "I look like a ginger skunk. This is ridiculous." She flung herself against her bed, knocking over several of the tchotchkes of her headboard shelf.

"Don't break a hip," Sylvia said, grinning from ear to ear.

"You hag." A not-so-silent warning.

Chapter 6 - Thom

One of the guards took him home after a second day at school. He held his new prize in his fist in his jean pocket.

He rushed into the house, past the array of oversized portraits of the family who usually lived here. They all looked Glamoured, not like the mundane humans he'd seen at school. Their skin glowed with perfection, and their mouths stretched into immaculate smiles. Humans with Glamour. Pretend fairies. They didn't do it nearly as well. Fairies didn't make themselves perfect. They twisted their faces and bodies into exaggerated beauty approaching the grotesque. Thom didn't like it, but at least it was art. The canvas on the walls around him purported to be art, but it was mimicry of a low class.

Dropping his backpack on the floor by the bedroom door, he crashed into the bedroom. He gingerly placed the mini-car that Ms. Hargrove had given him on the nightstand.

The blue paint on the mini-car was dull and flaking in the afternoon light, but the wheels rolled. He stared at it, unable to keep the growing smile from his face as he imagined being able to drive like all humans seemed to. He'd cruise over the earth, almost flying. He'd zoom past everything, leaving behind his parents, and drive to Tirt. Just like when Mother let him open the window for a minute and his hair whipped around crazily, he'd have all the windows down, plastering his hair into a tall forest.

"Chchchchchchch," he tried to mimic the sound of the car starting up. He felt weird and childish for doing it. But he was happier when he was younger, maybe if he pretended to be that young again, all this stupid stuff would go away. "Jjjjjjjjjjjjjoooooooommmmmmm!"

He pushed the car on the plush floor. "We're gonna escape!" he exclaimed. Just saying it aloud made him happier.

"Escape what?" came the stern voice of his mother.

Misery punched his stomach. "Nothing. I'm playing," he bit out resentfully.

Her face drooped and her eyebrows narrowed.

"Hello Mother," he ventured, hoping she would be distracted from his talk of escape.

"Hello Thomas," she said. "What's that?" She indicated the mini-car.

"My teacher gave me a gift today."

"Why?"

"I don't know." Thom held out the little car.

"I think I would like to drive one day."

Mother's eyes perked as she examined the prize in his outstretched hands. "Your teacher gave you this?" Her bony fingers floated over the detailed surface.

Something in the way her eyes pierced his car made him feel queasy, but an explanation tumbled out of his mouth. "Yes, Ms. Hargrove is a really nice lady. At first, she was annoying, she asked too many questions. But now she gave me this car, and she's not so annoying anymore," Thom unloaded.

"I don't think you can go back to school," Mother said slowly with a questioning turn of her head. Her eyes still hadn't left the car.

A brick dropped in his stomach. "Why not?"

"Your teacher is a witch." She pocketed his car.

Chapter 7 - Sylvia

Sylvia was excited to go to work on Wednesday. She wanted to see the effects of the little charm she'd made for Thom.

She called Chrysa on her way to work.

"At least I have a bit of my strength back," Chrysa said. "But it's pitiful."

"Welcome to the club!" Sylvia beamed.

"I decline your gracious invitation, my darling."

Thom wasn't in class.

She kept an eye on the door, hoping he would show up, but his blond hair never graced her classroom.

The clock ticked away the day to her growing unease. He could've run away. Her charm could have backfired. Why did she do that? It was not smart to give a child a charm. Her patrons understood that they were dealing with magic items. Poor little Thom had no clue. But her charms had never backfired! She was always careful.

She went to the office at lunch to see if there

was a number to call his house. She dialed the number, but it rang incessantly. She gave up on that and copied down his family's address.

She was her very own bomb when she drove to his house after school. The ticking in her head at every second passing was the most painful countdown to implosion she'd ever experienced. Her life was organized. She wasn't used to this sort of stress. What would she find? A sobbing mother? The cops? She would hate to think she was the cause of it.

The house was enormous, comparable to her friend Patty's home. It had a modern twist that exuded privilege and new money.

She knocked on the door, not bothering to smooth her hair. She fidgeted.

A man with a hollow face answered the door. His eyes widened just slightly as he examined her, but his voice was smooth. "What is your business?"

"I'm Thom's teacher," Sylvia said. She couldn't freak out. It wouldn't accomplish anything. She paused for a moment, collecting herself. "I'm here to check in on him. He wasn't at school today. Are you his father?"

"One moment." He left.

A woman with white blond hair and light blue eyes filled the doorway a minute later. She smiled, showing all her teeth. "Ms. Hargrove? It's a pleasure."

"Where is Thom?"

"He's in his room. Feeling unwell." She gestured into her home. "Come in for some tea." The main entry way was lined with pedestals and art. Sylvia didn't have an eye for that sort of thing, but it was grand.

The tension in Sylvia's body released, and she breathed out a sigh. Tea didn't sound too bad after this ordeal.

"I hope it's not too bad of an illness."

"Just the regular sort, I assure you," she said.

The tea was milky and had a slight almond flavor. It left a light airiness in her mouth, like she was drinking a cloud.

The room they occupied was a living room with imposing white walls. Above the fireplace hung a family portrait, but the people in it looked nothing like Thom or his mother. That scratched at her brain but she let it go, so relieved that Thom was okay.

"Thomas says you're a really good teacher."

"I always try my best. And I love my students."

"You gave him this car?" She held up the matchbox car charm.

The magic didn't look nearly as strong as it had been when she'd given it to Thom. Barely a hint of her teal magic remained. Sylvia hesitated. "Y-yes. I wanted him to know he was welcome in my classroom." Something felt off here. But she couldn't put her finger on it.

"Interesting," Thom's mother said.

She didn't know the woman's name. Just as she was about to ask, Thom's mother started again.

"Interesting that a witch teaches human children." Malice edged her voice.

Sylvia cocked her head to the side but didn't say anything. She stared at the sharp bones on Thom's mother's collar. They jutted out like knives in a butcher block.

Thom's mother laughed. "You're really that dense. You haven't put it together yet?"

The air around the woman wiggled like a mirage. That quality was usually the effect of Glamour. The pins in Sylvia's brain clicked into place. A fairy. Sharp fear closed around her neck. She managed to squeeze out, "But we have treaties."

"Yes, we do." The woman launched herself at Sylvia.

Sylvia rolled away, just barely missing her, spilling the tea everywhere. Something cut her arm.

"Mother!" cried a voice from somewhere else. "Please don't! I like her!"

Thom's mother didn't stop. She was a monster. Her teeth and nails sharpened. Her pale blue eyes bulged and wobbled. She crawled forward on the couch, like a macabre puppet on strings.

Sylvia pushed herself into a standing

position. She pushed her magic into her hands to give her the strength to flip the couch with the fairy on it.

The fairy yowled.

Sylvia ran towards the front door, skidding just in time to not smash into the hollow-faced man.

He was a wall.

She reached out around the room with her magic to find something... anything! A vase zipped into her right hand, and she launched it at the hollow-faced man.

He dodged easily and lumbered toward her.

"Get her!" screamed the female fairy.

Sylvia magicked another vase from near the door to her, but the hollow-faced man's head intercepted.

He crumpled.

The female fairy screamed furiously.

Sylvia yanked open the front door and scooted out of the house just as the tips of fingers scraped against her back. She whirled around to face Thom's mother and yanked the door shut on her fingers. Screams carved into her ears.

She jumped into her car and backed up hitting a large flower pot with her bumper. Her tires squealed as she made it to the road and turned sharply.

Chapter 8 - Thom

Mother cried hot tears. Her reddening face scrunched up like a walnut. They went to the faucet in the kitchen and ran cold water over her fingers. Magic didn't fix everything. Pain was one of those things that magic couldn't get rid of.

Perhaps that kept Folk grounded. They would not think themselves invincible if a slap to the face still stung.

"That, Thomas, is why we must keep the witches down," Mother hissed angrily.

"But she's nice," Thom said.

Mother whipped her hand out of the stream of water and held up her red and swelling fingers. "This is not nice." Each word came out in a heaving breath.

His fingers ached just seeing them. "Should we go get someone to help?"

Mother shoved her hand back under the faucet. "No, absolutely not. Your grandmother must never learn of this."

"But the guard knows," Thom pointed out.

"He won't tell either after his pitiful

display." Her mouth twisted into pure disgust.

They both watched the cold water run over her fingers for a long moment. The water was opaque, not crystal clear like the rivers at home.

His mother looked him directly in the eyes. "Promise me you will never speak of this."

"Why?"

"Promise me."

"I promise. But why?"

Mother's eyes bulged in disbelief, and her mouth hung agape. "Your father wants to be the next King. Your grandmother will never choose him if she finds out her grandson is a witch sympathizer, and her daughter-in-law was bested by a pathetic excuse of a witch. We would be disgraced."

Embarrassment burned on his face. Every time Mother stepped foot in Court, she could not forget that she was a common fairy by birth.

"I will be Queen," she said. "I've known it since I was little."

"Does that mean I will be prince?"

"Yes!" Mother's pale eyes danced with liveliness. "You will want for nothing. Servants at your beck and call. And the girls will come from far away to gaze at your beautiful face. They'll cut off their pinky fingers to just get the chance to win your affection." She grinned then and held up her right hand — the one untouched by the door. The Glamour that Mother always kept about her flickered for a second, and Thom glimpsed her real hand. The skin had a slight greenish tint, but he knew that. All fairies were some version of green — moss, forest, seafoam, emerald, algae. The startling thing was that his mother only had three fingers and one thumb on the hand. The last was a stub.

He blinked incredulously, and the peek was gone.

"Your grandmother does not appreciate drive. But I do."

Thom was stunned. "Perhaps we should go lay down."

His mother acquiesced, and Thom led her upstairs to the expansive borrowed bedroom.

He pulled the crisp white blanket around them and pressed his face against her back. In their cocoon, Mother laid motionless; he was glad he couldn't see her face. He imagined it would rot his soul, shriveling and collapsing like the maggot-infested carcass of an animal. He cried.

Chapter 9 - Sylvia

As Sylvia pulled into her garage, an agitated David Rather paced on her porch. His eyebrows pressed together, forming a hard line on his forehead.

She kept steady, put her car into park, and left everything but her purse in her car. Her heart rate had slowed on her way home, but she didn't think she could take any more. She gulped the spit gathering in her mouth and waved with a big smile plastered on her face, hoping to abate his tension. "David! What brings you to my side of the street?"

"I know you're a witch," he said bluntly.

Dread punched her stomach, and she opened her mouth to say something. Not twice in the same day, please.

"Don't worry. I've known since I moved in. I'm not here with any vendetta," he said, and then added, "Though witches are unstable and crazy." His jaw moved just slightly like he was gritting his teeth.

Sylvia's mouth thinned, but her stomach leveled out. He was clearly an asshole, not a murderous fairy.

"My mother and my sister were witches, so I think I have the authority to say something about the matter," he said with an unapologetic shrug.

"I am a witch, and I don't have a say?" Sylvia asked. She raised her eyebrows.

"Not if you're crazy, no, you don't," he said.

Sylvia crossed her arms over her chest. "Why are you here?" she asked.

"The fairies have come to town," he said, as if that would explain everything.

"Witches have treaties," Sylvia asserted. It felt more like a plea.

David huffed.

He reminded Sylvia of a student about to throw a temper tantrum. It was usually best to let them work out their own anger. David was no different; it would almost be cute to watch him. But she didn't really have the patience to watch a full-grown man lose his temper.

Then he said, "Fairy Court."

She raised her eyebrows. If it was more than Thom and his family, there was truly something to worry about.

"It's the Fairy Court, that's who has come to town," he said.

"How do you know?" she asked.

"It's on the internet," David said, as if that had been obvious.

"You can't believe everything on the internet," Sylvia said. "Lots of crazies." She said it with annoyance, but if he was right, there was definitely something to be worried about, more than rogue fairies attacking.

"It's some 100-Year Hunt," David said.

Sylvia thought for a long moment — brain processing much slower than she wanted to. The Fairy Court was a collection of old fairy families — each represented by their own royalty — who ruled over all fairies. Long-dead witches from the Mundane Realm sought them out to garner a deal to protect witches from random fairy attack. In exchange to sate the fairies' need for magic, they promised that every 100 years the Fairy Court could enter the Mundane Realm and freely hunt witches in a given city or town. No outside entity was allowed to interfere; if not for this stipulation, the elves in Europe would have quashed the tradition long ago.

Sylvia was only a teenager when the last Hunt was held in London. She heard secondhand stories of almost every witch in the city being sucked dry of her life force. The thought was terrifying, and Sylvia was surprised that none of the witches she knew had mentioned it. It was as if they had all forgotten.

She tried to remember what year the last Hunt took place. It was 1915; Sylvia remembered because she had received a beautiful doll that year with brown curly hair and green eyes.

Her stomach dropped; it was 2015. The Hunt was here. Thom's mother was the first fairy who had tried to kill her. The evidence was clear and chilling, like ice on the surface of a lake. She slipped down under. She would surely die, unable to break through to the surface.

How had she not remembered it? How had she not left? How could she have been so daft? "What does the internet say?" she asked with a solemn voice.

"Not much, but that every person of witchblood is eligible to be hunted," he said.

"Which includes you and... that's why you came to me?" Sylvia asked.

"Yes," David said,
 not the least bit abashed.

"Couldn't you just leave the city?" Sylvia asked.

"I tried this morning after reading about the Fairy Court. I tried to drive out, but as I made it to the Newhall Pass, I was suddenly heading south again. But I saw other cars having no problem driving sorth. I'm surprised I didn't cause an accident," he said.

"Who are these people who're talking about it on the internet?" Sylvia asked.

"Mostly magical whack-jobs, but there are one or two women claiming to be witches in Kentucky that say the Fairy Court announced their Hunt location on Halloween," David said.

Sylvia gasped, remembering the powerful feeling that espoused in the air that night. Chrysa's accident was probably an unexpected side effect of the Fairy Court sequestering L.A. It all seemed so clear now. She wanted to laugh bitterly, to bemoan her incredible stupidity at not realizing what year it was. But to be fair, it was all so long ago that it was easy to forget. She suddenly wondered why she had a fancy smartphone if she wasn't going to use it to put important dates on it, like 100-Year Hunts that might kill her. That'd be a good idea.

She frowned, and her bottom lip pouted just slightly. "What's your plan?"

"My plan was to get you to save me," he said without a shred of embarrassment. Sylvia kind of liked that.

"Well, the first thing to do is call everyone," she said decisively, like a PTA mom on a mission. "I'll go get my phone tree."

Within two hours, Sylvia had assembled a fair amount of witches in her living room. Each woman eyed David warily before finding a seat on one of Sylvia's couches or chairs. Sylvia, ever the good hostess, had set down a platter of fruit she'd cut up.

Penelope — the breast cancer survivor — and her three powerful daughters had arrived first. The young witches ate chocolate ice cream that Sylvia had scooped into blue glass bowls.

"Hi," Sylvia said to the witch. "You're looking well." It was true. She found it hard to look Penelope in the eyes. The mudslide of guilt sludged over her. She shouldn't have abandoned her friend like that.

"I feel well," Penelope admitted. She managed a small smile. "But now... this." Her eyes watered slightly, but she blinked and smiled harder.

"We'll survive," Sylvia said. Her friend's feigned courage stabbed into her heart. She'd do everything possible, she promised herself. She couldn't let the Thins down again.

"I already feel like I'm living past my time," Penelope said. She looked at her daughters.

"They're young."

"I want you to treat them as if they were your own." Penelope looked levelly into Sylvia's eyes.

Sylvia met her gaze and nodded. She turned her attention to the other witches in their company

There was Patty, a married witch with a wealthy but often absent husband from Pasadena; she and Sylvia were good friends from years ago. There was Wendy from Culver City; she was the last to arrive because of traffic. A few other witches that Sylvia didn't know well were present too. Chrysa lounged on the loveseat. When Sylvia had called her, she had not sounded surprised. Now, the resignation pulled down her face in ways that she had never seen on her friend.

Sylvia positioned herself in front of the fireplace, feeling at odds with the space which was usually so comfortable. Probably because there were so many people in her house. "So I'm sure you all were told why you're here. It's come to my attention that the 100-Year Hunt is taking place in Los Angeles. I have already been attacked, and I was lucky to get away."

She received solemn nods from most of the witches. This was no small thing. In history, the 100-Year Hunt often left almost every witch in the city dead, permanently. It turned out that none of the women had remembered that it was the year of the 100-Year Hunt.

"I think it was a widespread Glamour," Chrysa said, like a mouse. She was so much quieter when she was weak.

The idea was almost preposterous, but the Fairy Court might be capable of something like that, especially with all the witch souls they had stolen over centuries.

Glamour was a fairy's natural inclination, making their world more beautiful, hiding the ugly, while not actually changing the true form of an object or being. It was essentially the ability to make an illusion, to mess with the mind's perception. It was a basic fairy skill, something even their children did instinctively, like Thom. But something so large-scale such as mass witch forgetfulness seemed a hair complex.

The women discussed the possibility of this worldwide Glamour. Wendy, a witch historian, spoke the most, and she became increasingly animated.

The conversation was going off-topic, so Sylvia cleared her throat and said, "Ladies... this is all beside the point. We need to figure out how we're going to survive this or maybe stop it."

"I don't think we could stop it," Wendy said with finality. "The treaty signed with the fairies actually is a good deal. It's a crime for fairies to come to the Mundane Realm and attack witchbloods, though I don't like being in Los Angeles right now."

"Then how do we not die?" Penelope asked. Her voice trembled. She knew what death's door was like, and she didn't want to go back.

"We fight," Chrysa said.

"We run," Patty said.

"Maybe we think first," Sylvia said, hoping to steer the group away from rash decisions. She did this all the time with her sixth graders, especially when they were in groups and the onus of responsibility was distributed. "What do we know?"

"We're gonna die," one witch said with terrible resignation.

"That doesn't feel right," Sylvia said. "It can't be that hopeless."

Another witch stood up abruptly. "I'm going to try to escape, and this is just a waste of time," she left. Two others followed her.

The resigned witch ate some fruit from the table, comforting herself from the perceived inevitability.

"Preparedness is the best tool," Sylvia said firmly. "And information is the best way to achieve an acceptable level of prepared." She looked each of the remaining women in the eye to show them her confidence. She wanted them to know she had control of the situation. But she didn't feel that way.

"What information do we need?" Ellie, Penelope's middle daughter, asked. Her black hair was pulled back into a loose ponytail. She tapped her fingers on her legs. She seemed ready to go out and do something. Sylvia admired that.

"How not to die," Penelope said and put a hand on her daughter's forearm.

Sylvia started spouting the things she thought might be useful and counted them out on her fingers.

1. *How to reliably spot a fairy.*

2. *Where the fairies were congregating.*

3. *Methods for debilitating a fairy or killing one if necessary.*

4. *Possible methods for escape from LA.*

5. *Places that might be safe to hide.*

6. *Is there a way to hide one's witchblood?*

7. *Is it better to stay in groups for strength or does that make them too much of a target?*

The conversation waxed and waned. Sylvia pulled books from her shelf, and they scoured them for mentions of fairies. They amassed a small amount of information about fairies and the 100-Year Hunt.

Some fairies were naturally inclined to malcontent. Dark-aligned fairies tended to be solitary creatures, and they were the original reason for the treaty. The fairy court had promised to make it illegal in fairy law to attack witches, unless it was during the Hunt. In exchange, they got unfettered access to the power of witches once every 100 years. Without an official treaty, it was very realistic that the elves in Europe would interfere. Balance in the Magical Realm was of utmost importance to them.

Since the treaty, the Fairy Court's strength grew tenfold. As pseudo-immortal beings, witches produced a large amount of magic. Their souls were like little factories. Fairies drew their magic from the environment. They didn't produce it. So possessing a witch's soul was like buying an annuity if not overdrawn. As the fairies consumed more witch souls, they'd get more powerful as the Hunt continued, making it harder to fight back, especially for a weak witch like Sylvia.

"It requires decisive action," Sylvia said.

"We're gonna die," Chrysa said. "It only gets harder as time passes."

"I wonder which witches have died already," Penelope said.

"Probably the ones closer to their base of operations," Sylvia said. "Which is why we need to figure out where that is."

"My friend Gia didn't answer her phone when I called about this meeting. And she still hasn't called back," Wendy said. "She lives in Little Tokyo." She looked down at the floor. "Maybe they're headquartered there. Or near there."

The pressure in the room increased as the women realized what conclusion Wendy had drawn: Gia was dead.

"I would try to contact every witch you've ever known and find out where they are," Sylvia said. "In the meantime, we're safer in groups. And we should practice some defensive magic."

"I've got no magic to use," Chrysa said. Bitterness soured her voice.

"Then you might not be a big target?" Sylvia said, trying to give her words an optimistic turn. She asked if Maria could make her a protection charm with a tremendous amount of luck.

The young woman got to work, using the found items that Sylvia had collected in her den.

The rest of the women gathered around Sylvia's defensive magic book. Sylvia had never needed it, because her life was decidedly not dangerous. She suddenly appreciated how incredibly lucky she'd been at Thom's house. Moving a couch, throwing a vase and slamming a door hardly seemed like combat magic, but those small actions had saved her life. She learned three new spells that might save her life.

The first was a hide in plain sight spell. It wasn't so much a spell as the absence of a spell. It involved the rhyme "What humans are, soul in a jar." It helped a witch withdraw her magic into a tight core, so her aura lightened or disappeared completely. With Sylvia's small amount of magic, it worked quite well. For a girl like Maria, it wouldn't be effective. When she had finished an array of luck charms enough for everyone in the group, Maria ignored that spell.

Maria took to the next spell quickly. It was more of an attack than a defense but luckily was included in the book, essentially an energy ball. A witch would concentrate her magic in her hand until it was too much then release it. Maria started trying it right away, until Sylvia reminded her that she'd like her home to remain intact.

They moved to the backyard, and Maria blew a hole in Sylvia's lawn. She smiled big.

Sylvia couldn't help but see the stark similarities between Maria and her mother. She sported the darker skin that Penelope had inherited from her Puerto Rican mother. Both their mouths were wide-set. And they both spoke English in a slightly off way that most folks couldn't pinpoint.

Ellie's and Loni's olive-toned skin, the narrow noses and the straight hair doubled their mousy dad's. They followed Maria's example with smaller holes.

"The magic in this spell is a bit unruly," Ellie commented. Her thick arms hung limply around her plump body. She looked empty and far away most of the time, and that unsettled Sylvia. It felt as if Ellie was experiencing the world in a completely different way than Sylvia did — something full of wonder and odd colors and puzzles.

Sylvia turned her attention to Penelope next. She directed her friend through the method of the spell carefully first.

Penelope needed very precise instructions or else her magic had the tendency to blow up in her face — or a tree, as Sylvia had seen on one occasion.

With a truckload of concentration, Penelope managed to singe the grass. She smiled softly. "It's been a long time since I've tried anything that dangerous," she said. Her magic was extremely fiery compared her daughters' powerful but stable magic — Penelope rarely used it, becoming a non-practicing witch. It was a rarity among their kind, but Penelope was neither a light or dark witch. If she had light magic, she would have orderly magic: usually less powerful but with a large amount of organization which was thusly suited to complex spells with many parts and required concentration and adeptness. If she possessed dark magic, her magic would fight with the strength of her emotion — shapeless and requiring a lot internal motivation instead of method. But Penelope had both types of magic in her, and it wreaked havoc on all of her spellcasting.

"I'm surprised you were able to do it at all,"

Chrysa said in a dull voice.

Sylvia elbowed her and turned her attention elsewhere.

Wendy made a respectable effort, knocking off the branches of a shrub.

Sylvia barely made a dent in the grass. She decided this wasn't her best shot, but she still memorized the method, just in case.

Chrysa did not attempt the spell. "Might as well try to get some sort of reserve," she offered as an explanation.

The last spell was designed specifically for magical opponents because it clung to their magic and pulled it down. A restraining spell for magic. This didn't require so much magic, but a lot of concentration and mental acuity and the removal of the spell was simple for the caster. Sylvia hoped it would be right up her alley. She was not disappointed. She tried the spell first on Maria, since the girl had so much magic. Sylvia imagined an anchor attached to a net and surveyed what she saw of Maria's magic to find the best place to latch on where it would throw her magic off balance. She spoke the rhyme: "Weigh down, way down." She felt little bits of her magic flit over to Maria. They attached themselves and grew, sucking in Maria's magic to hold her down.

Maria suddenly shook and struggled to steady her footing. She smiled through gritted teeth. "Oh this is weird," she said. She staggered.

"Try it on me," Penelope said. "I have a

theory." She braced herself as Sylvia concentrated on her desired goal. She said the rhyme and again the same thing happened, except Penelope didn't stumble. She laughed. "I was right. This only works on powerful magic," she said. "To me, it feels like a chipmunk is clinging to my shirt. A slight annoyance, but doesn't do much."

Her daughter was still swaying to keep her balance.

Sylvia disbursed the spell for both mother and daughter. "That's good," she said. "More information, so we don't waste this spell on weaker fairies."

Chrysa told everyone that she had more defense and fighting spells at her house, and everyone decided to break off into their own smaller groups.

Penelope and her daughters went to Chrysa's house to learn more spells and protect each other that night.

Wendy and the resigned witch would stick together. Patty would stay at her house and barricade herself in with her maids and security guard. Sylvia had David, and she realized they were most disadvantaged, her being the weakest witch in the group and him being only a human with witchblood. As a witchblood human, he had magic but was unable to use it. She figured though that he was very watchful and probably could see auras better than her — the ability to see magic was a benefit possessed by human witchbloods —

so they might have fair warning.

When the witches left, Sylvia locked all the doors and told David to put the blinds down. "We have the benefit of being close to invisible," she said. "Since I don't possess much magic and you have virtually none. Just a smidgen. That might be our saving grace in this Hunt." While David's unusable smidgen of magic made him a less likely target of the fairies, they would still kill him to get at it.

She and David read more of her books to find information. They poured themselves over the books, like melted ice cream through the exhausted hours of the night.

The knowledge they gathered this time was much more profuse than earlier that evening with all the witches around. This always happened with her sixth graders. She tried to keep them in smaller groups so they were more effective.

Fairies were elemental creatures so they tended to stick with their element of specialty. If you took that away, they couldn't replenish their magic quite as quickly. That information could make a large difference in their fight to stay alive. She wondered aloud if it was possible to find out a fairy's specialty element. And quickly. After she flipped through three books for the quandary, it turned out that she could make charms that would glow when in the presence of a fairy with that specialty. She retrieved her lost items box and picked out appropriate items to represent the elements: animal, plant, earth, sky, water and fire. Fire was a rare element for a fairy to specialize in because fairies generally gravitated to the less-wild elements. The fact that the Fauna Family was so good with the animal element was indeed a rarity, and their family's reputation for personality types was also unconventional. They weren't known for being reserved — quiet and classy — and so received the scorn of the other families. Similarly, fire-specialized fairies were few and far between. They tended to be fanciful and especially violent. Sylvia wanted to know if there was one in her vicinity, so she could get the hell out of dodge. She wrote notes for each item and put everything in a bag so that Maria could spell them the next day.

Onto her next question: how to spot a fairy at all. She scoured the books, and there seemed to not be any true physical identifiers. They — for the most part — were as varied as humans. Perhaps their features were generally sharper, but there were humans with sharp faces. And a fairy would Glamour themselves to look more human anyway, to hide the greenish hue of their skin.

So it would stand that maybe Glamour was the way to pick out the fairies. Any concentration of Glamour would be enough to find them. She thumbed through the index of a spell encyclopedia. Fairy dust, she smiled.

Fairy dust was actually a specially-concocted powder that detected the use of Glamour. Fairies certainly didn't make it, contrary to popular belief. They hated the stuff. So when preteen girls imagined fairies sprinkling fairy dust everywhere, they couldn't be more wrong. Sylvia loved this cultural misunderstanding. The fairies in these fables were just dusted and discovered, and they were trying to rid themselves of the dust by flying around wildly.

The recipe for the dust involved the collection of some unusual ingredients, including ground dwarf beard and hibiscus flower nectar.

Traveling into the Magical Realm while L.A. was cordoned off would probably not be the wisest of ideas. Or even possible. There were probably a foray of fairies waiting across the Veil to jump on the poor witch who tried. If one hadn't tried already. There had to be some way of getting some, though. Ground dwarf beard was not an easy-to-come-by ingredient. Most of the things existed in the Mundane Realm, but dwarf beard would have to be brought from the Magical Realm.

David had an idea for this, funnily enough. "We could contact a witch on the outside of the city. She could get it for us."

It was a marvelously simple idea and Sylvia wondered why she hadn't thought about it. But when she called witches outside L.A., none of them wanted to risk going to the Magical Realm at such an uncertain time, and Sylvia tabled the idea.

Chapter 10 - Thom

When Mother took him to Court, Thom tried to be his best. He didn't want a repeat of the day before.

They floated around the big room like clouds, tethered to each other with the unyielding strength of his mother's hand around his.

He didn't want to look at Mother. Instead, his focus tightened on a tapestry hanging from the ceiling.

The scene it showed was from a well-known bedtime story. A young fairy in the hands of three witches in a dead part of the forest. Their grotesque faces darkened with deep shadows. His mother told him the story sometimes:

Once, a long time ago, a young fairy girl did not want to listen to her parents. She was never back for dinner on time. She skipped past the borders that her father warned her not to traverse. She played jokes on the elder fairies, snickering with laughter when their faces displayed shock.

She was bad in every sense of the word.

After one particularly cruel joke in which

she dumped a bucket of pond scum on her father's head, she danced away from her mother's reach.

"Why do you always do this?" her mother asked.

"Why not?" the young fairy responded. Her face was gleeful!

Her mother tried to grab her again.

She skittered away into the forest, laughing the whole way.

The forest got darker and deader as she reveled in her grand joke. She didn't notice that she had wandered into a part of the forest that she'd never been.

"Oh, a delicious fairy," came a creaky voice.

"Young and supple. Always the best for stews," said another gravelly voice.

"Perhaps I'll use her skin for my new dress," said a third thin voice. "Green is my color, don't you think?"

The young fairy was no longer laughing. She looked around to find who was talking. But all she saw were rotting tree trunks and brown leaves. Where was her green and alive forest?

The witches pounced on her from nowhere. Their yellowing nails dug into her green skin. Their breath was foul, like death. They snarled, like a pack of wild dogs.

The fairy was caught. She screamed for help, but she was too far for her parents to hear. She had gone past their borders. She gave up, knowing she would be late again for dinner. She regretted all her jokes.

The witches devoured her.

Thom never particularly like the story. It made his stomach hurt. He imagined their gross teeth tearing into his arms, stretching him out, away from his body. He clenched his fingers until the feeling of teeth left him.

He wished he was home with Zoranna. Maybe then his stomach would calm.

To his dismay, the Court functions continued with absolutely no regard for his desires. Fast-paced music filled the room.

Thom imagined the notes dancing in complex patterns through the air and around the bodies of the fairies as they wordlessly began to dance the familiar Tree & Grass pattern. Thom loved this one. When other fairy children were around, they would dance this one whenever a musical fairy belted out the familiar melody. There would be screaming and laughing and running and pulling. But Thom was the only fairy child in Court today, probably the only one in Los Angeles.

He hated being here. He hated being alone.

Mother told him to stay out of the way of the dancers as she joined in.

The Court fairies and Mother were not smiling. Their movements were all precise.

Both sides of both lines of dancers started crouching. The fabric of their velvet and gold-trimmed Court tunics — the latest human-inspired fashion in the ever-changing Court — crushed in folds of their bodies. They swayed, linking arms, and brought themselves up to their full heights. They would rush forward, breaking into partners and spinning around. Patterns of grass or bark blossomed on the skin of the dancers. In the lengthy spin, green hair unfurled atop each of their heads. They were great big trees in this cave of a building. When the fairies began the next part, Thom stared in awe. Each of the women looked like a tree; the men were the lighter-toned grass. It was Glamour, but it was as if they had a forest inside the room.

Thom and the other children never used Glamour in their fun. They hadn't been taught to control it yet. He wanted to know how to do that now. It was so free and beautiful. But still the fairies weren't smiling. It was as if they had no clue how wonderful this was. It was the essence of magic.

He wanted to learn how to do that.

When the song ended, the dancers wordlessly went back to their conversation partners and resumed as if nothing had happened.

Mother came and took his hand again, pulling him to another conversation that he would undoubtedly find just as dull as all the rest of it.

He wanted to dance with Glamour following his lead, displaying brilliant greens and woodsy textures of the outside, spinning around until he was giddy with light-headed laughter.

While Mother chugged through the

pleasantries with the Court healer, Thom watched Duke Puck.

Sparks danced in his dark hair. His eyes were wide. His voice boomed like thunder. "I found her in the oriental district. But she wasn't exotic like those kitsune. I wouldn't have minded a little tango with a fox woman. But this witch was plain, by all accounts, and how she begged! These witchbloods are damned weak. A bit of a challenge would be appreciated, please!"

The Duke's slight and dark conversation partner nodded quickly. His head bobbed so vigorously that Thom worried it would pop off and tumble to the ground. "It's a shame. But at least you can collect a fair supply of magic. Though to you, I'm sure it is pittance." He wheedled. His voice wheezed. Thom didn't recognize him.

"We've been too easy on the witches. Maybe on all the Folk. Power grows on the backs of the lesser. We'll never beat the elves unless we're ruthless," said the Duke. His eyes bounced around the room unable to focus on anything in particular, sweeping over Thom.

He looked away.

War with the elves was subtle. Mother said it was like two children threatening to "tell" on the other.

"We need war," the Duke continued. "Posturing will accomplish nothing! They stay across the ocean, like scared dogs. But let me tell you, Maurel, we're cowering too. I have a hard time not being embarrassed. I swear if those witches knew how cowardly we are, they'd march right in here and take the jewels from the fingers of the King." The Thauma Family's King was the Duke's cousin, similarly thick and muscular. He was the youngest of the Kings and Queens. Mother told Thom to never look in his eyes. He saw conspiracy in even the brightest corners.

Maurel glanced in the direction of the Thauma king. He seemed nervous. "I think the King is more adept than that." He tugged at the duke's elbow before the man could speak further on the subject.

Thom snuck a peek at the Thauma king, who cast a heavy-lidded glance at the duke and Maurel.

Mother yanked his arm, pulling him to another conversation. His father was talking now. He had on an easy smile. His eyes set on Thom. "Oh, what a delight. Lady Estrelle, meet my son, Thomas."

He bowed his head at the busty woman, barely able to see her face above her humongous chest.

The lady's voice squeaked. "You're a very lucky child, Thomas. Not many parents would bring their child to an event with as much action as the Hunt. It's quite a treat."

"We like our son to —" Mother started.

"Nothing but the best education for our son," Father interrupted. He reached in front of

Mother and pulled Thom closer to him.

The wrenching on his arm sent a jolt of twanging pain up his arm. He caught his balance and moved his feet to ensure he didn't fall.

Father shaved his face daily, though he didn't really need to. None of the fine hairs growing out of his chin darkened or lengthened. His red full lips framed his sharp teeth. They shined in the way pyrite misled greedy fairies. Of course, the Lodes family fairies were experts in all sorts of minerals, and only the other families or unclaimed fairies might misunderstand his smile.

"They pulled me from school," Thom said. As soon as the words left his mouth, he knew he wasn't being good. But he suddenly didn't care. He might try to be good for Mother, but Father? He traveled separately to the Court every day, not wanting to enter when they did. He barely talked to them throughout the festivities, only pulling him over to boast. Thom hated him.

Mother's hand became a vice around his.

Before Lady Estrelle — of the Flora family — had a chance to comment, Father seamlessly made up some sort of excuse that Thom didn't care to hear.

He didn't care he'd be scolded later either.

Chapter 11 - Sylvia

Sylvia called in sick for the next two days of work. She didn't want to risk dying just because she wanted her students to do well. She did feel a little bad about it, even still. Substitutes these days were top-notch — at least sometimes. She hoped she got a good one as she emailed the school her lesson plan.

She and David scoured the internet. David was good at it. He knew how to find all the right chat rooms. The fairy court was in Downtown L.A. Apparently, they didn't know about the Mundane Realm enough to know that no one was in Downtown L.A. It was certainly not the hub of L.A. even though geographically, it was fairly central.

"Oh no," she said, "Wendy's friend Gia." She was dead, no doubt remained for Sylvia. The thought depressed Sylvia for a long minute, but she shook the negativity away. She had to concentrate and save everyone, even if she was the weakest. Thinking about the dead witches did not help.

"So we've got to find out what's going on

Downtown, maybe plan an attack," David said. He leaned forward in his chair.

"An attack?" Sylvia said. The thought jolted her. "Why?"

"Running and hiding and defending doesn't always work," David said. He looked directly at Sylvia now. "You've taken charge. A leader considers all his options. And the fairies won't expect an attack."

"I can't," Sylvia said. "I've always been against violence."

"That energy ball spell you taught them was violent," David pointed out.

"That is self-defense," she said.

"So is this," he said. "Plus, violence is violence. Even if it is in defense. Hell, the fairies might even see the Hunt as a defense on their part."

"You're making me regret sharing that spell now," Sylvia said glumly. She hoped no one would die because of her. The guilt she would feel, she didn't even want to imagine it.

"Sharing it was the best thing you could have done," he said.

He was resolute, and Sylvia wondered what course of events had led him to this line of thinking. And, for that matter, what course of events led her to her stoutly non-violent line of thinking?

She considered an attack — to see if it was something worth contemplating. Immediately, she imagined witches dying, and she shut it down.

She had David do more research on spotting fairies. Witches from everywhere chimed in on the internet chatter to provide their support and any bit of information they had.

One post — among many with the same sentiment — on a witch forum read:

Posted: 11-02-15 1:15 pm PST By: CherylsWhimsy

This is so absolutely unfair to all the witches in Los Angeles. My heart goes out to you all, fellow witches. I live in Bakersfield will gladly offer my home for any witches that manage to escape and need a place to stay. This is a disgusting practice. I'm so surprised that witches agreed to it, even back during the ghastly medieval times. Witch hunts are inhumane. This has to change!

Sylvia's heart swelled at the concern, and she hoped she would make it through. If not for herself, for all the people wishing her well. Though she knew it was probably hopeless. She wondered why she was staying as positive as she was. Years as a teacher had made her stoic in the face of a crisis. She could handle tantrums, meltdowns, bribes, destruction, self-destruction, and smooth talking. She'd seen so many conflicts that might seem small and insignificant in comparison, but to those children and parents they were incredibly important at the time. One mother had even tried to get Sylvia fired for giving her daughter detention. Nothing happened, but she admired the mother's fire. Sylvia knew how to handle trouble.

They sat and read and passed the time with hysteric calm. The kind of calm that was false and foolhardy but also necessary.

At four o'clock, Sylvia realized that Mrs. Potalecky would usually call at this time and inquire if Sylvia had any new charms. But the call hadn't come. Sylvia thanked her lucky stars that Mrs. Potalecky wouldn't insist on coming over and inadvertently risk her life.

Sylvia didn't know if her house was a beacon of magic in a sea of mundane, but as a witch, she was never too hard to find. Maybe they should've been at David's house. She suggested it.

"I don't know, maybe. I suppose that human witchbloods are less noticeable than witches, yeah?" he said. "You sure you can handle being at my house? It's not quite your OCD paradise."

"I do not have OCD," she said indignantly. "I can handle anything."

Sylvia ended up packing an overnight bag with some clothes and an assortment of useful trinkets and books. She took her time to place everything in her bag with care and order, putting the boxy and sturdy things on the bottom.

David's home was more of a teenage boy's room than a grown adult's mortgage-fueled house.

Cups of noodles littered the coffee table, along with an unhealthy helping of old rice on a permanently stained plate. Sylvia wondered how this man sustained himself. This was disgusting. The outside of his home looked pristine, she would never have guessed that this was — in fact — his space. It seemed outlandish to say the least. Science magazines and internet printouts of witch sightings spread out on the floor over the right side of the big gray armchair.

"Excuse the mess," David said. He was clearly not embarrassed by the state it was in.

Sylvia was about to go back to her home, but pride stopped her. She could handle anything. She would prove that.

David showed her his rifle collection. She stared at the barrel of a particularly menacing rifle. She wondered how many times he'd contemplated using it on her. How many times he relished the thought of killing a witch? He still seemed apt to do it if he didn't need her and her connections.

When she was appropriately settled in her relatively clean guest room — keyword is "relatively" with three gurgling and algae-filled fish tanks — she decided to brave it and ask, "Why are you so against witches?"

"Hmm?" he asked. The question didn't seem to register at first with him, but then his mouth hardened. "Both my mother and my sister were witches. Are, I suppose." He said it with odd finality like that was all that Sylvia needed to know.

But Sylvia had students like this who would only tell a little of the answer in class. She learned how to pull the answer out of them after years of practice. "What were they like?" she asked. The key was to ask a series of open-ended questions.

David breathed in sharply like he didn't want to answer. "Typical witches."

Sylvia raised her eyebrows. "How so?"

"Crazy bitches."

"What makes you think that?"

"Do you think you're gonna connect with me? We're gonna have some moment that humanizes me? And then, you still don't like me, but you'll forgive my assholery?" David spoke with clipped words — a staccato musical cadence. "Call me when the Hallmark movie ends."

Sylvia drew in a slow breath and pursed her lips. She held up her hands and said, "Okay."

David left the room, and Sylvia looked at the fish. The tanks looked very green and unkempt, but there were many fish inside: fish with feelers in the dark crevices, small bright fish schooling together, and an algae eater making slow progress on the glass of the leftmost tank.

Piles of books and papers avalanched when Sylvia tried to sit on the edge of the bed. She jumped up before more than one book and a sheaf of papers made it to the floor. Discomfort gripped her brain dripping into the wrinkles — a disgusting occurrence — but she tried her best to remain positive — at least there was no old food in this room.

She picked up the mess off the floor and set off on the task of organizing everything into respective sturdy piles along the inner wall of the room. Dust wafted in clouds as she smoothed the bedspread.

For some inane reason, they ate dinner together. Sylvia wasn't quite sure why. But they cooked in silence, passing each other's bustling with their own contribution to the meal. To his credit, the refrigerator was not as disgusting as she had feared. Sylvia made mashed potatoes with chives and a vinegary side salad. David sauteed some chicken breast.

They wordlessly made extra space at David's cluttered dining room table by just pushing everything away.

The clink of the forks and knives against the plates was their conversation until David said, "You think we have a good chance?"

The earnest question threw Sylvia, making her push back on the ground. The chair squeaked. "Uh, there's always a chance."

"Magic sucks."

"I don't think so."

"It makes witches crazy," David said.

"A very small subsection maybe," Sylvia said, narrowing her eyes skeptically. Magic sometimes muddled a witch's brain. They got a little "magic happy," as it were. It was often coupled with the eccentric stylings of the human myth of witches: cauldrons, cackles and coarse hair. Mix in the occasional easily-thwarted evil plan and warts arising from forgotten hygiene, and a crazy witch was born. But a witch really had to severely overuse her magic for that to happen; Chrysa hadn't gone crazy and she had really depleted her stores. "Witches aren't bad."

"100% in my family," David said.

"What's your mother's name?"

"None of your business."

"If you're badmouthing witches, it's my business."

"I'm a victim," he said with a prissy tone. "I was almost boiled alive." He was taunting her.

Sylvia was about to have some retort back about the use of the word "victim," but the other sentence processed. "V— boiled?"

"Wanna see my scars?" he asked. His eyes were bright, and his lips stretched wide over his teeth. Delightedly vicious.

He didn't wait for Sylvia's answer but instead leaned back to slammed his heel onto the table. The plates jumped. He pulled up his jean leg to reveal mottled and shiny skin.

"What do you think of your precious witches now?"

Sylvia reached out to touch the bumpy skin, but she stopped herself. "What happened?"

"Witches happened," David said.

"Not all witches do this," Sylvia said. "Not

104

even close to a small percentage."

"Happened to me."

"I'm sorry. I wish it hadn't."

"Your apology does nothing."

"It does something."

"What?"

"It expresses that this is not normal. You were hurt by someone not in their right mind."

"Because she is a witch."

"Because she is a being," Sylvia said.

"You're full of bullshit if you think witches aren't bad," David spat.

"I don't think I'm bad. Or any of my friends," Sylvia said firmly, though she felt like cowering next to David's unshakeable angry and determination. "Or my mother."

"I think you've got crap in your eyes," he said.

"Imagine if I held the Salem witch trials against you," Sylvia said.

"That's protection."

"That's insanity too," she insisted. "Witches died then."

"Humans did too. See? Humans are still victims. We are disadvantaged."

"You have a room full of guns. Don't tell me you're disadvantaged."

"You can throw fireballs and shit," David said.

"Bullets are faster."

"You don't need any tools. Humans earned

our tools. We made them. We invented. You just have your power. You didn't work for it."

She didn't know what to say. David was maddening and perhaps slightly accurate, but she didn't feel privileged over humans. They were just different.

Both of them left it at that. Sometimes conversations shouldn't be continued, because it would just serve no purpose. Nothing could ever get done with a man like David, she decided.

Sylvia went back to the guest room in silence.

It reminded her of her childhood, staying at her uncle's house. He lived in the Midwest, and she'd take a train to see him every summer because her parents worked all the time and couldn't go with her. The train in the late 1910s was busy and rowdy. She enjoyed the action. Every time she went, her uncle would pick her up from the station in his Sunday best. It made her so happy to be that special to him. She loved sitting in the room he'd haphazardly fix up for her and imagine what it might be like to be a farmer like him.

She remembered visiting him in the 1950s again, and he picked her up in his red pickup truck from the airport. His hands shook, and his skin was sun-spotted. His house now contained more creature comforts. He even had a TV, even though in the 1940s he'd sworn in a letter to her that he'd never get one. Even then, she stayed in the room he still kept cleaner than the rest. Its pensive vibe put her at ease. She would imagine a simple life where she wasn't a witch and that she'd be in her fifties, visiting her elderly uncle.

But as time wouldn't have it, she barely looked out of her twenties. Her uncle never mentioned her slow aging, though. He still took care of her like when she was the cutely dressed little girl. He made her grits and biscuits. He asked what was going on in her life.

She never told him that she was a witch. Would he believe it anyway? Her father hardly believed it, and he knew since Sylvia had been born.

How sad it must be to be her uncle or dad, watching their relatives never change as the ravages of time got them. She wondered if David was bitter about that. Knowing the possibilities, but being limited by his body.

The fish tanks trickled along steadily despite Sylvia's many frantic thoughts.

Chapter 12 - Thom

Adjusting his eyes from the bright day outside to the sudden darkness of the tunnel to the Court, Thom stomped, letting the echoes of his steps reverberate off the concrete walls.

It was his first day back at Court. Father had insisted he stay home after "his little scene."

Thom didn't think he'd made a scene. He stated fact. It wasn't fair, but he hadn't minded staying home. It was more of a reward than punishment.

Mother pushed open the gray metal door to the Court. Something was different. Instead of the usual milling and mulling, it was organized. The gray stone floor cobbles arranged themselves in a geometric pattern featuring concentric circles starting near the middle of the room, the focus of whoever Glamoured this room was changed. The fairies were similarly arranged facing the center of the room. The colors and textures of their clothes seemed to paint a pastoral scene.

Thom gazed between the bodies of the much taller crowd to get a peek at their focus.

A woman with gray eyes and stringy brown hair barely stood with her hands bound. Her red and brown long skirt was tattered, and blood smeared down her cheek. Her eyes flitted around as if looking for a sympathetic face. They landed on Grandmother. "Please, I just want to live."

Thom's stomach twisted. He thought of his teacher Ms. Hargrove.

Grandmother didn't say anything, just glanced at the Thauma king.

Thom looked up at his mother and asked, "Are they really going to kill her?"

Mother didn't answer. Her attention was completely on them.

He knew what the hunt was, but he hadn't actually thought too much about the witches. And he was getting that same icky feeling in his gut that he had when mother ordered him to stay upstairs at Ms. Hargrove's arrival at their house.

"My king!" Duke Puck strode towards the Thauma king. "I have brought a gift, for your personal harvest."

A murmur went through the room. "He went hunting himself?" "Who are his subjects?" "I wish I had thought of it."

Thom squeezed forward, letting go of his mother's hand.

The Thauma king smiled. It was small and polite. "I thank you, Duke."

Duke gestured toward the witch who shook her head vigorously, whimpering "please." He seemed to be waiting for something. "She is yours."

The Thauma king's gold embroidered tunic glittered in the light of the room. He merely smiled back at the Duke.

Thom looked between the two fairies, wondering what was going on. There was guile, finesse and restraint, but he didn't know to what end.

After a long moment, the duke's face fell. "Very well," he said. He flicked a finger at the witch. Lightning — disjointed and thick — careened towards her.

She shrieked.

The sound pierced Thom's ears, and he wanted to crawl into a ball. It hurt so much.

Amber magic ebbed out of the woman. It lit up the room with caramel tones, streaking in every direction.

The feel of magic was comforting, like Zoranna's embrace after he was crying, warm, safe.

But here, now... the magic ripped at the witch's skin, leaving it shining through the disjointed cracks. She wailed, unable to speak anymore. The noise twisted around Thom's ears, like the incessant warbling of morning birds being squeezed and squeezed until finally they were pancakes of their former selves.

Pain gripped his insides. He looked around to see how the other fairies were taking this.

Bored faces, bright faces, awe-filled faces. Mother had squeezed forward too. "It's the leeching," she said, not taking her eyes off the woman. Leeching was the letting of the magic, before the core — the center of the witch's being — was harvested.

The witch collapsed, gasping raggedly for breath. Her gray eyes rolled around, staring at the ornate wood and stone ceiling. Blood leaked out of the cracks in her skin. With barely a whisper of a voice, she said, "Please. At least let me become a ghost. I'm not ready to cease." She closed her eyes, and a tear oozed out.

Thom felt rooted into his spot. He didn't think anyone else had heard, but he couldn't break ranks and try to help her. He couldn't even use magic. He was useless, helpless.

The duke made a show of harvesting the vestiges of her magic, sparks and jaunts of lightning flying every which way. His lightning penetrated her chest. The witch's body convulsed. He pulled out her core with a lightning cage that contained it like barbed wire. The amber core was dense. The witch was lifeless.

Sorrow tightened in Thom's throat, and a strangled cry escaped his mouth.

The Thauma king locked eyes with him. The disapproval and appraisal laid heavy in the room, more eyes pointed at Thom.

He shrunk, hiding behind his mother, hoping they would forget him. Her fingernails dug into his skin.

Luckily, the duke seemed unaware of Thom. "For your pleasure, my king," the duke said, presenting the lightning-encased magic.

The Thauma king waved away the lightning, as if it were a fly, a mere nuisance to him. He reached out and grabbed the core. His body stiffened as lightning wrapped around him. It coiled around him like a great big snake.

Thom didn't understand. He looked at the duke, who wore a grin as big as the sun.

A collective gasp dominoed through the room as the Thauma king fell to the ground, mere feet from the dead witch.

Mother grabbed Thom's shoulder and pulled him away from the crowd to the edges of the Court room. "He killed him," she said. Her face was a mixture of wild, awe and fear. "That bastard did it right in front of all of us." She smiled. "He's got guts."

"Why did he do that?" Thom asked. He still didn't understand what he had just witnessed. The witch died, the king died. Everything felt weird.

Mother's eyes fixed him. "And you!" she exclaimed, then lowered her voice. "People are going to think you sympathize with them! Never — " she gripped his arm hard "— ever, ever, do that again. We're lucky Duke Puck is a crazy son of a bitch. Everyone has already forgotten you, I hope." Mother sucked in a sharp breath, turning her attention one again to the crowd. "The duke is king now."

Thom's stomach twisted. He had just witnessed an assassination. He didn't know what to think.

Father came over to them. His face was similarly awe-filled as Mother's. "I am surely glad to be born into the Lodes family. The Thauma family changes too much and the treachery is astonishing. I am glad we are steady and secure like the rock of a mountain."

"Does this help us?" Mother asked.

Father shook his head. "We just need to hope that someone takes King Puck's place soon. He is touched in the head. That is good for no one." Then he smiled. "But it was interesting." He left them to speak with Grandmother.

"That was terrible," Thom said.

"That was fun," Mother corrected. She and Father were very different from him.

Thom's face burned. He didn't like it one bit.

Chapter 13 - Sylvia

By Saturday, the resigned witch was no longer in contact with Wendy because she had insisted on going home by herself after the second night. Sylvia tried to contact the witches that had left her meeting prematurely on Wednesday. None answered their phones. She hoped they'd made it out of Los Angeles, though that didn't explain why they didn't answer their phones or let Sylvia know how to escape. She accepted that they hadn't made it.

"You're being stupid," David told her. "They're picking us off one by one, while we cower in waiting. They just get stronger with every soul they suck dry."

"Why don't you fight them then? Huh?" Sylvia bit back. It irritated her that she couldn't protect anyone.

"You might think I'm dumb, but I'm not," he said. "I can't take them on by myself. Or else, believe me, Sylvia, I would've already. I don't plan on dying soon."

Sylvia had nothing to say. She didn't want

to think about it.

But David checked the Internet chatrooms and found that the numbers weren't good. Some estimated that as many as 150 witches had been killed. That was a high number. She didn't even know 150 witches in her entire life.

Would hiding be that effective? Knowing that so many had died already wasn't comforting. Perhaps they should try to run.

David agreed that it was worth a shot. He snorted, making a snide remark about how she was finally doing something he had told her.

They didn't prepare, didn't call anyone, and just hopped in David's car. The lack of preparation was unlike Sylvia, but the dead witches had panic rising in her throat. She had to do something — at least try — she figured. That desperation made her reckless.

They cruised north on the 170 for a few minutes. Sylvia rolled down her window and let the wind rip at her hair. It felt a little crazy and wild. Not at all appropriate for a woman her age, but she nurtured this feeling. If she was going to save all the witches depending on her, she needed to take risks.

Once on the 5 for a while, she rolled up the window, and her hair was a nest. But she wanted to feel the wind again.

"We should probably keep the windows closed now," David said. There was a hint of a smirk in his voice, and Sylvia turned to confirm her suspicions. He was laughing at her. He thought she was silly!

She pursed her lips trying to keep a smile away. "Have something to say?" she said playfully.

He took his eyes off the road for just long enough to throw her an amused look. "Nothing at all, Fido," he said.

She laughed loudly. "Woof woof," she said. The silliness was a welcome change.

They reached Newhall Pass fairly quickly. The freeways separated and came together here. It was quite an engineering feat, the bridges and tunnel conveying the multitude of commuters. Sylvia liked the grandness of it. She didn't often have reason to be here, but she admired with awe when she did.

She watched for signs that fairies were around or that Glamour was in place. She did not see any signs. She let herself hope.

Hope is a dangerous thing, because the next moment Sylvia was blinking confusion from her eyes. Their car was gently drifting onto the right shoulder.

David's eyes drooped as if he was in trance. Sylvia yelled and grabbed the wheel before they skimmed the concrete wall. She kept a firm grip on the steering wheel and elbowed David in the chest.

"Wha--? Huh?" he said. His voice was unfocused.

"Watch the damn road!" she shouted.

David snapped to attention. Once she was

sure that he was in full control, she relaxed her grip on the steering wheel and eventually let go. They sat in silence for several long minutes when Sylvia realized that they were going in the wrong direction, heading back towards L.A., towards home.

David must've realized too, because he asked, "What happened?'

Sylvia shook her head. "I'm guessing Glamour coupled with a control hex." It was powerful stuff. That scared her. The fairies had to be putting out an enormous blanket of magic for that kind of widespread control. She thought of all the witches who died for that kind of strength. That kind of consistent magical output was gross, frivolous and terribly wasteful. Like gambling a house to win a car. She had to imagine that magical power wasn't the goal of this. It was fear-mongering, terror-mongering.

There wasn't much to say, so they made their way back to David's house.

She was convinced, though, that hiding alone and terrified was not the correct course of action anymore. That's what the fairies wanted. They wanted them scared and alone, hoping to be the lucky one passed over.

She called everyone and expressed her worries. They would go to Patty's house, since it was big enough.

When she and David left the house, she expected the streets to be barren, like a desert. But it was business as usual. She wasn't sure if she should feel disappointed or enthralled. Disappointed, because no one would even notice if she died. Enthralled, because her town would still be intact when this was over. She loved L.A. for all of its quirks and unbeatable weather.

Two cars passed the house as Sylvia and David packed their few things into his car. Sylvia tried to play it cool, but she used the hiding spell just in case. She felt like she couldn't trust anything. She ran back inside to retrieve the fairy specialty charms that she had charmed the night before, and, at first, she barely looked at them. Just as she got to the threshold of the front door, she looked down at the charms in her hands. The fire charm was glowing. Her eyes snapped up.

A tall, lanky and blond man strolled just ten feet from David. He had his hands shoved in his pant pockets. His dark eyes crinkled around the edges when he looked at David, and his mouth pulled into a toothy grin that was anything but friendly.

He did not look in Sylvia's direction. She had a chance! But she froze, not knowing what to do. She'd never needed to fight to live.

David looked up at the man, and even from her distance, she could tell the exact instant when he imagined his death in excruciating detail. He also froze.

Even his fighting instinct was failing him.

The fairy stared at his victim. Everything

was still for a long moment, which gave David false hope that he was not going to die in a matter of seconds. But the fairy's wait was more a let-me-enjoy-your-fear-for-a-second pause.

Sylvia knew it was up to her. She stuffed the charms in her pockets and sidled down the lawn. The fairy was too captivated with David's wide eyes to have noticed her yet.

Fairies didn't have auras like witches did, but the air around them became fuzzy and hard to concentrate on for too long. And with the amount of blurriness hanging around this fairy, she figured that the restraining spell would have a fair effect on him.

Under her breath, she whispered the words to the spell: "Weigh down, way down." She released the magical darts towards him. That's when he turned and bored down into her soul. He looked a bit disappointed but still hungry. When her spell hit him, his left shoulder jerked like someone had just pulled him backwards. He was quickly stumbling to maintain balance.

Sylvia thanked her lucky stars that she had guessed correctly that the restraining spell would be helpful. She stepped toward him with shaking limbs. She wracked her brain for a spell that might debilitate him. The only one that came to mind was a spell she and Chrysa had made up more than a few years ago. They'd cast it on each other and blather like idiots for a few hours before it wore off. She pointed her index finger toward him and said, "A drunken stupor is for humor."

The fairy stopped cold. His head swayed, then a wide smile broke out on his taut face. He laughed. It was as if someone had cut a string in his mind and unleashed a torrent of bouncy balls. With the restraining spell and the drinking spell, he couldn't even stand. He rolled on the ground laughing. "Y-you're... so weak!" he exclaimed between gasping laughs. "I... can't be... lieve that... you... undid me... like this."

Sylvia smiled, very pleased with herself. "Where are the fairies headquartered in Los Angeles?" She used her authoritative teacher voice.

"Opera... house," the fairy said.

"What are your plans?" she asked.

"Eat all the witches I can," he said viciously, then burst into laughter — an egocentric hyena.

"How'd you find me?" Sylvia asked.

"The fat lady with all the charms," he said. He seemed particularly pleased with himself.

Sylvia frowned — Mrs. Potalecky — and was about to ask another question when the fairy's head sort of disintegrated. She let out a strangled scream. Terror stopped the brunt of the noise. But the loud boom was not stopped. Sylvia's brain was scrambled, but she took a panicked moment to process. David was holding a handgun. The fairy was clearly dead. No one was outside yet.

Her decision was made. She ran toward the car, roughly grabbing David's shirt and dragging him with her. She shoved him at the driver's door and ran around the other side to rip open the passenger's seat. Was she trying to escape from a murder scene? Definitely, yes.

David put the car in reverse before Sylvia could even buckle up.

"Why'd you do that?!" she half-screamed. She twisted her whole body around and craned to get a view of the body. The Glamour was dissipating, revealing a green-hued, much thinner, much shorter fairy under the façade. That was the fairy's true form. She didn't think she'd ever seen a fairy like that. Fairies tended to only die alone and thus their bodies were never associated with their public persona. They used Glamour so much that only in death was their true form revealed.

"He was going t—" David said.

"Why would you do that?" she yelled with hardly-controlled rage.

"Someone had t—" he said.

"That was a life," Sylvia said. Her fingernails dug into her jeans.

"I would do it again," David said with calm resolution. "When you were finished asking questions, what would you have done?"

"Spelled him!" Sylvia said.

"With what? I'm sure none of your spells are lethal," David said. "Imagine when your spells wore off. He'd be pissed. He'd know what we look like. Could you live with yourself if that fairy came back and killed one of the three daughters of that woman?" He meant Penelope, she realized.

Sylvia looked down, ashamed.

"That talented blue witch girl." Maria. "She dies because you thought a sleeping spell was enough," David said accusatorily. He took his eyes off the road for a good long second and looked Sylvia directly in the eye. "That could've been your fault. This is why I don't like witches."

She shook her head. "We can't just kill indiscriminately."

"He said his plan was to kill all the witches he can, Sylvia. I don't know how much more clear it needs to be for you," he said. He made a last minute right and hopped on the freeway.

Chapter 14 - Thom

Grandmother took them to a cafe in Santa Monica.

The air was thick and salty. Humans whizzed past on wheeled shoes, bikes, and their own feet. The smell of local food surrounded them in a cloud of meat and sweet sauce.

Wind chilled his body, and Thom pulled his jacket closer to him.

Mother pinched his side.

He twisted his body away from her hand. "Thank you for bringing us here." When he saw her approving face, anger seared in his face. She never made any sense.

Grandmother smiled. "You are a credit to our family."

"Of course!" Father piped in.

"He's our son after all," Mother said.

Thom wished he could kick them.

Grandmother rolled her eyes.

Pride surged in Thom's chest. He wasn't the only one who thought that way about his parents. It felt good that an adult, the Queen, shared an opinion with him.

"Puck's coup was... unsavory," Grandmother said. Her pale pink lips pressed together, the wrinkles deeper than when she smiled.

"Entirely inappropriate," Father agreed quickly.

"Shocking really," Mother followed suit.

It was like watching a troop of goblins playact being heroes. It was painful, the embarrassment.

Grandmother sighed slowly. "Enough. You two annoy me."

Mother — who had been about to further agree — closed her mouth abruptly with an audible clash of her teeth.

"Mother," Father said to Grandmother. "We are just —"

"I have avoided choosing my successor for many years."

Mother and Father both straightened in their seats. It reminded Thom of the time he was in the Flora capital city, joining his parents in the spring festivities. Zoranna was with them that time, and she took him out into the city. The streets of the giant city were alive with masters of magic. Some were merchants, blooming vibrant pink flowers before accepting coins from a housekeeper for their creation. Some were performers, battling vines against the most pliable tree Thom had ever seen to the delight of all sorts of Folk. One master seemed separate from all of it. Thom stopped amidst the crowd to watch the old fairy conduct his hands in front of a small patch of tall grass. It was the only unkempt plants that Thom had seen since his arrival. But as the fairy worked his magic, the stalks of the tall grass swayed, stood straight up, and leaned in time with his hands. No one was giving him coins, but Thom watched for several long minutes, mesmerized by the uniformity and control. His parents were just like those stalks of grass, at attention, ready for commands.

A waiter brought the ribs to the table, and Mother stared daggers into him.

Thom wringed his hands and did not grab the delicious-smelling food, remembering his manners — Zoranna had drilled him.

When the waiter was gone, Grandmother began again. "I have avoided choosing my successor, because I wanted to ensure my safety."

Father and Mother both trained their eyes on Grandmother. They seemed to be at a loss for a response.

"Yesterday has proven to me that I need to make other provisions," she said, reaching for a rib.

"You think you will be killed like the Thauma king?" Thom asked. The second Grandmother finished retrieving her food, he zipped to pick his own. He took a bite of the meat. It was so soft that it just fell apart in his mouth.

The sweet and tangy sauce covered his lips, and he licked it up. Humans made delicious food.

Grandmother took her napkin and wiped it on his face. The paper was rough, and she pressed too hard. "Hopefully not after this," she said. "But the world is not how it used to be."

She was speaking directly to him now. He swallowed the meat in his mouth and the flavor dissipated in his saliva.

"There used to be honor. Not just coup here and murder there. It's terribly dull. We used to make things happen with finesse," she looked out at the sea. Her ember eyes flamed but reflected back the blue. "We're getting further and further from what really matters. We, fairies, need to be strong. In-fighting will only further divide us."

"Don't we always fight?" Thom asked. "Mother says it keeps us on our toes."

Grandmother shot Mother a look. "Your mother sees the world as a gauntlet."

"I do n—" Mother started.

"Quiet," Grandmother's voice cut like steel against a pillow. "She always wants to fight. Even now when she will get exactly what she most desires."

Mother's face perked, and she drew her shoulders back.

"It is her nature. And there are benefits to being like her. But a future king cannot want war for the sake of war." She pointed to father then. "A future king cannot also say yes to everything, lie and agree just so that he seems desirable and good."

Father did not respond, but his face fell and grew red.

"A future king must know when to fight, when to lie, when to make nice, when to wait, when to be honest, when to be kind. Your one-dimensional parents can never do that. Do you understand that?"

A terrible weight crushed in on him, and he nodded because what else was there to do?

"Unfortunately none of my other children are much better than my son," Grandmother said. "A good queen does not make a good parent. I suppose I am not as skillful as I had hoped."

Father's face dipped to the deepest crimson that Thom had ever seen it.

"Luckily, it skips a generation."

"To me?" Thom asked. He wondered where his grandmother was going with this.

"To you, correct. Very astute. Somehow, you are the one grandchild who has managed to be free of those nasty traits — arrogance, hostility, stupidity and docility." Grandmother looked at his parents again. "I have decided to name Thom my successor, with you two as regents."

Mother's eyes bulged.

"I don't want to be successor," Thom said, looking for Mother's approval at the statement.

Mother shook her head then nodded.

Thom knitted his eyebrows together.

"Yes, you want to be successor," she hissed through her teeth.

His face burned. "I don't think I do." He wasn't as good as he wanted to be. He didn't care. He didn't care.

A pair of seagulls squawked with their piercing screams over the beach. He watched them spiral down towards the sands where a beach picnic sat unattended. The bigger of the seagulls pecked at the food and snagged a diagonal cut sandwich half — fanning its wings to claim the food. The smaller seagull gouged at the larger seagull. They screamed and ruffled their wings. Finally, a family in puffy jackets that made them look like tire sales mascots shooed the birds away in a flurry of feathers and hands. The youngest one cried as the parents threw out the food.

"It's not like you have much choice in the matter, Thomas," Grandmother reminded him. "I have made arrangements."

The comment pounded into Thom's chest. She was the cruelest of them all. He hated her too. He just wanted to climb trees and have Zoranna hug him. He wanted to be away from these rules, away from Mother and Father and Grandmother with their schemes and demands. He didn't care about power. If he never learned how to use magic, he would be happy. That's how much he didn't care.

He didn't talk to any of them the rest of the afternoon. He didn't eat any more of the ribs.

Their deliciousness was tainted and sullied.

Mother and Father eagerly accepted their future roles. Their faces were all smiles. Their questions were all platitudes. Like Grandmother had not insulted them terribly, like that didn't matter one bit now they would be regents.

He hated it all.

He saw the kings and queens of Court. They wore stuffy clothes and were forever assaulted with frivolous niceties and gifts that meant nothing. And like Puck, assassins and ill-wishers stalked every corner. It was not freedom. It was the opposite. Power was nothing.

A heavy weight pulled down his limbs. Not even the car ride back to their "borrowed" home cheered him up.

As Grandmother and his parents made plans for the next day, Thom stalked upstairs and slammed his bedroom door with every ounce of strength that he had. The noise wasn't satisfying. Air caught the door and pillowed it.

He groaned.

His body felt like it would burst from the anger and pressure. No one cared about him.

He wanted Zoranna. He had to go see her, no more waiting for her return letter.

Chapter 15 - Sylvia

Neither of them spoke when they arrived at Patty's Pasadena mansion. He pulled up to the overgrown ivy gate and pressed a buzzer. Sylvia yelled through the open window that it was just her and David. Without a word in response, the big heavy gates swung in towards the house to welcome the two witchbloods.

The front gardens were magnificent. The driveway split into two sides to give way to a path-lined fountain with the most precisely managed hedges. Amongst the hedges, there were a brilliant array of red, yellow and orange flowers that contributed to the awe-inspiring overkill of the place.

"Rich people," David said shortly.

Patty came out of the house wearing an Hermes robe, made out of silk with a beige cherub design repeated throughout. She looked concerned. "You're the first to arrive," she said.

"I might've been the closest," Sylvia reminded her solemnly, getting out of the car.

"Let's get inside," David said gruffly

through the window. "We had an encounter with a fairy." He parked the car alongside the house while Sylvia recounted the story for Patty.

Just as David rounded the corner of the house, Patty's blue eyes shot to him, and she said loudly, "That's awful."

David didn't stop, but his eyes lingered on both women as he passed.

Patty's house was filled with stuff. Rich and expensive stuff. Little knick-knacks and hard-won trinkets. Patty had done some world traveling, most witches did nowadays. Except she went in impeccable style and wealth. Sylvia was a little jealous. She could mostly only afford places with neon open signs, not some place that laid claim to being a favorite spot of Beyonce or Prince William. She was sure Patty could go to any of those places.

Patty had recently gotten a beautiful mahogany armoire that Sylvia had come to see and help lift. It was in the entry way. It was a grand entry way, but still normal and welcoming. No antique swords hung on the walls, which was, of course, the defining factor of "not normal."

In the kitchen, Patty instructed the two housekeepers and one guard with an abridged version of why there would be an eclectic group of women coming to the house. "But no one else is allowed in," she said. Despite her age and experience, her voice trembled through the tail end of the lecture, Sylvia noticed.

Everyone was properly introduced. Leticia,

the head housekeeper, sported crisp white gym shoes and a neatly pressed uniform that she had clearly bought from a uniform store. Her gray and dark brown hair was pulled into a tight bun. Everything about her was serious. Mora, the assistant housekeeper, might've been Leticia's daughter, though neither of them mentioned it. She was dressed in the same uniform, but her shoes were a worn but clean pair of converse. She was crisp but somehow very warm. Jonathan, the guard, seemed peculiar. He drawled in a half-hidden country accent and had the swagger of someone who had been in some position of authority. His uniform was definitely custom-made, it even had a company logo.

David didn't bother hiding that he had brought guns with him.

Jonathan grew rigid and wary at the sight of them. "Mrs. Greene, are those weapons sanctioned? Shall I check them?" he asked.

Patty looked at him, then at David. "Use your judgment."

Jonathan examined the guns, ensuring that each had its safety on before returning them to David.

Sylvia didn't want to draw more attention to the guns than necessary, so she said, "Where's Mr. Greene, Patty?" Patty's husband was often away anyway, but she liked to inquire to be polite.

"I sent him away. Told him that he couldn't come back to L.A. until I called him," she said. "He always misses out when something is happening." The thought seemed to please her, and she smiled.

"That worked?" Sylvia asked incredulously. Thomas Greene was a very singular man. Stubborn was the way Patty had always described him.

Patty gave a little smile and shrugged her shoulders. "When you threaten divorce to a devoted husband, it works."

Rooms in the same wing as Patty had been made up for all the witches they anticipated. Sylvia put her stuff down in one and left immediately. She didn't see David in the hallway, so she followed Patty back to the kitchen.

"I think one of my patrons is dead," Sylvia said quietly to Patty at the kitchen counter.

"What? No!" Patty said. She patted Sylvia's hand. "I'm so sorry. What happened?"

"That fairy that David killed. He said that's how he found me. She hasn't called me for several days either. She always calls," Sylvia said.

"If they can find a human with your charms, they're going to find us," Patty said. Her eyes darted around, scanning the windows for anything lurking outside.

Sylvia nodded. What else was there to say? What could they do? She wondered if she should just resign herself to the fate. Lots of witches died during the Hunt. That was unfortunately the point. But maybe that needed to change. Since the treaty with the fairies, there hadn't been any sort of governing body for the witches. They hadn't needed one. Most witches respected one another and followed the local laws, as opposed to some universal witch law. But perhaps if they banded together they could stop the horror that was the Hunt. Her whole body ached just thinking about it.

Penelope, her daughters and Chrysa arrived within the hour. They hadn't encountered anything but had needed more time to gather their things before driving over to Pasadena.

Loni, Penelope's youngest, had bloodshot eyes and huge bags underneath them. She didn't handle stress well. She shook and started crying without anyone saying anything to her.

Sylvia put a reassuring hand on the girl's back. "We're all trying to protect you, honey."

Loni's face broke, and she let out a terrible pained noise. "That's the problem! I don't want anyone dying for me."

Sylvia rubbed her hand over the girl's back. "I think any one of us —" she glared at David momentarily "— would do that for anyone else here, honey. We want to make it through this."

David was on his laptop at the kitchen bar, already doing more research. He didn't look like a man who had just killed someone. Though, what did a killer look like?

Sylvia set Loni on the task of cutting onions for the stew that Patty was making to distract herself. She showed the girl how to curl her fingers so, at most, only the knuckles touched the knife. It'd be terribly ironic if someone lost their fingers during the Hunt to... onions.

The onions burned both her and Loni's eyes. Sylvia laughed and told the girl it was her job now. She hated when onions made her cry. It was stingy and she just hated the sensation of crying. She'd seen too many tantrums and meltdowns from her sixth graders to see the value in a good cry anymore. Crying accomplished nothing, at least for her, and though she sometimes still did it, it wasn't cathartic. It was a gut reaction to circumstances.

Chrysa had regained some of her magical supply. She sat at the kitchen table and frowned.

Ellie, Penelope's middle daughter, took a seat at the bar and looked at nothing in particular. Ellie had always been the shy one of the family. She hid behind her mother when she was little and faded into the background as she grew older. The distance that always existed between her and everyone else was odd.

When Ellie started to pull the leaves off the plant on the counter and fold them, Sylvia sat across from her best friend at the table. "How's it been?" she asked.

"I feel useless," she said.

"Everyone makes mistakes. You had no idea."

"This is the mistake that'll probably kill me," she said.

"I'll probably die too," Sylvia admitted — quietly — more freely than she had ever been with herself. "We've lived long lives. I'm more concerned about the young ones."

Chrysa shook her head. "You might be selfless at a time like this. But I want to live, I really do. There won't be any consoling thoughts from me."

"What do you think we should do?" Sylvia asked.

"I wish we had left L.A. before all this," Chrysa said wistfully.

"Let's think in terms of actual possibilities," Sylvia said. "We could go far, to the farthest reaches of L.A. and hope that the fairies have too much to do to consider attacking us. Maybe the time would run out?"

Chrysa didn't answer. She probably thought it was pointless to still discuss options.

"We could hunker down here. Take a stand," Sylvia said. As she said it, she looked around the room — wondering who would have what it took. Only David, and she didn't like his methods.

Chrysa shrugged. "It's a plan like any other."

"We could try constantly keeping on the move," Sylvia said. "Get an RV, only stop for gas, never present a lasting magical presence. Maybe they won't notice us." The idea was certainly out there. But perhaps it was worth a chance. She quickly ruled it out when she realized that any fairy they passed would surely know. It would be a chase.

Chrysa looked out the window and didn't respond.

David turned away from his computer suddenly and said, "There's a rumor on the internet that if, during the Hunt, a witch goes directly to the fairy court and asks for immunity, it must be granted."

"What?" Sylvia asked in disbelief.

"It's a rumor," David clarified.

"But it sounds like what the fairies would do," Sylvia said eagerly. "About pomp and circumstance and honor and rules."

Penelope — who had mostly been quiet up to this point watching Patty and Loni cook — said, "The court fairies participate too. Hunt, like it's a sport." She spit the last word.

Sylvia nodded glumly. Her mind had fast-forwarded past "fairy court" and had zoomed to "immunity." She looked out the window with Chrysa and watched the plant life outside in silence.

The greenery reminded her of the time she went to Guatemala six years ago. She had stayed in Guatemala City to see Iximche, some pyramid-like temples an hour and a half outside the city. While the ruins had been amazing to see, her favorite memory from the trip was actually meeting a Guatemalan grandmother at a shop in a street market. The old woman described herself as a step-grandmother, as she had married into the family after all the children had been born, but before the grandchildren came. She loved them dearly, was even helping out with one of the children's street shop. And she was a witch, a powerful one, though she would never have told her family.

Sylvia had stopped her whole day to talk with this woman. They had exchanged the usual pleasantries. Sylvia told her about how it was to teach sixth grade with its constant rehashing of city history, consonants and vowels, numerical expressions and highly mediated art projects. Sylvia found out the woman used to have another whole family in Mixco, the second biggest city in Guatemala, but she had stayed much younger than them, and eventually she had to fake her own death because she had never told her two sons about her magic.

Before she and the Guatemalan step-mother had parted ways that day, the old woman had offered this advice: "I wish I had not hidden. I love my new family, but I would still love to be with my sons." She explained that once she hid, she grew fearful. It made her weak, made the hard decisions even harder.

Sylvia concentrated on the waxy green leaves of a bush outside. She breathed in and out slowly. She felt her magic swell in her body. She wanted to know what she wanted to do. Her magic felt tumultuous and wild. Her meager amount of power was ready to do something. But she didn't know what. Was it hide? Was it run? Was it stand steady?

She couldn't tell. It was all just a mish-mosh of mixed emotions with a whole lot of fear in there for good measure. She wondered if the rest of the women's magic was this unstable right then.

Ellie put down her seventh destroyed leaf and said, "I think it would be nice to be a plant."

The odd statement broke Sylvia's meditative concentration; why would the girl want to be the thing she just destroyed? Every conversation with her was like this — serenely making outlandish statements. How did Ellie stay so calm while everyone else seemed terribly tense amidst this life-shattering situation? She asked the young woman.

Ellie shrugged. "It'll turn out okay," she said. But she said it with quiet confidence. "Not the best outcome, but better than others."

"Why do you think that?" Sylvia asked.

"I know," she said. "I see it."

Did Penelope's daughter just admit to having precognitive ability? So nonchalantly? It startled Sylvia. The power of Penelope's daughters. The Zaragoza line of witches was truly remarkable. And everything was going to turn out fine? Was that something possible? "Really? What do we end up doing?" she asked. "Are all of us okay?"

Ellie pressed her lips together and didn't look Sylvia in the eye, the girl rarely did. "I don't think I should say anything," she said. "If I tell you, it's possible that it changes, and my mom and I have discussed that we do not want that. None of the other possibilities have been good, so I said things to change them, but this one is acceptable." Tears threatened to fall from her eyes on her otherwise dull, unemotional face.

The new knowledge didn't relax Sylvia. What was good enough? What would they do? But if Ellie thought she couldn't say anything, Sylvia figured she shouldn't pry. She asked instead about the precognitive ability.

Ellie said that she'd always had it, but she hadn't known what it was. Precognition wasn't visions for her, she explained. It was like memories. Constantly altering memories. The closer the time, the more clear and real it was. The farther off it was, the less certain and fuzzy it was. Like remembering babyhood was tremendously hard, so was remembering the far future.

Sylvia asked why she hadn't seen the Hunt.

The girl said, "I was having headaches for the last year. And it wasn't quite working right. On Halloween, that dissipated. But I didn't really understand the future memories until you called us to talk. And they were constantly changing, so it's hard to get a good grasp on what's going on until there are less options, and the time is closer."

"They had the Glamour on us for that long?" Sylvia wondered aloud.

Ellie shrugged.

Sylvia wondered what it was like to have

memories of the future. It had to be cool... but confusing. Her grasp on reality had to be so rooted to be able to tell the difference. Witches with precognitive abilities sometimes couldn't handle it. It was a great and terrible gift. A particularly famous precognitive witch by the name of Crazy Cassandra had been known to throw herself into dangerous situations, because she saw it in her visions. Despite her penchant for danger, Cassandra died of sickness, back in the 1800s. Sylvia had seen a few excerpts about her in magical history books.

"Do you like it?"

Ellie gave another shrug.

Sylvia excused herself and wandered around Patty's huge house, with her permission. She entered one room, and an oboe prominently featured in the center, though music sheets were strewn about carelessly. She remembered then that Patty had mentioned once that her husband played oboe. It was such an odd choice, Sylvia had thought and that thought crossed her mind again. She'd never met Mr. Greene. But Patty still would occasionally gush over how romantic he was.

She made her way up to the room that Patty said she could stay in. She thought about unpacking, but she had an inkling she'd be packing soon again and decided against it. She admired the large bureau opposite the bed. She thought it might be hand carved. She opened it and was greeted by neatly arranged designer handbags.

Each was in pristine condition. Prada, Louis Vuitton, Gucci. Sylvia wondered why she had never seen Patty with them.

She lay down on the bed and tried to sleep. She figured out pretty quickly that wasn't going to work. Sleep was obviously not the answer. She decided to wander some more.

In the hallway, she heard Penelope's normally gentle voice take on a rough tone. "No, Mark. You can't come." Sylvia knew she shouldn't snoop, but she planted her feet in the wide hallway and magicked her ears so she could hear better.

"I don't care what you think you can do," Penelope said.

"I have to protect my family," Mark's voice came out tinny through the phone speakers.

"I will not forgive you," Penelope said.

"You'll be alive."

"You heard what Ellie said."

"I don't care," Mark said.

A click and the call was over.

Sylvia unrooted her feet and scurried her way downstairs — being caught would mean she'd have to say something. She passed the sitting room next to the entrance hall. Maria was sitting inside, poring over a book.

Sylvia drifted over to her. "What are you doing? Homework?"

"I'm not even thinking about homework," she said in misery. "I'm trying to memorize as many spells as possible."

Sylvia sighed slowly. "Spells are like mermaids, Maria. You can see as many as you like, but if you can't catch one, there is no point."

"What's the point of catching a mermaid?" Maria asked.

"To get their scales? They're good for some spells. Highly sought after," Sylvia said. She waved her hand to dismiss the thought. "Anyway, I was saying that you should practice them instead of read. Very few witches can read a spell and do it right the first time."

"You did that with the restraining spell," Maria pointed out.

Sylvia shrugged. "I'm good at that sort of thing, because I'm very careful and even if I mess up, my magic is weak. But if you think you can do that, do one of those from memory," Sylvia gestured to the book. "Any one."

Maria stood and put a plastic cup from the kitchen on the table.

Sylvia reflexively took a tiny step backward.

Maria stared hard at the cup. She actually made a scrunched up face as if she was concentrating so hard.

Sylvia couldn't help but smile, though she could immediately tell that Maria wasn't going to succeed. The only thing to do was be prepared if it went awry. She subtly put a containment spell around both Maria and the cup. The spell was invisible, but she could sense it and that was enough. Plus, she didn't want to overuse her magic. She hoped she was judging Maria's level of restraint and safety correctly.

The cup sagged a bit. Sylvia wondered what the young woman was trying to do. Perhaps a melting spell, but that didn't seem so useful in their present predicament. A little flame appeared on the plastic. Sylvia came forward flapping her hands at the flame to put it out. "Whew," she said. "Don't want burn down Patty's nice house... or anyone's house for that matter." She added a smile to assure the young woman that she wasn't mad.

"I was trying to make it into a flashlight," Maria said with an over-exaggerated frown.

"A flashlight?" Sylvia asked. She almost laughed. The spell was not what she needed at all.

"It's useful. And for practice, I thought it was a good idea," Maria admitted.

Sylvia thought for a moment before she said, "I think the starting point is to figure out what kind of spells you might need, considering your power level and your skill level. What do you think?"

Maria huffed. "I don't know. What do I need?"

"Depends on your goals, I guess,"

"I want me and my family to survive," she said.

"At what cost?" Sylvia asked.

"Any," she said.

"Even if you had to kill someone? Even if you had to let a demon lay claim to your soul?"

Sylvia asked. She wasn't trying to be mean, but the girl was starting to cry. The demon example was extreme, but she'd heard of it happening in the last Hunt. And killing was already happening.

"I don't know, I don't know," she said, grinding her teeth to keep her concentration.

On the table, there was a tray with a decanter of some sort of alcohol, Sylvia guessed. She removed the decanter and picked up the silvery tray. It probably wasn't silver, but all she needed was some metal substance, preferably shiny. There was a spell when she was a kid that she loved doing, and she thought it might actually be helpful for the hunt. A non-violent attack. Sylvia liked that better than a violent one, though she didn't like the terminology "attack." Burst spell was a much better name for it. Though a rose by any other name would smell as sweet, an attack by any other name would still technically be an attack. But phrasing and terminology was oddly important, because intention was impactful and an important consideration; magic tended to follow a witch's focus and intention more than her words. Intention first, that's what Sylvia lived her life by.

She showed Maria how to concentrate her magic and create a burst of light that left a person temporarily blind, even if they were wearing sunglasses. It was mostly for getting away suddenly, but it could be followed up by a stealthy attack, she supposed. It'd work best against a powerful but clumsy or frenetic opponent, she figured.

When she was a kid, she liked the brightness and she'd sit on their kitchen door's wooden stairs and do the burst spell on an old spoon. Her mother always hated when she came inside with her long dress covered in dust. Since she didn't have siblings, that was her fun. Once her mom had her start working on charms to sell, she didn't do so many fun spells. Her family was better off than the average family. Her dad made enough to support them all, which wasn't common at the time, but that was because he was too old for war. And her mother sold her charms to buy the family nice things from the catalogs and the door salesmen. Sylvia got to keep her earnings from the charms. She bought books. It was a simple time.

It took a bit of explaining and demonstrating for Maria to get how to do the spell. There wasn't a rhyme for this one, she just had to imagine what she wanted, a bright burst of light to come off the surface. Sylvia also explained how to put it on a delay of sorts, so she could throw it and have time to cover her eyes. For the purpose of practice, they did not throw the tray and instead put it down on the nearby couch. Sylvia let the light fade from her eyes, then had Maria try it. After two tries, the young woman got it, and Sylvia was very pleased. No moral dilemmas with that sort of spell.

"So, once they're distracted," Maria started. "What would I do next?"

"Whatever you're prepared to do," Sylvia said quietly. "I have no place saying what you're comfortable with. What do you think you'd do?"

"I don't know," Maria said.

"Well, y'know what? We should practice non-violent, non-deadly and deadly spells, so you're prepared for anything. The kind of decision you will make will be made, but if you don't have a wide skill set, that decision might be pointless and ineffective," she said. "Did Chrysa give you more spell books?"

Maria nodded and showed Sylvia the array she had.

Sylvia skimmed the titles and her eyes settled on "Everything You Need to Know: Combat Magic." It wasn't particularly used, and Sylvia figured that Chrysa had received it as a gift, because combat wasn't necessarily her friend's specialty. Chrysa's specialty was telekinetic for the most part with some transfiguration and fire in there. She thumbed through the pages and found something that was deadly but not gruesome. Some of the spells seemed like they'd cause a mess, and she didn't think the young woman standing next to her was prepared for something like that. It was a suffocation spell, anatomical. Perhaps her sister Loni would be best at this one, but Sylvia thought Loni was much too young to teach her something like that without her mother or her asking for it directly. "This one," she said aloud to Maria. "Read this, and the reversal."

Maria took a long minute to read it. Her fingers clenched.

Sylvia felt so sorry for the girl. Maria had not grown up in war, and it made her unprepared now. Of course, she'd been growing up around the time of the Afghanistan and Iraq wars, but those had never impacted daily life for Americans, unless their family members had been soldiers.

Sylvia was old enough that she'd seen enough of the world and knew what type of person she was. She was prepared to do her all for kindness and good. And even still, she didn't even know what she would do if the time came in the next week that she might have to use deadly force. In a way, David had done the hard work for her with the fairy earlier that day. And that allowed her to be properly outraged and feel innocent of wrongdoing. She wondered what she would have done otherwise, and she had no idea.

Sylvia was confident she could do the spell without testing it, because she had a knack for that, but she knew Maria did not have that skill. She sucked in a sharp breath. "I want you to practice it on me," she said.

Maria shrunk away with a pained look on her face, like it was something she didn't want to do.

"You want to know how to do it, right?" Sylvia asked. "Just keep that reversal in mind, and I'll do my utmost to reverse it myself if need be. But I'll only do that if I think you can't do it."

"How're you so sure that you can reverse it?" Maria asked. She looked doubtful.

"I understand magic and my limits very well," she said. If nothing else, Sylvia was competent. She took to most things quickly. Made Chrysa jealous, and made Sylvia a little arrogant, but that was tempered by her weak and meager magic supply. However, Sylvia wasn't as confident in her ability to reverse Maria's spell as she was letting the young woman believe, but she had to put herself on the line. It was a calculated risk to hopefully benefit the whole group if need be, if Maria would make a decision like that down the line. "You should at least try."

Maria breathed in and out slowly. She had to take this very seriously, or else something could go very wrong. Sylvia was glad to see this. A determined student was always her favorite type.

After a quick moment, Sylvia felt a terrible tightness in the front of her throat, but it wasn't quite cutting off her air, just made it uncomfortable to breathe. She shook her head at the girl. "Not on the right spot," she said in a huffy voice. "Do the reversal, it's a bit uncomfortable."

Maria stared hard, and Sylvia felt no change. Maria raised her eyebrows in quiet question.

"Still there," the older woman said.

She considered undoing it herself, because she surely would've suffocated by now if the spell had been done right. But Maria had to learn it herself.

"I'm not quite getting how to reverse it then," Maria said.

The reversal involved pulling only the suffocation spell away from the throat, but magic was clingy and didn't always want to let go. If even a bit remained, it was still somewhat effective. She explained to the young woman how she usually brightened the appearance of her own magic by spending a moment focusing on it before reversing it.

Once again, Maria concentrated.

The spell peeled away, Sylvia could feel it. She breathed in, pleased and relaxed. She smiled and gave the young woman a thumbs up. "Very good!" she said. She loved when her mental tricks worked for other people too. Maria was a light witch, so their magic's temperament was likely similar.

Light magic witches didn't take quite as easily to destructive spells. Chrysa was a dark witch, and her magic was more rough and powerful and unwieldy. Dark magic usually was. That was what made Maria's super powerful light magic so rare. Light magic was more controlled, calmer by nature, and usually weaker but precise. A powerful light witch was unrivalled, but on average, dark witches were more powerful and effective. It had something to do with the wildness of their magic. "So," she said with a big grin. "Now for the placement of the initial suffocation spell. It should've been further back."

Maria nodded with an eager but calm demeanor. Determination was great to see.

The Zaragoza family was truly remarkable, Sylvia thought. Their grandma was a well-known witch. Sylvia had met her a few times. The woman lived in Santa Barbara and she ran an interesting consulting business that specialized in negotiation. Grandma Maria Zaragoza was a talented mind control witch, which wasn't technically hard, but the finesse and subtlety the woman possessed was well-regarded. As a professional courtesy, Ms. Zaragoza didn't use her ability on other witches, at least that's what she told everyone. Sylvia could never be sure, because Zaragoza's talent was essentially unnoticeable. Of course, regular humans just thought she was very convincing, and that's how her business thrived. Sylvia thought about Penelope and her three daughters' skill sets. They were a force to be reckoned with. If anyone would survive this, they would. It was sort of the obvious outcome, if there were witches to survive. Chrysa was her next pick for survival, only because she had accidentally used up her current supply of magic on Halloween and had not quite recovered. At her full power, Chrysa was easily the pick, because she had so much experience and so much power. And her impulsiveness was probably an asset when fighting unknown opponents.

Sylvia's own cautiousness was perhaps a detriment when quick decisions were required.

She liked to be careful and surviving the Hunt might not actually call for that, once put in a directly deadly situation.

Maria tried the spell again, and Sylvia felt the tightness again, but she didn't quite understand the effect until she was getting lightheaded. She held up her hand and immediately did the reversal spell, because she wouldn't be awake in the next moment.

Sylvia sat down on the ground and let the dark spots from her eyes clear. After a few moments, she said, "It would've knocked me out. I had to reverse it." She was glad she was actually able to undo the young woman's spell.

Maria dropped to her knees. "I'm so sorry," she said. "I didn't realize!" She put her hands out to comfort Sylvia or help, but she didn't know what to do, so it just looked silly.

"'Ts okay," Sylvia said. She smiled to reassure her. "I think we learned somethin'."

"What's that?" Maria asked. She looked so upset.

"We have a knock out spell!" Sylvia said with vigor. "You cut off the circulation in the arteries in my neck. No blood was getting to my head. I would've been unconscious in a second or two more, I'm sure!" Her voice squeaked.

"You seem a little off-kilter," Maria said. "Are you sure you're okay? I really don't like hurting people."

"Can't think quite right, right now," she

admitted. "But it's a valuable spell." Then she put a hand on the girl's shoulder. "Still not in the right spot though. Artery inside of windpipe."

"Sorry," Maria said and looked down at her hands.

"It's alright, we got a secondary spell out of it that you might like more to use," Sylvia said. She stood up, bringing the young woman with her. "Once more though! You're getting the hang of this." Sylvia was surprised at her own enthusiasm. She was hiding her shaking very well.

"Are you sure?" Maria asked again.

"Definitely," Sylvia said, feigning confidence. While she was trying to exude bravado, her hands shook imperceptibly. She steeled herself for round two. A teacher must take risks — usually her risks weren't so life-threatening.

Maria concentrated again. And right away, Sylvia couldn't breathe. She held her hands up, so Maria would know to do the reversal. It was extremely painful and terrifying to not be able to suck in a breath. Fear seized up her limbs, and Maria was taking too long. Sylvia was so concerned about not being able to breathe she couldn't remember the reversal spell. She stopped attempting to breathe and focused on the spell. Just when she was going to reverse it, her breathing came back. After a moment of stick-still confusion, she gasped for air.

"Oh god," Maria said, rushing forward.

"Was it that bad? You didn't seem that under duress."

Between gasps, Sylvia managed to squeeze out, "I was keeping calm for both your sake and mine." Her eyes were tearing, and she looked up with a weak smile. "Never going to volunteer for that job again. Suffocation was terrifying and painful."

"I am so sorry!" Maria said profusely. After that, she refused to test anything on Sylvia.

Sylvia's body fidgeted because of the intense panic; she thought overall it was a good method, though she certainly wouldn't do it again. She was way too old for it. She hoped it was enough for the young woman, but she suspected that the girl would not use the spell. She was not a destructive person. Sylvia knew that Maria was the type of witch to use her magic for great works. She was good, through and through.

However, what happened in the next hour proved that her sister Ellie — the awkward and quiet middle daughter — was nothing close to that.

Commotion brought both Maria and Sylvia to the front door.

A husky man with soft features and big arms stood red-faced with his foot blocking the thin-armed Penelope from closing the door.

Sylvia's heart raced. She wasn't ready to be attacked so quickly. She needed more time.

"Dad?" Maria said.

Sylvia expelled air like a compressor.

"You can't do this to us," Mark growled.

"I've decided, Mark," Penelope said. Her normally subtle Puerto Rican accent came out strong.

"I need to protect my family. We're married, Penny. We vowed to stick together through thick and thin. I want to help. I don't want to be shut out because I don't have magic."

"You can't do anything close to help," Penelope said coldly. "You'll just get in the way."

Sylvia had never heard her friend like this. How could she talk so dispassionately?

David came up next to Sylvia and asked loudly, "What's going on?"

"What about him?!" Mark almost shouted. It seemed like an artery might pop in his temple.

Without missing a beat, Penelope said, "He's a warlock. He has magic."

Her friend lied so seamlessly that Sylvia drew back. This was different from how she usually was.

"There must be something I can do," Mark said firmly. "I can't sit in that hotel room any longer and wonder if my family will be alright."

"You can make sure you're there for us when this is all over."

"This isn't right. You're lying to the gi—" Mark started until he swayed and stumbled. As his thick body lumbered to the floor, an invisible pillow seemed to catch him and soften his landing.

"Dad!" Maria shouted as she ran forward to

155

check on him.

Ellie walked up to him out of nowhere. "Sorry, Dad."

"YOU did this?!" Maria shouted angrily.

"Yes," Ellie said. Her face was innocent. It was peculiar — for Sylvia — to see the utter blankness on the young woman's face. Even her more conniving students would have some glimmer of shame on their faces when they admitted their wrongdoing.

"WHY?!"

"Dad was going to get himself hurt. There is no point in all of us being in danger unless absolutely necessary," Ellie said.

Penelope nodded in that way mothers did — a slow nod with a tilt and the subtlest of smiles to express approval without outright enthusiasm.

"Mom?!" Maria's eyes bugged out of their sockets.

"We need to protect Dad," she said gently.

"By making him faint?! This is so stupid," Maria said. She kneeled down and shook her dad.

Penelope put her hands on her oldest daughter's shoulders and held her firmly. "Just wait. We should discuss this in private."

"I'll bring Dad," Ellie said before spelling him to float in the air as if on an invisible conveyer belt.

The family disappeared inside.

Chapter 16 - Thom

He left before sunrise, while the air chilled him through his jacket. The sky was cloudless, and the navy blue lightened to gray blue.

He would make it to Kentucky and then somehow cross over into the Magical Realm to Tirt. He didn't know how yet, but he set his jaw.

Getting out of the house was easier than he had expected. The house was silent as he crept down the stairs and out the front door.

He walked east on the sidewalk. It's all he had to go on. There was a park in the distance, maybe he could climb some of the trees before continuing, get a good look around. Mother hadn't taken him there, telling him he should be mature — no more climbing trees.

A woman pulled up next to him in her shiny black car. "Hi darling," she said in the high-pitched voice that adults used when they spoke to children. He hated it.

Thom didn't look up and just kept walking.

The tires of her car crunched against the pavement of the road. "Where are you going, honey?"

He knew he shouldn't tell the truth. He was running away after all. "Home," he said. It was innocuous enough.

"Where are you coming from?" she asked.

Where did human children walk home from? "School."

"Honey," the woman's voice got sharp and low suddenly. "Now, I know that's not true."

Thom glared at her. How could she know?

"It's Sunday, before sunrise. No kid walks home from school in the morning."

He had no response; he walked harder, letting his shoes slap the ground.

"Where do you live? I can take you home," her voice was high again.

"I live in Kentucky," Thom said, hoping maybe she would drive him there.

She continued to follow him. With one hand on the steering wheel, she dialed on her phone and brought it to her ear. "Yes... I want to report a runaway... Yes, uh-huh... No, I'm not his mother... He's just wandering on the street... Okay, will do... How long?... Thank you."

"Who did you call?"

"The police."

The fairies didn't have police, but they had the Guard. He ran then, not wanting to be caught. His legs and lungs burned.

She was still following him, not even breathing hard, because all she had to do was let the car roll. "Please stop," she called to him. She and the police were going to bring him back to his parents and his grandmother.

Anguish tightened his stomach. He sprinted for the park at the end of the block. If he just reached the trees, he could hide and escape this woman.

He tripped on a crack in the ground, flying forward onto his hands and knees. His leg jolted from the impact. His hands burned, and tears filled his eyes. Getting off the ground was harder than he'd anticipated. Pain gripped his knee, making it hard to even bend, and he limped in the direction of the park.

"Please stop," the woman said. This time her voice sounded more desperate. Her car came to a stop, and out she stepped.

Thom made to run again, barely three steps into the nerve-shattering jog, her hand was on his shoulder. "Let me go!" he screamed at her, knowing it was useless but doing it anyway. If he could kick her, he would; his leg hurt too much.

The police came with their pressed black shirts and wide stances. The uniformity was more imposing than the hodgepodge of outfits that the Guard wore.

The shorter man kneeled down and looked into Thom's eyes. "Where are your parents?"

Thom pressed his mouth closed. He didn't want to go back to his parents, but he also didn't want these uniformed humans to have him either.

The woman and the police officers talked out of earshot for a few minutes and the tall one left to knock on the door of the nearest house. Thom inched closer so he could hear what they were saying.

"I just didn't want to hear on the news about a kid found dead, y'know," the woman said.

"You did the right thing," the short police officer said. "Thank you, ma'am."

The Right Thing, the phrase struck Thom as important.

The woman smiled and said something else that Thom didn't catch.

"It's standard procedure, ma'am," the officer said. The woman sighed relief and hopped back in her car.

She had done The Right Thing.

The sun rose above the horizon by the time the officers were knocking on the door of his family's "borrowed" house. Apparently the police had found out which one was theirs. He didn't know how.

The short officer held Thom's hand. "We're just going to have a conversation all together. Nothing to be worried about. Do you have anything to tell me before your parents come?"

"No," Thom said, still hoping that maybe something would change.

But his father answered the door. His sharp face sharpened as his eyes flicked from Thom to the officers and back again. "What is this?" he asked. "Why do you have my son?"

"We found him trying to run away, sir," said the short officer.

Thom stared into the dark entryway. It felt like the entrance to a cave, dark and foreboding. He did not want to go inside. He wanted to be back with Zoranna.

Smiles and apologies welcomed the officers into the house.

Thom's throat tightened as he was pushed inside.

The short officer mentioned The Right Thing again.

It echoed in his brain like some taunting mantra. Thom started to cry. Father set him with a glare, but that didn't stop the tears.

The officers stood in the entryway taking up so much space. Maybe they would just leave without talking to Father too much. Maybe everyone could just forget him.

Thom stared at the pictures on the walls of the other family through watery eyes. Glamour immediately warped the images until they resembled Thom and his parents — his father had seen it also. Thom couldn't figure out whether or not he was glad.

"Has running away been a problem in the past?"

"No, sir," said Father.

His fingers grasped Thom's shoulders so tight it hurt. Tears streamed down his face. They were going to say he was bad. And he still would not see Zoranna.

"What's with the tears, son?" said the short officer. "A man doesn't cry." He smiled, like that was supposed to make his harsh words any gentler.

"They're going to make me king," Thom blurted in a whine. "And I still can't see Zoranna."

The officer chuckled. "King, you say? I think I'd like to be a king."

"A real king," Thom spit out. Adults were all the same. No one took him seriously.

The officer's mouth made a flat line. He smelled like coffee and sweet things. The smell was overwhelming, and while he might've usually enjoyed it, the saccharin scent made him want to throw-up. He felt absolutely terrible.

Thom backed up, hoping they would leave now. At the least, maybe he could just go to his room and cry.

Chapter 17 - Sylvia

The weekend passed at Patty's Pasadena mansion. Sylvia spent most of her time with Penelope's daughters. It had been decided behind closed doors that Mark would be kept sedated in Patty's panic room for the duration of the Hunt. Maria stalked about grumbling. Loni seemed even smaller and birdlike than she had been before. Ellie was a stone — unchanging and stoic.

When Sylvia sat down with Ellie, she wasn't sure what to say.

The young woman stared out the window, humming to herself. She nodded her head to the beat of her hums.

"Are you seeing the future now?" Sylvia asked. Everything in her body was set on edge. How did one deal with someone so... off? Was it even fair or kind to think that she had to "deal" with Ellie?

Ellie did not stop her staring or nodding. "No, I'm waiting for you to talk."

Sylvia let out an uncomfortable laugh. "Well, uh, I was thinking that..." She trailed off, because Ellie seemed not to hear — eyes still focused outside. "You're listening?"

"Yes, but you haven't really said anything."

Sylvia felt her face getting hot, but she continued talking steadily, hoping some of it was being absorbed. She explained the burst spell, describing the intricacies of the visualization. She kept stopping, checking Ellie's eyes for any sort of recognition.

When Sylvia asked Ellie to do the burst spell, the young woman took the silver tray abruptly and did a little hand motion. Tendrils of mauve magic danced to the tray. A blazing flash of light blinded Sylvia, and it took her a moment to recover. Sylvia had not been expecting that. "You were paying attention?" she asked incredulously.

"Of course I was," Ellie said. "It's rude not to."

"You weren't looking at me."

"I use my ears to hear, not my eyes," Ellie said. "Can we do some more complex stuff? I like the light trick. It's just... I want something more forceful."

Sylvia realized right then that Ellie had already considered what she might need to do and had decided to do it. It was refreshing to see such decisiveness. Though the rough manner in which the young woman was expressing that caused Sylvia to be taken aback, until she considered the situation. Her family was in mortal danger... but — Sylvia reminded herself — Ellie had always been like this, awkwardly abrupt and painfully direct, even since childhood. "What are you thinking about?" Sylvia asked.

"How I will save my family," she said.

"What do you think you're gonna do?" Sylvia asked. In the group, she knew both Chrysa and Patty enough to understand their roles and limits, but these sisters — as young as they were — would be wild cards when a fight inevitably began. While Sylvia wanted to protect them at all costs, their group's survival depended on the skills and power the Thin sisters possessed. Having children fight with her? It would've been preposterous a week ago. And now? She was actively helping them learn spells for violent protection. It went against everything she had ever stood for: letting kids be kids and being kind even in the face of adversity. But she didn't want to be unprepared, and she didn't want to break her promise to Penelope. "Proper planning prevents poor performance." She didn't know when she picked up that alliteration, but it stuck with her and sort of became a motto.

"A lot," Ellie said without hesitation. "More than my sisters would."

"That's bold, Ellie," Sylvia said, genuinely surprised.

"Like my mother, I understand the finality of death," she said, looking directly into Sylvia's eyes. Then she looked back out the window. "Maria told me that you taught her a spell that she could use to kill someone. I need something like that."

Sylvia literally took a step back. It was so blunt, and now she felt like she was a monster. Teaching kids how to kill someone. "It's not like I wanted her to use it, but I thought she should have the skill, in case she decides she needs it."

"I'm not saying you're a bad person. You're not. You're taking responsibility," Ellie said. She leaned to the left and then to the right. "I want to know. And I'm fully prepared to use such a spell." Her voice was steady and even.

Sylvia nodded. "Did you have a spell in mind?" She wondered how she could help the young woman when she was already quite good at sight-reading.

Ellie pushed the combat magic book into Sylvia's hands. It was open to a spell on laceration. "This one," she said. "And..." She flipped a few pages. "This one." The second was a burning spell.

They were deadly and gruesome. Sylvia wondered how such an innocent young woman would choose these first. And then she remembered Ellie's attack on her very own dad and her newly-revealed precognitive ability. She had perhaps seen these spells in the future and decided she needed to know how to do it to make that future come true. That took a lot of foresight and bravery. Sylvia doubted she would prepare herself like that. Ellie would do what it took.

It turned out that Ellie had already practiced both spells on a pillow from one of the upstairs bedrooms. She could easily do both spells, but the control required for precision was a bit more finesse than Ellie had yet achieved.

Sylvia helped the girl focus and aim better with the laceration spell. Together they created the ideal mental image for Ellie to use to concentrate and only cut what she wanted to cut. It didn't take too long before Ellie had become precise enough to cut only the thread holding together the seam.

The rate at which the young woman took in information and internalized it was astounding. Sylvia felt almost useless as a teacher. Just before she'd get to the meat of an explanation, Ellie would remark the point or demonstrate the skill discussed. Sylvia was impressed and a bit envious, if she was being honest with herself — probably something she should do more.

When they moved on to fire, neither of them was equipped for the task. Both were light witches, and when Sylvia suggested another, less chaotic spell, Ellie flat-out refused. Sylvia told the young woman that she'd think on it and that Ellie should go relax for a bit. Ellie left carrying another book under her arm.

Sylvia brushed aside the gray hairs that had fallen from her bun and sat on the couch. Sunlight streamed in through the windows, and dust particles hung in the air, only visible in the rays of light.

Fire was not so much a substance as energy in one of its more wild forms. It was hungry and destructive, which was slightly different from the way electricity was. Admittedly, electricity was wild too, but it did not consume everything like fire tried to do. Fire was much more suited to dark magic, like Chrysa wielded. She — like the fire she commanded — was a force of nature. And Sylvia didn't try to change that. Was there a way to not change fire and still have some semblance of control over it? She didn't know.

She fingered the lace of a crocheted throw draped on the couch and examined the complex pattern that resulted in the beauty of the delicate piece. It was a form of organized chaos. Thread went in every which way, seemingly disorderly up close, but when she examined from further away, it culminated in an orante piece. Controlling fire might be like controlling all the threads — crocheting one thread until a blanket of fire is created. She knew that was not how Chrysa would think of the process, but she was a dark witch and handling the wild nature of things came instinctively for her. She met passion and craziness with her own passion and craziness.

Sylvia moved off the couch and went out the front door. In the middle of the driveway, she sat and began testing her theory. Stones on the pavement dug into her. She blocked the annoyance from her focus. She only called to being the tiniest bit of fire. She channeled its nature into a fiery tendril. Little blips escaped the tiny fire column but, for the most part, she was able to direct it.

Penelope came outside and sat with Sylvia. "I hear you're helping my daughters."

Sylvia hardened her mouth but nodded. "Yes, if you would like me to stop—"

"Thank you," Penelope said, putting a gentle hand on Sylvia's shoulder. "They need it, and I can't help."

For as long as Sylvia had known her, Penelope rarely did magic. Eventually Sylvia had plucked up the courage to ask why. Penelope explained through a half-sour smile that she had been born with a mixture of light and dark magic, something that Sylvia had never heard of. It seemed quite impossible. Penelope explained that when she was a girl, things exploded around her all the time. The orderliness of her light magic coupled with the wildness of her dark magic caused things to break. She accidentally caused a lot of fires, which is why her mom moved to Santa Barbara to a beach house. Eventually she just had to learn not to use magic and actively contain it. The few spells she could reliably do were small and took a lot of effort. It was why Penelope looked so amazingly young, despite technically being 50 years old. She never used her magic, never ran even close to empty, so she never aged. Now, Sylvia smiled at her friend and said, "It's a pleasure to help your daughters. If you want me to work on certain things as opposed to others, let me know."

"I trust my daughters, and I trust you," she

said.

She was really a mother, Sylvia thought. And the kindest and gentlest she knew. Penelope had learned self-control at a young age, and that permeated in all her relationships.

Penelope left Sylvia to her fire experimentation. Sylvia felt an overwhelming sense of love, and she couldn't help but smile, despite the situation that they were in.

The air was cold, and she decided to work on a second tiny column of fire. She practiced for several attempts and had them spinning around each other as if in some elaborate mating dance. She added a third column and a fourth. In thirty minutes, she had what resembled a curtain of fire. It bent to her will and did not randomly burst from her control.

She found Ellie and had her practice it too. Together, they perfected the method, as best they could in such a short span of time.

Over dinner that night, each of the Thin sisters explained what they had spent their Sunday on. Sylvia was struck by how normal everyone was acting. It was as if they weren't actively being hunted. It made her hope that maybe they could live out the rest of the week in Patty's mansion and emerge after the end of this week, unscathed, unscarred.

Chapter 18 - Thom

Mother locked him in his room for the whole day. Not even the windows could open.

Father had yelled, and Thom earned another stinging red handprint on his cheek.

He was so powerless, so weak.

He wet his pillow with salty tears.

"I hate them," he said quietly. "I hate them."

Sadness and hopelessness swirled in his entire body, making him feel uncomfortable in every position. He stared at the little blue car.

Maybe he should just let his parents get their way. Maybe he should just stand quietly behind them at Court and wait for the rest of their visit to come to an end. Maybe he should just ignore how ghastly it is here. Maybe he should just stop caring that he liked his teacher, that she was a good person. He didn't want to see her harvested like the witch at Court. He didn't want to see any of the witches harvested. But maybe he should pretend he didn't care. It was easier.

It wasn't The Right Thing, he realized with such clarity.

He picked up the little blue car and pushed it on the dresser. He followed the car's path, not letting the wheels leave the surface. He rolled it down the side of the dresser and onto the floor. The little wheels squeaked.

The Right Thing was impossible. Fairies killed witches. It was for survival.

He pushed the car up onto the wall. The wheels scratched the paint, leaving parallel trails of light gray.

Was it really survival? Thom had never killed a witch, never harvested her soul. Yet he was alive.

When his mother brought him some dinner on a thin white plate, he said to her, "How many witches have you hunted?"

She pushed the plate toward him, the fabric of the white blanket folding underneath it. "Your father's workers have gotten four so far."

"But you've never hunted?"

"No, I don't need to."

"Why not?"

"We are able to pay other fairies for the work."

"Do all fairies hunt?" he asked.

"No," Mother said. Her ice blue eyes narrowed on him.

He was surprised she hadn't chided him for his frivolous questions yet. "What do those fairies do?"

"Who?"

"The ones who don't hunt?"

"They work. There are many ways to harvest magic."

"How?"

She explained to him about mining, the magic present in the rock. It clung to the hard sediment and minerals. As the laboring fairies hit it with their axes, it was released for harvest.

At home, he heard the clink, clink, clink of the axes during all waking hours, echoes and vibrations from deep mining. It grinded on his brain, one of the many reasons he liked to be outside. The incessant noise could drive any fairy to madness — perhaps that explained his parents.

Mother left him. Her voice had been gentle and patient, much different than she usually was.

Going home early was hopeless, he knew now. The humans had found him so quickly. But maybe he could do The Right Thing while he was here.

Chapter 19 - Sylvia

Late in the night on Sunday,, after they had cleared their plates and sleepily crawled to bed upstairs, Sylvia woke to blaring alarms sounding throughout her room and, as it turned out, throughout the house. The confusion of sleep lingered on her eyelids, but she sharpened herself and jumped out of bed — not quite the spring chicken.

She raced to the next room and shook awake Chrysa, a notoriously heavy sleeper. "Chrysa! Wake up!" Her friend tangled herself up in the sheets trying to get up.

Both women went first to the room with the Thin family. Each of them was groggily pulling on a jacket. Penelope helped her daughters before herself.

They met Patty in the hallway.

On their way down the stairs, Jonathan the bodyguard bounded up the steps. "Intruders, ma'am," he said, slightly breathless. "Three people. I advise that all you ladies head to the safe room."

"I'm not going," Sylvia said in a brazen state

of mind.

"God damn it," Chrysa muttered. "...Me neither." She pushed her way through the group and glared at Sylvia.

Usually this dynamic was the complete reverse, though Sylvia didn't begrudge her friend's eccentricities like Chrysa seemed to now. She wasn't sure if she should be angry or feel guilty for dragging her friend into it.

"I'll stay out here too," David said, readjusting his rifle on his shoulder, as he joined the group. None of them had heard him walk up, but they had bigger problems at that moment.

Penelope ushered her half-protesting daughters after Patty who offered no heroics. No one expected her to anyway.

"What now?" Chrysa asked with an unimpressed voice.

"Do you have any of your stores of magic back?" Sylvia asked in return.

"Hardly anything," Chrysa said. "Rob took everything I had. But I could do some small stuff."

There was clattering coming from the kitchen. Jonathan the bodyguard did not offer to investigate. He kneeled behind a large vase in an alcove of the staircase. David staked out a spot behind a couch with its back to the ornate handrail at the overlook.

Sylvia stood still and wide-eyed like a kid caught stealing a classmate's prized mechanical pencil, and they all witnessed three slightly odd-looking people, two men and one woman, stalk into the entryway below.

The woman sported curly red hair, much like Chrysa minus the few new gray arrivals. She wore fitted blue jeans and a lacey top. Her face was angular, and she wore a smile like a mask.

The first man was unusually tall and dark-haired. His features were square and sharp. He might've been a model in his black v-neck sweater and slightly distressed jeans. Sylvia wondered when he found the time to look up human fashion when he Glamoured himself.

The second man was much less visually impactful. He was fit, though.

"Ah, we knew we'd sensed witches," the model fairy said. He smiled slowly, and there was delicious viciousness in those teeth.

An odd thought crossed Sylvia's mind and she wondered if fairies ate meat and if they were prone to ripping apart their meal. Just so she had an idea of what to expect. She figured they did eat meat with the same restraint as their elaborate court functions, but their sharp predator teeth left her doubting.

"Leave us," Sylvia said, figuring it was worth a shot.

She received a sneering laugh in return. "No," the female fairy responded with strict matter-of-fact-ness.

"We'll fight you," Sylvia said, managing to sound much more sure of her words than she felt.

"We're strong. Why don't you just leave us alone?"

"My dear tuna fish," said the model fairy. "You barely register on our meter." He gestured at Chrysa. "She, however, seems like quite the store."

"I don't taste good," Chrysa said flatly. Her usual vivacity was completely gone. Sylvia couldn't tell if it was because she was still so depleted or if the situation deemed a serious response and, for once in her life, Chrysa was conforming to expectations. Sylvia figured it was the former option.

Sylvia looked at her three opponents, trying vainly to ascertain the strong one. Their auras weren't strong enough for her to notice, so she figured none of them would be stopped by the restraining spell. She didn't have the concentration for the suffocation spell. The energy ball spell required too much raw power, and for a witch of Sylvia's power level, it was truly a last resort. And the hide in plain sight spell was useless since they already knew she was here.

She wondered if she had made a mistake by insisting to remain outside the safe room. She certainly felt more helpless now than she did earlier. She was not one for rash decisions, and she surprised herself. She focused on the mental steps involved in the energy ball spell. The meditation helped her increase the effectiveness of the spell.

However, before her energy spell was complete, the red-headed fairy sent arcs of lightning toward Sylvia. She lunged forward, towards the fairies, away from the lightning. Oh god, she'd have to stop letting her body make decisions for her; instinct was certainly not going to bolster her survival.

The regular fairy reached for Sylvia, and she swerved out of his reach, rounding down the staircase and into the main entry hall. Now she was completely separated from her group.

A loud boom resounded in the entrance hall. It took Sylvia a moment to process before she realized that David had taken a shot. He'd hidden himself, and she had completely forgotten about him. He must've missed, because no one crumpled.

Sylvia decided to go for the energy ball spell again. She kept an eye on the fairies and subtly built her energy up. They might not even notice magic as unassuming and dull as hers. Her life's misfortune might be her biggest asset.

They instead were eyeing Chrysa, though the regular fairy was sure to throw casual glances at Sylvia. His glances were more like how one would glare at an annoying buzzing fly before absent-mindedly swatting it. Sylvia stopped her energy ball spell.

Chrysa stared dull-eyed at her adversaries. She yawned, still fighting off sleep. This was probably the worst time for her to battle. Though she was traditionally strong at night, sleepiness just made Chrysa grumpy and rash, contributing to her lack of enthusiasm. She was not the panglossian type of friend when she was tired. "I hate you all," she said. She stared near the center of the three fairies and conjured up a fire tornado.

All three fairies easily avoided the fire, but their backwards movement gave Sylvia enough space to dart back up the stairs. Her knees creaked in the climb. She was starting to hate her body. That was a fact she wrestled with in the most recent years. She'd always done as she pleased like the heroines in her cheap paperback novels, but none of those heroines had bones from the turn of the previous century.

Sylvia stepped behind Chrysa and decided to think instead of act. She knew one of the fairies was a weather fairy, because of the lightning. Too bad she couldn't tell what the others were. She didn't have the charms that she made, and she regretted taking them off earlier that night when they chafed her neck.

She'd have to figure out their elements for herself. They were definitely not fire fairies, as evidenced by their jumping away from Chrysa's fire. Maybe groups of fairies associated by element type. If Sylvia were to strategically hunt, she'd find partners with different skillsets. Were these fairies that smart? They still did not seem alarmed by Chrysa's power, which meant they were either too weak, too strong or too dumb to notice. She figured it was either too strong or too dumb, because if they were weak, they'd compensate like Sylvia consistently did. She was easily able to rule out too strong as well because she would've sensed their magical aura if their power was even close to Chrysa's level. So they were too dumb. And that led Sylvia to the conclusion that they were all also weather fairies.

Since they were weather fairies, she had a few options. She definitely didn't want to use earth magic on them. That was their naturally weaker opponent. Weather's naturally stronger opponent was animal magic wielders, for their quick wits and highly versatile magic style. Weather was resistant to change and slower, which was probably why the red-headed fairy was using lightning, the fastest of the weather elements. It was also highly unpredictable, hard to control and required a lot of mental energy. She might not notice a sneak attack.

And so Sylvia had a makeshift strategy that she hoped might work, but she needed the male fairies distracted as well. She whispered to Chrysa that she needed all three of them to be using lightning and be distracted by her.

Chrysa nodded. She began shooting streams of water at all three fairies. Not fire — her usual specialty. The fairies grinned in unison. Sylvia realized that her best friend had just created an ingenious distraction for her. Water was a natural conductor for electricity, which was what lightning was. And when the fairies had an opportunity like this, they would all wield lightning to attack Chrysa through the streams of water. Chrysa was letting them have the upper hand so Sylvia could do her work. Sylvia just hoped that her friend had a way of protecting herself.

Sylvia created the tiniest fire column she could conjure and directed it towards the floor and wall to slither like a snake. It was so small, it just darted like a shooting star. She let it grow slightly bigger once behind the fairies. None of them had noticed, each was taking turns trying to time a lightning strike just right to shock Chrysa before she disconnected from the stream. Her friend was very fast, and she was surprised she had the physical or magical energy for it. Perhaps her friend's definition of "not much magic" was different from Sylvia's definition.

Nonetheless, she weaved a fire curtain, slowly out of sight of the fairies. Since each fire thread was so tiny and the fairies were soaking wet, they probably didn't even notice the heat, or figured it was them warming up.

Sylvia was thankful that neither David nor the bodyguard had said a word yet, not spoiling her trick. It took her a good three minutes to weave the fire curtain. She did everything she could to keep from smiling when she finished. It wouldn't be right if the surprise was ruined yet.

Chrysa had corralled the fairies close together. Sylvia was thankful that even when the water streams hit her curtain, the magic-imbued fire was not doused.

She was thankful she had such a competent

friend too. It was odd to be thankful in such a moment, because she suddenly realized what she would be doing in the next minute. She pushed the thought away and just did it.

She directed the fire curtain like throwing a net onto the fairies. They screamed as their skin burned. Their clothes sizzled, still wet from Chrysa's water. They struggled, burning themselves even more. Sylvia held her magic steady. This spell didn't require a lot of power, but it did require a lot of concentration, keeping track of each small fire column. She drew the curtain closer and closer around them, but none of them cried for mercy. Perhaps fairies did not do that. Perhaps they didn't know it was an option.

The fire clung to them, no longer letting Sylvia control it. They were truly on fire now. It was terrible to see. But neither Sylvia nor Chrysa doused them with a water stream. The fairies rolled around on the ground, trying to smother the flames themselves, but the fire was magical, taking most of Sylvia's magical store, and it was not easily squashed.

When their Glamour disappeared, Sylvia realized that they were certainly dead. She stared at the small, green-ish, blackened bodies.

She recalled whatever remained of her magic in the flames and stepped forward to see what she had done. It wasn't right to look away. She should see the consequences of her actions, she was an adult and she deserved the truth of her being.

She hadn't known she was capable of such a thing. It was despicable, but it was also necessary.

She didn't cry. She wanted to, but it seemed dishonorable to cry for her lost innocence when she had taken their lives in such a gruesome way. They weren't crying so neither could she.

Chapter 20 - Thom

Thom straightened his shirt and held himself as tall as he could as Mother led him to Grandmother.

It had been easy to convince her that he wanted to talk to Grandmother. He was the future king, after all. And she was softer than she had been two days prior.

Thom cleared his throat when in front of Grandmother.

She seemed so tall. Her amber eyes glowed, and her graying hair seemed impossibly neat, not a single strand out of place. She smiled. "It is good to see you. Are you feeling better?"

Of course, Mother and Father would lie; they couldn't have it known their son had run away. No, they would hide it, like they did anything unsavory. In this case, it helped him, and he was grateful. He nodded. "The shock of your announcement must have affected me more than I knew," he said, using the words and cadence his parents used at Court. "And I would like to impress upon you, that I take the responsibility very seriously. It is a great honor to be chosen."

His mother squeezed his hand reassuringly. The sensation was warm and gentle, and it felt weird coming from his mother.

Grandmother let a little laugh escape her mouth. "They're teaching you the ways of Court, I see."

Thom nodded. He felt icky, speaking like this. It felt foreign and stiff on his tongue. "It would be a great honor to speak with you alone of my future responsibilities."

Grandmother flicked Mother away, like a horse lazily swatting flies with her tail. "You do not need to use such stiff language with me, Thomas."

When he was sure Mother was far enough away, he said, "What do you think of the Hunt?"

"It's a very successful harvest, probably more than any of our other harvests," Grandmother said. "I believe it is because our family was the one to organize it. Our family has a wa—"

"I think it's not the right thing to do," Thom interrupted in one big breath.

Grandmother's mouth hardened, and she sighed. "You are a child."

"Witches are alive, like we are," Thom said quickly, trying to make his voice sound as adult and authoritative as hers was. It sounded pretty good, he thought. Maybe they would listen to him. "They matter, like we do. We don't want to be hunted. How would you feel if the witches hunted us? Harvested our souls?"

"Thomas, we are hunted, every day, the elves encroach on our territory. They kill us, for nothing, because we are fairies and we refuse to be controlled by them," Grandmother said sternly.

"I've never met an elf," Thomas said.

"That. That is because we have protected our kind," Grandmother said. Her mouth was a hard, disapproving line. Her grandmotherly love has vanished. "We are doing so well that you do not even see them. That is success."

"How do we even know there is anything even going on?"

"There are occasionally diplomat parties sent to and fro."

"Why don't we hear about them?"

"Thomas," she said. Her voice warned of impatience. "You are eleven years old. Of course you don't know of many things that go on. Do not think you will outwit me, because you will not. I have been Queen a very long time. Your momentary guilt is nothing in comparison to the years of my life that I have dedicated to weighing options. If the Hunt wasn't necessary, we wouldn't continue it. You think you see one injustice and that outweighs the safety of all fairies? It doesn't. The witches have a fighting chance. And they agreed to this. We have a treaty that outlines this very practice." Her words were clipped and precise. She hadn't raised her voice, and he was grateful — for that and only that.

Thom drew back, feeling told. He was stupid, what made him think he could convince anyone of anything. Adults never listened, even if he were right. "I did not know there was a treaty."

"Yes, there is a treaty. It is why I do not feel bad in the slightest."

"Okay," Thom said. Another dead end. He was so useless. He couldn't protect his teacher, he couldn't go home, he couldn't stop the Hunt. He couldn't do anything.

Was anything worth the effort?

His mother collected him and made the rounds with the other Courtiers.

Yes, sir. I am very honored. Smile. Smile. Bow his head. Yes, ma'am. I believe my parents will be excellent regents. I am lucky to have them. Six more smiles. Attempt not to cry. Wipe his tears on his sleeve, discreetly.

Uncle came to talk to Father. Thom noticed the disgust on his face when his eyes wandered to Thom.

Maybe he should say something, work to establish respect. No. There was no point in trying to do anything for himself. He wouldn't succeed. Just be polite and quiet and a credit to his parents. It was all he could do. He felt ashamed. Ashamed that he thought he would be able to help the witches. He couldn't help them. He probably hurt them by getting Grandmother to feel more secure in her opinion.

He knew in his heart that The Right Thing

was no Hunt. But there was no way to make that happen. There was no point in doing anything. No point, no point.

Sorrow swallowed him up, sludging through his veins like sap down the side of a tree, but none of the sweetness. It was disgusting. The kind of sorrow that made babies cry. The corners of his mouth pulled down, and tears watered his vision.

He was glad that the glittering embroidered edges of the Court garb was barely visible. Its brightness would be a mockery to the failure he felt. Look at this shining Court, they all smile, confident adults, they had power, they had knowledge. He had nothing. He couldn't even use magic, beyond the instinctive Glamour.

"Future King!" King Puck exclaimed. "You look as if you might cry. Kings don't cry."

"It's a pleasure, King Puck," Thom said, barely managing.

"Doesn't look it." He laughed heartily.

It was impolite to point out someone's negative emotions in Court. Thom wished, just this once, that Puck would follow the rules. "I apologize."

"It's pleasurable to be king," Puck mused. "I get their smiles now. Before they averted their gaze. No more." He laughed even louder, as if to brag of his power.

Did the king not see that it was meaningless? They didn't care about him. Just as they would not care about Thom when he became king. Just like his parents did not care about him. Just like his grandmother did not care about him. Court was horrible that day.

Chapter 21 - Sylvia

Penelope and Patty worked to clean up the mess the next morning after the fairies had attacked; the bodyguard had left with a vehement "Screw this shit. I don't get paid enough" immediately after the fight, and the maids had the day off. Sylvia kept insisting she help, because she felt huge slices and jabs of guilt. But Penelope insisted, saying Chrysa and Sylvia had saved their lives.

Penelope did, of course, spare her daughters the task of removing the fairies. She was a mother after all.

The three daughters scrubbed the floor after the messy part of the job was complete.

"It smells icky," Loni said, wrinkling her nose. She pushed hard with her sponge.

"I know what this is," Maria said with the threat of a wail coming. She closed her eyes as she moved her hands, getting the soot off the hardwood floor.

Ellie didn't say anything. One might think she was sorting paper clips or some other mundane administrative task at the easy pace she fell into.

It bothered Sylvia and she squinted at the girl for a long moment before making her way into Patty's backyard and solemnly digging a shallow grave for the small charred bodies. Every part of her body ached. She didn't cry, but hopeless despair made her feel like she was falling. It was such an uncomfortable feeling that seemed as if it would last forever, and she was the one who did it. Guilt, she realized. It was a new feeling. Unlike the low-level guilt that she might've felt at times in her life. This was mortal guilt. The type that would stick with her until she died.

She laid in the grass afterwards, hoping the sprinklers would turn on and wash away the dirt. She didn't mind so much that it was chillingly cold outside. In fact, it felt like a punishment — as slight as it was — to endure it. That would theoretically absolve her of the guilt of murder.

"Sylvia," David's voice said sternly. His shoes scraped against the grass. "Are you wallowing?"

"I murdered today," she said.

"You saved lives today," David said with a sigh. He clearly didn't want to comfort her, but he seemed to want her to do something.

"Does that make it justifiable?" Sylvia asked, not looking at him but up at the dark sky.

"Yes," he said.

"I can't believe that I knew what I was

doing, and I still did it," she said. "This was not an accident. I set out to kill them."

"You had people to protect," he said. Before she could say anything else, he added, "Remember that rumor about going to the fairy court and asking for immunity? I think we should give it some credence, especially if you don't want to kill more fairies."

"I don't think I could kill any more," she said.

"The second time is easier, I'm sure," he said. "I used to do some hunting."

"You're a hunter just like the fairies," she said. Her voice had a lost quality to it. She hoped she could just disappear: floating in the great abyss of space or maybe falling into an endless pit. Either would be acceptably away from her life and these problems.

"You should act like the adult that you are, Sylvia," he said sharply. "You're older than me and don't have time for this nonsense. People need you."

"You're supposed to make me feel better, and you're not very good at it," she said, still not looking at him. She felt like throwing an attitude-laden tantrum like one of her sixth graders would. Maybe the self-indulgence would make him go away.

"Killing is killing. The only moral litmus test is whether it was necessary or not," he said. "That's why I don't hunt anymore. But I will defend myself and other good people."

Sylvia didn't answer but rolled over onto her stomach and pushed herself off the ground. Her elbows creaked, but she continued as energetically as possible.

She didn't feel any better, but she'd soldier on because she cared about her witch friends and even David... maybe. Damn empathy, never had it sucked more.

Inside the house, all the women were gathered in the sitting room. David stood awkwardly near the arch to the entryway.

Each woman was generally quiet. How loud could they be facing their imminent deaths? Sylvia was glad that calm pervaded. Hot-heads and panickers would require more of her energy and she was running low.

She sat on the edge of the coffee table and tried to work the kinks out of her back without asking for help. "Before I say anything, I kinda want to get a feel for where everyone's head is at. Patty? You want to go first?"

Patty first thanked Sylvia and Chrysa for their hard work — ever the cordial socialite — but she didn't feel safe in her own home. She wanted to find a bigger group.

Penelope said they needed to be proactive, because sitting around would just make them sitting ducks. She was taking David's role of the warmongering, leather-skinned citizen in the emergency town hall meeting.

Chrysa said, "I think Penelope has the right idea. But I might have the unpopular opinion that we should see if we can seek the fairies out before they find us. Role reversal, if you will."

"Maybe there's a way to leave LA," Loni said in her quiet, unassuming voice. "We just sort of believe everyone but Sylvia and David only tried once."

"I'd like to stay here," Maria said. She looked away from everyone as if she was embarrassed for the opinion.

Ellie shook her head. "We should go to the fairy court."

Sylvia did a double-take about Ellie's words. She immediately wondered if this was a genuine suggestion or her precognitive ability directing them. Now she didn't want to go, definitely not. The acquiesce was too odd. She wanted more pushback from the group to convince her out of her choice, to temper David's stone-faced enthusiasm. "Why?"

"You have already thought about it," Ellie said. "So I do not know why you are questioning it now. It is a good idea. Will they expect us to attack like that? No. The immunity thing might work. We have the upper-hand by aggressively taking ground." She shrugged before continuing. "My mom wants proactivity. And I think almost everyone here wants action. And I think Loni is a bit too wishful that there is a way out. I mean, I am not opposed to trying but for how long and how much magic. And staying here will just bring more fairies to our neck of the woods." Ellie finished her little speech and didn't look anyone in the eye. She stared blankly at nothing, and her face remained serious.

Sylvia didn't think she'd ever heard Ellie talk so much in one moment. She had to smile. When she realized she was smiling, she frowned — this was no time for joy. It was an emergency! "Does anyone agree with her?"

David raised his hand, so did Penelope and Chrysa.

After a moment of prodding stares from Ellie, her sisters half-raised their hands.

Sylvia turned to Patty. The woman didn't look prepared to fight. She wanted to be protected. And that was fine, but for Sylvia, Penelope's daughters came first. They were a new generation. And that was how it was supposed to be. Protecting the young was a natural instinct, and Sylvia appreciated the surety that accompanied it. There was nothing like love to motivate an originally non-violent person to commit acts they never thought possible for themselves in order to keep loved ones alive. Which also made Sylvia apprehensive. If love was so good and right, why would it make her feel better about murder? Which led to the idea that murder was perhaps not unequivocally bad?

She usually didn't mull over these moral conundrums because there were too many facets.

Now that she mulled, guilt made her feel worse for even trying to justify herself.

Without any more discussion, it seemed they were going to the fairy court. The question was now strategy and role assignments. Patty prepared to stay behind and fend for herself.

The three remaining adult witches and David discussed what they knew and their methods for achieving what they wanted.

It was unanimously decided that Sylvia and David would go on the first scouting mission. Their magic or lack thereof was the most unobtrusive and least noticeable. Arguably, they might be able to pass for human with minimal effort.

They'd go during the day, best to hide in plain sight and seem like tourists. They were going to investigate the LA Opera House. Sylvia had seen it a few times.

David did more research and found out that there were actually two opera houses next to each other. The Walt Disney one, which was the one she had originally thought it was, and the LA Opera in the Pavilion.

It was kind of a toss-up which one the fairies might've chosen. Fairies loved old grand things. There was power in a long-standing building like the Pavilion, which was opened in 1964. The Walt Disney Concert Hall was from this millennium. But fairies also liked garish displays of wealth and design. They'd go see both and discover whatever they could. They were flying fairly blind, so anything was better than nothing.

Through the rest of the night, Sylvia slept downstairs in the sitting room on the couch. She didn't want to be caught unawares if there was another fairy attack during the night. Even when she managed sleep, it wasn't good, restful, peaceful sleep. She tossed and consistently woke. She saw the fairies she buried when she closed her eyes, so she tried to keep them open until natural tiredness made them droop.

Her lost innocence made sleep less pleasurable. No one told her that would ever happen. She wondered how she'd made it through 114 years sleeping like a baby to end up like this — magic had made her life effortless. She could always sleep easily. Even during the first week of the Hunt, she'd slept mostly easily — she knew it wasn't fear for her life that caused the light sleeping. It was the guilt. It was as if an image of the fairies had been tattooed with permanent ink on the inside of her eyelids. She sincerely hoped that time would fade this. But tattoos didn't go away.

She decided to look it up on the internet on a computer neatly hidden away in a cabinet because, even as a teacher, she still had stuff to learn. She read an article about a science experiment to find out how people felt about killing in war and killing a regular civilian. And, of course, it stated that war killing didn't make people feel as guilty. But it said nothing of the lasting effects of guilt.

She cleared the browser history, feeling embarrassed for having searched that. She was already trying to end the pain of guilt. That just wasn't right. She thought she ought to feel it to some degree to honor those she killed. Those words "she killed" bit her mind hard — iron-clad jaws of only incisors.

She went back to the couch and tried to settle into sleep once again. It was mildly successful. She didn't wake until the sun was shining directly on her closed eyes. She didn't remember her dreams, but she woke with unease and an odd feeling of aliveness but in a dirty way. It didn't quite make sense. Her stomach quivered, and she knew food wouldn't help at all. Instead she went to the kitchen and sat at the breakfast nook.

The outside was bright — almost as a direct mockery of the unsettling feelings she had. She turned in her seat and force herself to look out. Patty's beautiful garden extended far and it was all green. She wondered if fairies could be hiding out there right then.

Maybe that would be good that she was the only one downstairs. Maybe the fairies would overwhelm her and eat her soul. And then her guilt would be absolved. Chrysa and David would have enough forewarning to be able to protect the rest of the group. She might like that outcome.

But she thought about why she had

murdered the night before. It was to stay alive and be able to protect those witches she loved. It would be a disservice to lose her life just a few hours after killing three beings. Sylvia, after all, was primarily about respect. She couldn't imagine disrespecting those that she killed so much.

Loni wandered into the kitchen. "Morning," the girl said.

Sylvia nodded. Even that particular salutation, which was objectively neutral, was too cheery for her current state.

Loni looked into the refrigerator. "Do you feel bad?" she asked.

"About the murders? Yes," Sylvia said. She didn't sugarcoat it. She didn't deserve to.

"My mom said you're hating yourself right now," Loni said.

Sylvia didn't know how to answer that, so she didn't.

Loni continued. "She said that we're alive because of what you and Chrysa did. Not that bodyguard, not that witchblood man. She says you did the right thing."

"Thank you," Sylvia said, not quite sure how to take the justification from an outside source. She still didn't feel it in her core. She didn't know what would snap her out of it either. If she should even attempt to snap out of it. A very vocal part of herself said she should feel guilt to punish herself.

The weight felt heavy on her shoulders, and she got up to see what food she could make for herself and the young witch. She whipped up some pancakes, and by this time, Maria was downstairs as well.

Sylvia retrieved fancy maple syrup from the pantry. She explained to the two sisters the process of getting maple syrup from a tree. Even now, she was a teacher. It calmed her. Let her forget herself. Be in control of a situation.

As she washed the dishes, she looked out the window at the flowers. They were all colors and she imagined they might smell wonderful, but did she deserve that? Any reward was too selfish. The soap smelled too sweet. She rinsed everything quickly and went to nap on the couch in one of the living rooms.

Loni laughed when she saw her. "It's the morning," she said.

"Never say no to sleep," Sylvia said. She added a watery smile and did not engage with anyone for the rest of the morning.

When she and David got into the car to check out downtown, she didn't say much. David brought a concealed handgun, and Sylvia was sure that was not legal without a permit. Maybe even with a permit. But she didn't cause a fuss, because she wasn't sure of anything now that she had killed sentient beings.

David drove, and she was glad for that. She'd been driving for the past 60 years; it was just not fun anymore.

Way before they reached downtown, she

used the masking spell and hid her magic. She didn't like to know that she might be discovered because of David, though. He had no way of shielding himself, though witchbloods were usually the last to be found out because of their negligible amount of magic. It wasn't even worth the time to hunt them, apparently. That's what her mother had told her when the Hunt in London happened.

Her mother — while very kind — always had a way of telling Sylvia that things were just the way they were and she ought not to strive to change them. Her mother liked being anonymous and normal. That's probably where Sylvia got her tameness from, her calm demeanor and quiet presence. Her mom never networked with other witches. Except for her family, she was the epitome of a solitary witch.

Sometimes, Sylvia wished her mom had been out there in the witch community, because Sylvia wanted to be. Now would've been a really good time to know a lot of witches. She was sure now that surviving the Hunt was a numbers game. The bigger the group one starts out with, the better their chances were. Banding together before fairies were strong with their stolen witch magic meant that strong witches could defeat the fairies. Every witch saved was a less powerful fairy. That was a tide-turning proposition.

Of course the treaty might end if the fairies no longer found it fruitful for them. Sylvia wasn't sure, and she didn't much go for politics.

Most witches didn't. Politics were boring and if done right, free from guise, which is something that might be hard for a witch — to have her magic potentially exposed. Most humans wouldn't believe it anyway; those that did were written off as crazies. That was a witch's greatest protection, the impossibility of her existence in the eyes of humans. Though it made Sylvia sad sometimes, knowing people thought she was just a crazy idea only for children's books. Witches were at least YA-worthy. She smiled at her joke.

The traffic was dying down since it was already 10am, but Sylvia was still impatient for the cars to get out of her way. She thought it'd be better if she just got her reconnaissance mission out of the way.

She wanted to wallow and carry on. She wasn't usually like this. She was usually perky and responsible. The desire to wallow was so self-indulgent. She shouldn't be like this. She was supposed to be more put-together than this.

She thought of her classroom and her kids. She'd always be put-together for her kids. She had to be. She had to control her energy for them. Children absorbed moods like sponges. And as a teacher, a room full of rowdy, grumpy kids was quite the predicament. She learned early on that calm and confident got the best results. She'd mastered that skill, so she didn't know why she couldn't do that now.

She sucked in a sharp breath. She'd fix this. She had to. It was not right for the others.

She forced a smile and stared out at the cars.

They parked in an over-priced parking garage. Sylvia stumbled out of the car and stretched her legs. Car rides certainly weren't the same as they used to be — her knees told her.

She attempted small talk, but David wasn't having it, so they walked to the opera houses together in silence.

Sylvia twitched like a cold Chihuahua as she tried to be nonchalant and observant. The more she tried to "play it cool," the more her body went crazy. She pushed the thoughts of controlling herself away.

The open space around the Walt Disney Concert Hall was bright and normal-looking. Los Angeles sidewalks were notorious for being devoid of pedestrians and this was no exception. There were a few business people and maybe a tourist or two. Certainly nothing comparable to a New York City street. And they were a little way away from the tall downtown buildings; the feel was light and airy.

They walked to the front of the Pavilion. There was a park that was mostly paved, but it still felt somewhat outdoorsy. There was nothing to indicate fairy activity. No oddly unfocused air caught her attention.

Inside the Pavilion, the windows rose all the

way to the ceiling. The chandeliers overhead were magnificent. Tons of little crystals hung down. It inspired awe. Sylvia wondered how her life would've been if she'd chosen to be a chandelier-maker, something she'd never considered. She probably wouldn't live in LA. She wouldn't be here now.

How she wished she wasn't here now.

Sylvia caught sight of a Pavilion employee, and magical pressure packed in. She eyed her — not openly staring. Her features were sharp like a fairy's. She wasn't getting a strong magical presence from her in particular, but there was something to this place definitely. The potential fairy employee barely looked at Sylvia or David, and Sylvia breathed a tiny sigh of relief.

The magical pressure felt very much like the time she was in the Magical Realm. She'd only visited a few times; because making her way there took so much energy, she generally didn't make the effort. Most of her friends were in the Mundane Realm.

Witches had the distinct competitive advantage of being able to seamlessly blend into either world. They could hold their own among the magical folk. But humans would not suspect anything of a witch in their world. Witches were descended from humans and so they did not technically belong in the Magical Realm, but witches who chose to make the Magical Realm their home did just fine anyway. She liked that adaptive trait.

When she visited the Magical Realm, she visited a friend who used to live in the Mundane Realm — an old friend named Orinda. She was quiet. When Sylvia talked to her, she kept her voice low and spoke only gentle things. She was an odd woman, and Sylvia liked that. Frail like a sprout. But she surrounded herself by powerful things, strong things. Her pet was a bobcat — a Mundane Realm original. The bobcat wasn't actually domesticated. It did love Orinda though.

The bobcat was essentially a large cat — though much stronger — with a short nub of a tail. Sylvia steered clear of it. She admired its power and grace from afar. Though one time, the bobcat rolled around on its back and begged for affection from her. She cautiously obliged.

Anyway, Orinda was a talented musician. She played flute and bass guitar, which she took up in 1993. Sylvia thought it so entertaining to see this woman rocking out quite successfully with her bass guitar. She wore thick linen clothes and had her hair wrapped in a super soft scarf. She was Polish. Old World Polish. She was probably 603 years old. Orinda said she stopped keeping track a long time ago. Sylvia supposed it didn't matter that much at that point. And even though witches were technically immortal if they were careful, reaching 600 years was quite an accomplishment. There were so many ways to die. And yet Orinda had managed to outsmart them all.

She had moved to the Magical Realm because the magic-rich environment treated her bones better — she said. Sylvia laughed at that explanation at the time, but when she did visit Orinda, she realized the difference. There was much less strain of living for magical folk in the Magical Realm. Magic was abundant. It imbued everything with energy instead of leeching it — like in the Mundane Realm.

The Pavilion had that same abundant feeling as Orinda's house. It relaxed her when she walked in — the calm before the kill in a lions' den.

This was it. No doubt about it. She hadn't known what to look for, but she certainly knew it when she saw it or felt it. She loved the feeling of this magic. Her body felt young and spritely. It was like relaxing in a hot tub after a long day of work. It had to be the souls of dead witches though, and that soured the feeling for her. It was disgusting.

"This place is interesting," David said, obviously trying to inject meaning into those words.

"Feels powerful," she said back.

They looked out the windows for a long minute before silently agreeing that exploration was in order. The only thing was that they needed some sort of reason to explore.

Sylvia meandered over to the employee she was sure was a fairy. "Hi," she said, putting on her teacher voice. "We were wondering if we could have a tour."

The employee looked back glumly. "Yes, ma'am. What parts of the Pavilion interest you most?"

"What do you like most?" Sylvia asked. "Me and my friend have never been to L.A. before. We're just checking out the sights. So we're up for anything interesting."

The employee showed them up to the balcony overlooking the window room. Sylvia realized why quickly. There was much less magical energy up there. Of course the fairy wouldn't bring them even remotely close to the court. And, in fact, would naturally take them to the furthest point away. And that's when she knew it was underground or close to it.

She made eye contact with David and tapped her nose.

They listened to the employee tell about some of the history of the place for a few minutes before going back down to the main floor. They also checked out the actual venue before leaving the building. She could tell that David was getting impatient, but it was necessary, she thought, to make sure they looked like tourists.

Outside, she made sure no one was looking then said, "It's on the lower levels. Or underground or something." She thought it was weird that the fairies were lower though. Generally, they liked higher, more open spaces. She wondered which family was in charge of the court. Then she remembered it was almost winter, and the Lodes Family were cave dwellers, so perhaps they had had some sway in the matter of choosing the headquarters for their fortnight stay in Los Angeles. The Lodes Family were unusual fairies, their like of deep and dark places was just the start of it. They weren't known for being power-seeking. They accumulated wealth and waited out the court squabbles. Or participated for a price. Their power lied in their resources. Sylvia had a modicum of respect for them.

They walked to the sidewalk and David motioned to the under-building parking garages. "We might be able to get access that way?" he said.

"I'm just worried about not having an escape route," Sylvia admitted, but continued walking forward. She had to gather as much information as possible. They walked past the parking garage entrance. They weren't doing a very good job of being spies. She felt so obvious. It hurt her heart, sending her stomach flipping and somersaulting. But maybe obvious was good? Tourists were naturally open and invasive.

Sylvia kind of enjoyed L.A. tourists sometimes, but they blended surprisingly well with the locals. Of course, once in a while she spotted a sock-and-sandal sporting tourist and it was a delight to see. She always wanted to talk with them and see if she could help them in any way. Tourists were cute and helpless.

She decided to go for it and just walk into the garage looking curious and looking up. She smiled like she was discovering something, even though it was just concrete slabs. Best to play dumb, she thought. It was slightly colder in the garage than outside and she thought that might be a good sign or a bad sign. The magical presence was stronger than in the great room in the Pavilion. She didn't look back at David. She almost wanted to pretend like he wasn't there, because she looked awfully suspicious. But he probably added to her credibility, because he was a man and the fairies were probably not looking for men, though they might later in the Hunt.

She went towards what looked like a service door, and double-checked her hide in plain sight spell to ensure that she wasn't giving off any magical energy. She wasn't. It was a weird feeling. She was sure that they would notice her. She pulled open the service door and musky air surrounded her like a soft blanket. The smell was old but comforting. She forged forward. Magic was definitely a strong presence.

She heard David behind her but dared not turn around; she might just run back outside and not return. The realization that she could very well lose her life at any moment hit her. Her fear was real and powerful. It reared in her body, almost making her fall back. She momentarily had no sense of up or down. She gritted her teeth and hunched forward. She couldn't control the fear, but she could move forward, tamping the fear down with sheer brute force. She passed a set of old spiraling steps downward to a cave-like room. It was blocked by a welded cage door with a locked entry. The magical feeling wasn't down there so she didn't pay it much attention.

There were pipes and conduits running along the wall. It felt industrial and abandoned. But there were signs of life. The floor was dusty but had shoe prints, lots of shoe prints. She must have been extremely lucky to have not bumped into someone yet.

And speak of the devil, she heard confident footsteps up ahead. She turned to run in the opposite direction, because she didn't know what to do. She ran into David and pushed him back towards the garage. He didn't know what was going on and stumbled. He was about to speak, but Sylvia managed to put her hand over his mouth before a sound came out.

Sylvia checked behind herself toward the industrial tunnel. She breathed out a sigh of relief but didn't stop pushing David away.

They made it to the garage, and Sylvia tidied herself. She walked over to a car. "David," she said. "I don't know. Is this the car?"

David was a bit slow, because he didn't catch up right away. He stared at her for a long moment then said, "No, I'm pretty sure we were in another garage."

"Are you sure?" she said as she watched what she was positive was a fairy come out of the service door and walk towards the outside. "I could've sworn that we were supposed to come back here."

David shook his head. "Just follow me. I know where the car is."

He followed the fairy to the outside. Sylvia snuck looks at their target while babbling some nonsense about how bright L.A. was. She couldn't concentrate on both tasks, but she was relatively sure it wouldn't sound like gobblety-gook to an unobservant bystander. Relatively sure.

The fairy made her way to a bench across the street from the Pavilion. She sat down and just looked around casually.

The behavior seemed odd to Sylvia until she realized what it was. The fairies had watch patrols, and they were fairly invisible. Sylvia was sure that if she saw that woman on the street, she wouldn't have looked twice or suspected anything. Fairy energy was subtle. Mostly anyone's energy was subtle when looking through Sylvia eyes.

Both Sylvia and David walked back to the car without saying anything once they were sure they were out of earshot of the watch-fairy.

On the ride back, she contemplated their options. Unfortunately, it would be highly suspicious if she and David came back there and acted like tourists again. They had been obtrusive enough to be annoying and be noticed. Anyone with a good memory for faces might recognize them. Maybe they could come in disguise, and if the fairies on watch were not looking closely they might make it in. However, once in the service tunnel, all bets were off.

The biggest crux of their issue was to get their whole group into the tunnel, which would be even harder because a group of women would draw any fairy's eye, especially since most of the witches in their group were so powerful that they would not be able to hide nearly as successfully as Sylvia. Her only idea was that they had to get to the tunnel without being seen. That sounded just as impossible as the rest of it.

Chapter 22 - Thom

A letter from Zoranna arrived, and Thom ripped it open. He almost tore the paper completely in half to get at the words that Zoranna had written him. He unfolded it in frantic hands.

First he skimmed, just to assuage his excitement. On the second pass through, he savored each word:

My little Thom,

I've heard a lot has happened while you've been away. It seems we will have new lessons when you come back.

You are there for only a short while longer, and Thom, I will be so proud if you came back with your parents, not before them.

The trees will be here for your delight, they can last centuries. You have your entire life to climb them and get leaves in your hair. A week or two will pass quickly in comparison. And a big house is more for the exploration!

Be strong. Be kind. Even to your parents.

I love you always,
Zoranna

Thom's heart swelled, imbued with the strength of his governess's words. The walls of the bland white bedroom seemed suddenly brighter and easier to deal with. He smiled at the small blue car Ms. Hargrove had given him. He pocketed both the letter and the car before bounding downstairs with the biggest smile on his face. He could do anything!

Mother smiled at him. "Zoranna always knew how to cheer you up."

"I will be good and kind and strong."

Mother put her thin fingers through his blond hair and messed it up. "I love you, I hope you know that."

"I love you too," Thom said. His feeling was still high, but it came down a rung. Did he know that she loved him? Or was Mother being more careful because she would be regent one day? And he would be king one day. They would have to do what he said.

With his exuberant mood sufficiently leveled, he went outside into the backyard. It wasn't what he thought a human's yard would be like. When he saw pictures, they were green with trees and hot dogs and smiling faces. This backyard consisted of gravel. It was, perhaps, why his parents magicked the family to leave for two weeks — the familiarity of stone, the resemblance to home.

His stomach twisted. He sat on a rough white rock protruding from the sparse gravel landscape. Good. Kind. Strong.

He could do anything. He could do anything. His face scrunched up, beating the words into his bones and etching it into his mind. He would live up to Zoranna's expectations. He just had to figure out how.

At Court that afternoon, he followed instinct.

When Mother launched into a conversation with the Court Master, Thom's eyes flicked from face to face, following the bounce of the conversation.

"But you have to think it's inappropriate," Mother said, referring to a rapidly spreading rumor about Sir Gerard taking Miss Elaria on a mundane "date" to see Hollywood's stars in the ground; Mother explained it was nothing spectacular, just pink stone in the shape of a star in the ground — not glittering points of light that would make him wonder about the human's ability to create their own magic.

The Court Master — an eccentric bespectacled fairy with grandiose ideas for Court fashion and music — waggled his eyebrows. "I say, let lovers be lovers." He was notorious for "bedding" — as Mother called it — every eligible maiden who would have him.

Thom always wondered what they would do in bed. He knew it was scandalous from the way fairies spoke in hushed tones about it. Perhaps it involved eating cake and talking loudly about anyone that caught their disapproval. Or maybe it was nakedness — always a state of scandal. He had heard of sex in hushed whispers and tittering laughter. Adult fairies overcome by passion, unable to keep their hands off each other. Red blossomed on his cheeks.

Mother's eyes turned icier, but she smiled. "Gerard is no lover. You and I know better than that."

The Court Master oooohed. "Dazzling Sadina—" Thom had trouble imagining his mother befitting the description of dazzling "— we must not gossip."

Thom knew that was precisely what the fairy wanted. His overtures were part of some joke that Thom didn't understand, but it left him with a distinct dislike of the blue-haired fairy.

Mother rolled her eyes. It was not something she would normally do at Court, but the Court Master inspired a loosening of the pomp. "He makes every effort to become titled. It is disgraceful. Throwing his wealth of magic around as if it would impress Elaria." Miss Elaria was not titled as of yet, her family's title was still with her childless great uncle. It would pass first to her father and then to her.

"Reminds me of someone with blue eyes and white blonde hair," the Court Master said with a smirk.

Mother shrank back. "I love my husband," she declared defiantly.

Thom furrowed his brow. Did she really? Certainly, his parents wanted the same thing, but would he say it was love? Love was Zoranna's warm embrace whenever he pushed his face against her colorful skirts. Love was her letter. Love was safety. His parents were not safe together, only dangerous and sparking — a crackling fire in a hearth with books too close.

"As a flower loves dirt." He was needling Mother. It often happened to her in Court. Just as she regarded Sir Gerard — a magic-rich farmer trying to become part of the Flora Family nobility — with disdain, they disdained her. "Only to grow on top of."

She would cry to him when they left, Thom realized. Maybe he could say something. "Mother loves Father," he said with definiteness.

The Court Master's black eyes danced with amusement at him. "What makes you say that?"

"Father would've never given up the chance to marry a titled fairy for Mother unless he loved her. And Mother... Mother always listens to my father. She hates being told what to do, but because she loves him, she respects him," Thom said. The words piled out of him, forming just as they came to his lips. His reasoning was sound. It even assured him.

Mother sifted her fingers through his hair. When she gripped it, the unsettling noise of hair on hair traveled through his skull to his ears. It was her tense but thankful affection.

Thom smiled. He had made a point. He was strong.

Chapter 23 - Sylvia

Before they attempted, Sylvia thought that more organized training was required. She even had Penelope, David and Chrysa come. Chrysa grumbled that she didn't need "training." She did air-quotes. David said, "Training this, training that. Might as well have some elaborate training sequence montage for fucksake. Magic on, magic off, motherfucker."

Sylvia narrowed her eyes at him, but he was smiling in a self-satisfied way. She pressed her lips together and cajoled them into it anyway. That was her special talent. She could get anyone to learn. Even though she certainly knew less than Chrysa, the teacher role was one she was comfortable with.

She had them do all sorts of things, practicing spells that anyone knew how to do. Sylvia coaxed everything out of them. It was good for her to focus on them, and she enjoyed it. She was way too into her mind.

She was processing some ethical issues, and it took up a lot of headspace. She was teaching these women to be soldiers. Mortal battles with real consequences for their bodies, minds and consciences. Was it the wrong decision to teach them? It wasn't like she was actually in charge of them, she reminded herself; they had free will. However, she had a habit of taking control, and that nudged at her brain. Even Chrysa and David were participating. Sylvia sometimes liked her subtle I'm-in-charge vibe. It certainly had its perks, but with great power comes great responsibility. She especially didn't like responsibility when she felt so blind. She was a ship's captain in the storm of a lifetime. Wind and rain were crashing against the windows of the bridge. Her crewmembers came in soaking and went out with new orders. Some disappeared without a word. She just wasn't sure if this was a tragedy or a triumph. Miracles happened, but many ships sunk.

David's exasperated voice jolted her from her thoughts. "None of this is of any use to me. Can I just go?"

She shook her head and refocused. Her attention needed to be on her pupils. She was pleased to see that David was asking permission to leave. It meant she had control over her makeshift class. Control was good. She wracked her brain for things that David might be able to learn. "Chrysa!"

Her friend raised her eyebrows.

"David, you, redirection, now."

Chrysa rolled her eyes but acquiesced and explained the basics of redirection to David.

Redirection was less of a spell and more of a technique. The redirector would subtly alter incoming spells to change their direction just slightly. It was a very effective defense tactic for weaker witches, though Sylvia could not really utilize it fully, since she was often flying as blind as a human might be. Redirection did not work unless one could see the spell. Theoretically, though, if a human were able to see magic, redirection was a technique they might be able use. Since every being possessed some level of magic, it was life itself.

David took to it remarkably well, slighting altering Chrysa's fire, though the edge of his sleeve singed.

Sylvia raised her eyebrows in question at him.

"Cool, but not as effective as my guns," he asserted.

She'd take it. She called Maria over.

Maria knew how to give herself impeccable balance. It helped with her dancing at school. Sylvia had gone to one of her performances a few months ago.

Her grace was unimaginably beautiful. She did contemporary dance, so the whole thing flowed — emotions in physical form. Maria expressed yearning and thoughtfulness in her spotlight dance, like a mind tinkering on a problem. It was admirable. She knew balance might be a valuable trait for everyone to have in the crises they'd face soon enough. She pulled Maria aside and told her as much.

Maria nodded seriously and demonstrated to everyone how to spell themselves with balance. It took continued concentration, which was incredibly hard to maintain during a dance, much less a battle depleting one's magic, or else Sylvia might have thought it would be worth permanently spelling themselves like this. Instead it was probably best for special feats, momentary needs for incredible grace and balance. Sylvia figured it might come in handy for someone in a linchpin moment.

Next they worked on Sylvia's and Ellie's mini fire tubes. Loni and Maria took to the spell. Penelope fetched water for her daughters. She beamed with pride at Ellie taking the lead and explaining it to Loni. Ellie had an odd way of explaining. At first she said, "Well, you make the fire go into little tubes." When that drew a blank stare, Ellie made a tube shape with her hands, "Like this." Still blank. Ellie furrowed her brow and said, "Make fire." That Loni understood, but the fire was more of a ball shape. Slowly, Ellie walked her little sister through the steps. When Loni got the hang of the fire tubes, Ellie shouted, "There you go!"

"She looks happy," Penelope said quietly to Sylvia. They kept their eyes on the young witches.

"She likes to help and do good," Sylvia said.

"Yeah... she'd do anything for her sisters,"

223

Penelope said and her voice trailed off. She gave a watery smile. "I'm very proud of her and her sisters."

Chrysa slinked up beside them. "I don't like this spell," she said. She smiled lopsidedly.

Sylvia laughed. Chrysa's dark magic did not like to be controlled in such specific, small ways. It didn't like to be tidy. "Didn't think you would. You can change the spell any way you like, but I know you're already good with fire, so I wouldn't try to do something you're not good at," she said. "At least not amidst a war."

Chrysa shrugged her shoulders. "I'm taking a page out of the Book of Sylvia and trying something new. Might come in handy. Even though I hate it." She made an exaggerated frown at her friend.

"You're the best!" Sylvia said with a heaping of sarcasm and a bit of genuine pride. "Taking my words to heart." She loved when people changed just by knowing each other. It was a very magical type of interaction. The magic of human connection made living with the humans worth it, because it rubbed off on her and even Chrysa.

After everyone had a good enough grasp on the fire tubes, Loni showed them all a simple healing spell that she said even non-healers could do. It was only for cuts and scrapes, minor things. Everyone paid very close attention while the young girl walked them through the words and visualizations.

Sylvia used the spell on a scab she had on her hand. She didn't remember getting it and it didn't hurt, but she watched the skin go through the natural healing process at an accelerated rate. She brushed the scab, and it just fell away. It was satisfying to see her skin beneath, though her skin wasn't smooth anymore. A nasty side effect of aging.

Patty excelled at the minor healing spell. She brandished her hands about, extolling her magic hands. Her many rings weighed down her hand and made it look more bony and delicate than it should. She also introduced everyone to a metal heating spell she used all the time for cooking. Stoves weren't good enough for even consistent heat, Patty explained with absolute seriousness. Sylvia wasn't sure what help it would be, but she learned it nonetheless. She had to set an example, and honestly, it could possibly be useful in some way.

Maria had a keen interest in the metal heating spell, so she and Patty talked about it together.

Penelope even taught everyone a spell she knew, though she didn't demonstrate. She was particularly good at describing the process. She gave exact and precise instructions. Sylvia figured every spell that Penelope ever did had to be done carefully. She wondered how the woman handled it.

The spell was a simple one, admittedly. Just

a second of very accurate vision. Sylvia tried it and was amazed at how vibrant everything became. It was like it was all magnified and bright and overwhelming, actually. She wondered why this spell had been created, because it made her nervous and immediately caused a minor headache with so much visual stimulation. Ellie took to that spell surprisingly quick, though, and she held it much longer than anyone else. She looked around the room with wide eyes and a giant smile. "Everything is beautiful," she said. "Mama, you should've taught me this one before." Ellie went over to her mother and they began talking to each other. Sylvia guessed that Penelope was teaching her the few spells she knew that her daughter didn't.

The depth and breadth of the spells and magic that this group of women knew was extraordinary. Now, most of it wasn't useful, but it hit home to Sylvia how diverse her community was. These were close, long-time friends, and they had never shared this much. It certainly wasn't like there was a witch school for them to learn the same curriculum. Sylvia wondered if she should create it, though; this wealth of knowledge was too valuable to not be shared. Or maybe a witch symposium or something. She smiled. She liked it.

Some witches wrote down their spells in books and some even had them published like Griselda, but there were so many unshared. Tiny, made-up spells that Sylvia would never have imagined for herself. Spells for teeth-brushing and hair-combing, dish-washing and litter-scooping — witches definitely liked their cats. She loved domestic magic. How laziness reached new heights, and witches discovered new ways to exist in the world. To do such human things in such witchy ways. She loved cultures melding together and creating a new culture.

She was distracted by her own mind until she remembered what fortnight it was. She shook the thoughts from her head. She had to concentrate. No time for flights of fancy. This was the Hunt, and she had killed and she still might not survive. She had to remember that. She had to get out of the clouds. Clouds served no purpose now. Soft and fluffy and wet and absolutely useless in battle.

The group took a rest for dinner, and David was clearly the odd man out.

"I think we should go tonight," he said.

Penelope shot an angry look at him. "Let me enjoy this night with my daughters in peace... sir." She had paused and said the honorific with specific care, clearly expressing her disgust with his warmongering.

Penelope's erraticism — ping-ponging between bellicose and hysterical — worried Sylvia.

"While you witches are having your hippie-dippy, let's-all-learn crap, the fairies are getting stronger and that's not good. The longer we wait, the stronger they get, because they're killing more witches and taking their power," David said without an ounce of care. "You're letting that happen. We need to take action. We need to kill every single one of them."

"David, you need—" Sylvia began.

"It's very unlikely that all of us will survive," Penelope said quickly. Her voice caught on 'survive.' "So please give us the dignity of spending our last night together in peace. Without this talk of killing and violence. I want my daughters to have happy memories." Penelope looked on the edge of tears and her hands were shaking subtly.

Penelope's words hung in the air for a full minute after she said them. Sylvia surveyed the three daughters. Maria and Loni reached out their hands to their mother to comfort her. They knew that death was something she was so scared of and had seen up close.

Ellie looked ready to cry. "Potentially... potentially our last night," she said weakly. This much emoting was rare from Ellie, Sylvia noticed.

She wondered what it was like to stare death in the face and understand her frailty. It was something witches didn't grasp quite right, because their lifetimes could be so long and indefinite that death was an afterthought. For the oldest witches, there was sort of a casual welcoming of it even. But Penelope wasn't that old, especially because of her lack of magic use. It was something she knew intimately. And even though Sylvia was scared of it, it was still an abstract concept to her, to not be living anymore. Even killing those fairies did not make her understand it. Even being forced to fight against death did not make her understand it.

Witches didn't necessarily die like humans. They could preserve their souls if enough magic existed at the time of their body's death. They became ghosts of sorts. No real physical presence, though in the Magical Realm they still wreaked some havoc. And in the Mundane Realm, they sort of haunted places—at least in the humans' perspective. Any witch would know that the apparition talking to them was their old friend; witches weren't scared of ghosts. Most of Sylvia's friends were still alive, so she didn't interact much with ghost-witches, though she had come across a few in her time.

Back in the 70s when hiking had been one of Sylvia's hobbies, she was in the Rocky Mountains on a camping trip. She had pitched her tent and was making the water in a nearby river dance over to her. She had been very wasteful with her magic in the past. And even now sometimes.

But her peaceful nature communing was interrupted by a helicopter overhead. It was nondescript and clearly not going anywhere near her. But she hemmed and hawed and said aloud to herself, "Technology always trying to ruin things."

"In my time, there were none of those flying machines," said a voice oddly close to her.

Sylvia turned to be face-to-face with a half-visible apparition. She was wearing a long beige dress with long sleeves. It looked very pioneer to Sylvia. "Hi," she said. "What brings you out here?"

"Eh," said the ghost-witch. "Always been out here. Died out here, and had nowhere to go so I just stayed. Gets lonely. Haven't seen a witch in these here parts in a long while." Ghost-witches weren't bound to certain locations, but certain witches just didn't care to leave.

"I'm just hiking and getting fresh air," Sylvia said.

"Women these days going out by themselves. It's really an odd thing how the world changed," she said. "Saw two women come by this river not a month ago. They wore long pants and wore their hair in braids. And they seemed not to care for the trappings of a man. Kept cackling about how much fun they were having."

"You think that's a bad thing?" Sylvia asked.

"It's a thing I'm not used to. Women succeeding without any men helping them along," the ghost-witch admitted. "It grows on me as I think about it. Only women are witches, and I'm sure there are more things that only we can do."

Sylvia never went back to that camping spot and never saw the ghost-witch again, but she had beamed with pride for the rest of that day. She felt unique, special and capable, thinking that she was a witch able to do things no man could do, despite her relative weakness in comparison to her witch counterparts. She finished the hike with a good pace and high spirits.

As she remembered that conversation, she thought about how it still applied to their current situation. How they were capable, perhaps even more capable, and that death was not necessarily the only outcome. And not necessarily narrowly avoided. They could perhaps achieve their mission of surviving with flying colors. They could excel and thrive, not just barely survive.

She told the women and David the story of the ghost-witch in the Rockies.

David rolled his eyes dismissively, but the witches nodded in hopeful camaraderie.

The rest of dinner was much more cheerful, especially since Sylvia was careful to stop David from making any unsavory comments. She was still unsure of him. His tendency and willingness toward violence did not sit well with her. But he was helping keep the group alive, just like anyone else. And it wouldn't feel right to just let him fend for himself.

She still thought it best to have some safety measures in place in case he did anything to jeopardize the witches. None of the safety measures she thought of seemed suitable. What was she supposed to do? Restraining David would tie up Sylvia's ability to help in a fight. But continuing on as if he was full part of the group didn't make sense either. What it came down to was they had to get to the fairy court and ask for immunity. When they left, David could go on his merry way. Ideally, they wouldn't have to fight at all. They might be sneaky enough, she supposed. It did not seem as if the fairy court's headquarters were closely guarded. The fairies certainly didn't genuinely believe any witch would try to make her way there, as evidenced by the fact that she and David had made it so close with no preparation— in hindsight their lack of preparation was a really dumb idea, so many other things could've happened. Going to ask for immunity still might not be the best way either. She knew that the Hunt would end on Saturday. They just had to manage until then. They'd managed so far fairly well. She'd only encountered four malevolent fairies. And the ensuing "battles"— if she could call them that— were solved relatively quickly. There were no dramatics or injuries on her side. She wondered if that was luck or skill.

She witnessed four deaths, even participated in most of them. After a lifetime of not seeing any sort of combat, it was a surprise that she was chugging along fairly calmly. Three of those four deaths had been her doing. Her mind had already started to make her forget the horror. It made her feel crappier that her bad acts weren't constantly haunting her. She felt as if she should be punished. But she wasn't being punished. She was in a way rewarded; the group looked up to her and continued to let her lead, and even her brain forgave her. She should be disgusted. She should feel worse.

She turned her attention outward again and heard the tail end of some joke that Chrysa was telling. She didn't bother to laugh. She'd just wait for the next one.

That night they double-checked all the locks and put chairs underneath the door handles. Patty volunteered to stay up to watch. Sylvia was grateful that she volunteered, since she said she wasn't going to the fairy court at the behest of a rumor. She said she might go if Sylvia and the other witches were successful.

But by the mere virtue that Patty was refusing to go meant they had very little confidence in the chances of success for their mission. Sylvia wondered if she was the smart one in this dilemma. Maybe, but Patty's house had already been attacked once, a second time was almost guaranteed. She wondered how Patty would manage by herself. She wasn't a weak witch by any measure. And maybe Patty's safe room was enough. But magic was powerful and creative and could often foil human technology, which had no magical defense built in.

She thought it was weird that human inventors would invent so many things and not even have a clue to the existence of magic. Many of their machines were easily replaced by simple spells.

And then, what about an inventor with magical powers? She might be the most powerful of them all. A lot of witches didn't bother too much with technology since they had magic. There was the occasional computer nerd. Sylvia had heard that Ellie liked programming or coding or whatever it was. But Ellie was certainly not the average witch. Sylvia could see her going places. Any of the Thin sisters, actually. There was so much potential. She hoped they all lived to see it come to fruition.

She made her way into her room and put a chair under the door handle. The room was a bit chilly, so she kept her day clothes on and crawled underneath the covers. She could hear the Thin family in the other room talking. She couldn't make out their words, but each voice was distinct. Penelope's voice was low, slow and measured. Maria was booming and powerful. Ellie's squeaked occasionally and was a bit high. Loni's was high as well but much quieter and not squeaky. Loni whispered even when she was being loud. That breathy quality was relaxing to Sylvia. She thought that Loni might be a very good doctor. Everyone figured she would be one day.

Most witches didn't become doctors. They did not purport to understand traditional medicine when their supposedly "homeopathic" — read 'magical' — stuff worked. But Loni was an actual healer with a natural gift for healing. She wasn't just using little convenient spells. It was real healing.

Sylvia turned on her side and pulled the blankets with her. It felt cold for a minute before her body heated up the cold parts of the blankets and sheets. She shivered to build some heat. She liked warm.

When comfortable, she closed her eyes. The female fairy from the night before, the one she had killed, popped into her mind. Her bouncy red hair lost its luster after her death. And then the other two fairies. The look of agony of their faces was unbearable. But she kept going.

Sylvia desperately tried to clear her mind from those thoughts, so she stopped trying to sleep. She thought back to her childhood of the time she went to the bakery and managed to steal some bread. Even to this day she felt bad about it, but she never told anyone, not her mother, not Chrysa.

The wife of the baker worked the front desk at the bakery. The inside of the building was very warm compared to the outside. Sylvia relished the warmth and pulled her coat tighter. The baker's wife was turned around, so Sylvia tiptoed up to the counter and stole a fresh hot roll from a basket near the baker's wife's accounts book where she meticulously kept track of everything. In town, the baker's wife had a reputation for being nit-picky and particular. But Sylvia's mother told her that the baker's wife was not being difficult on purpose and that Sylvia shouldn't participate in the nasty talk about her.

Still, Sylvia grabbed another two rolls and stuffed them in her jacket pockets, justifying her theft by reassuring herself that the baker's wife was particular. The heat of them comforted her. She said hello to the baker's wife and went on her way. No one caught her. Even so, as she walked away, her heart pounded out of her chest.

She didn't know why she stole the bread. She was a bit hungry, but she could've easily gone home and asked her mother for some. She even had a coin or two in her possession, but still she went and took some. In the woods on the way home, she took one roll from her pocket. It was covered in pocket lint and she haphazardly brushed it off before chomping down. She ate the second one in the same way, without regard. She wasn't hungry for dinner that night, but no one suspected a thing. She never stole again, but that did not excuse the act. What demon had possessed her? It was more of a rhetorical question. Demons were real, but certainly didn't possess people to steal bread. No, this was all her. Even 100 years later, that was one of the memories that stuck out to her and bothered her. She felt like she had been atoning ever since, and now she had something new to atone for.

And this was much worse, definitely not the memory train she wanted to be on. It was just leading her back to the same old thoughts. She should be resting; she had to protect the witches. If not with sheer force which everyone knew wasn't her strong suit, then with wit, because she knew she possessed that — more than the average witch.

She thought about each of the Thin sister's futures. It almost felt as if those girls were her own daughters, especially now. She had watched them grow up. She played in the garden with Maria, crafted alongside Ellie, and talked about poetry with Loni. It had been wonderful to see that, since she was sure she'd never have children of her own. She just didn't think she had it in her, to be a mother was a big responsibility. But she loved kids.

Her kids were in her sixth grade classroom. Some of them visited her, even when they went up some grades or moved on to other schools.

She smiled and exhausted herself with thoughts of them.

She fell asleep. At first her dreams were full of children. They happily went about their lives, playing in the sandbox or bossily telling the other children what to do. Sylvia liked the bossy children if they were nice. Other children drew pictures. Some children read books. They were doing things they liked. But the image dimmed. A dark presence came, ruining the happiness. It destroyed everything and everyone with a curtain of fire. When the dark presence was revealed to be her, she woke with a start. She was the darkness.

Her heart beat rapidly and roughly, but she eventually calmed herself down. This time she tired herself with thoughts of Chrysa and eventually fell asleep. She dreamed of Chrysa, but yet again the dark presence came and ruined everything. She twitched awake. She tried three more times that night before getting a solid, dreamless sleep. That was exhaustion.

Waking in the morning was the most sad and hard thing to do. She was so drained and the weight of the day pressed down on her. She didn't want to do this, maybe they could just stay holed up. It was only four more whole days until they could just be free. They could last.

Patty had not seen anyone through the night. The entire group sat down for breakfast. No one was perky. No one wanted this day to happen. The immediacy made it too real. Death was a real possibility, a likelihood. Maybe it was better that they didn't, because no one wanted to say aloud that anything could happen.

Ellie looked sharp, though — maybe the only one of them, even David seemed sluggish. She ate two portions of breakfast while reading a combat defense book and committing the spells to memory.

Sylvia hoped that she wouldn't have to use such haphazardly acquired spells. The danger for backfire was high. She mentioned it but didn't push the issue. Ellie was old enough to make her own decisions, and she very well might save them all. Sylvia was too selfish to pass that opportunity up, as terrible as it was. So instead she practiced the spells with Ellie, they probably understood ten more spells. And maybe one of them would save them all. She had to hope.

She imagined scenarios of what they might face when they got there, but her brain wasn't committed to it. She only imagined extremes, very empty corridors and no fairies until they got to the room or fairies every ten feet, a literal army. There was too much to consider. And she was better on the fly. They had done a lot of preparing, now it was time for action.

With that thought, something rapped on the kitchen window from the garden. Framed by background greenery, the fairy's angular face was odd. Then she saw the other six fairies and she froze. Everyone did. Sylvia recovered quickest and got up. She stood in front of the table and blocked her fellow witches from any potential attack with her body. In hindsight, it was very unlikely to be effective. Her body didn't take up much space, and everyone was seated around the table, not in the table. She was essentially protecting the table. That wasn't a good sacrifice. Goodness, she was tired.

Her heart pounded, and she thought of what she would have to do. She didn't know, she didn't know. There were a lot of them. Witches were strong, but seven fairies? If they were hunting buddies, they had strategy and group cohesion. Sylvia had her motley crew. What was there to do?

If any of them was a plant fairy, outside was not the way to go. She looked down at her fairy alignments charms and saw that plant, earth and sky were glowing. Definitely not an outside battle, but inside wasn't much better at all. With earth fairies, any sort of metal was extremely dangerous, as were jewels and any sort of stones. Patty's expensive cutlery could potentially be a problem, depending on how strong the earth fairies were. Sylvia had even heard of earrings being a problem unless they were entirely plastic, which earrings rarely were. But that was only the most powerful earth fairies.

Sky fairies did best during extreme weather, but they were dangerous both inside and outside.

She decided that inside was ultimately best. The plant fairies would be at a disadvantage. The sky and earth fairies could potentially be dangerous in either place. She could weaken at least some of the party with this strategic decision.

The entry way seemed like the only option.

Her mind was racing. She felt light-headed from the zooming thoughts and bombardment of ideas. It was ridiculous. It almost paralyzed her, but she couldn't fight this battle in her head.

She translated her mental energy into physical momentum and got all the witches and David away from the table. They didn't turn their backs but instead backed up slowly. Sylvia coached them calmly. "We can do this. We've got it in us. We will be fine." Inside she was screaming to herself that they definitely couldn't do it. There was no way in the Mundane Realm or the Magical. She told them to go to the closet area of the entry way, so they would have cover on their backs.

The fairies stalked closer to them too, magicking the door wide open. It made a loud noise as it slammed open, and Sylvia noticed that Loni and Penelope flinched. Neither of them liked loud noises. Ellie, however, didn't pay any attention to the noise. That girl could be so robotic sometimes. There was no such thing as shock for robots, except electrical shock. But when Sylvia saw Ellie smile so big about something she was happy about, it seemed impossible that the same girl was a robot. She was so vibrant sometimes.

This was not the time for frenetic, unfocused thoughts. She had to focus!

The fairies entered the house and advanced, but no one did a spell. It was as if they were all suspended in disbelief. Like maybe this fight wouldn't happen if they just continued to slowly slink in the same direction. Like some West Side Story snap battle. Sylvia could get on board with that.

But when the witches had backed themselves into the corner between an armoire and a dresser, chaos broke out, because David fired a gun that she hadn't known he was carrying. He nipped the shoulder of a female fairy, but she didn't go down. Goodness, he was a terrible shot. This fight would be over already if he was a better marksman.

The clipped fairy snapped to face him, like a rubber band that had just been let go. She seemed ready to launch herself at him, but nothing happened.

Sylvia saw the intense concentration in her face, indicating that she was magicking; the other fairies were now doing the same.

Sylvia tried the suffocation spell on a fairy close to her, concentrating on the fairy's neck.

Patty's new armoire broke up with a loud crack. Mahogany branches came out towards David. Maria screamed.

Sylvia lost her concentration, but she couldn't help either of them. The other fairies would pounce if given half a chance.

Sylvia refocused on her magic. The fairy was downed by her suffocation spell in a minute. The Glamour faded, and she was a monster.

Maria fired an energy ball at a rather short fairy, who dodged handily. Ellie used a fire curtain on two fairies at once. Loni used the bright flash spell to distract a fairy coming towards her mother. Chrysa threw fire at a fairy who was throwing lightning at her. The magical embodiments clashed in the air, and the result was beautiful and violent. David shot another bullet, only to miss because of encroaching branches tearing into his flesh. Patty conjured up a protective bubble around herself. She expanded the reach of her bubble and was able to collect Penelope, who had taken off her shoe and thrown it at a sword-wielding fairy, who momentarily seemed dumb-founded. Huzzah! He then aggressively walked towards her. His sword met with the semi-transparent barrier but did not pass.

Sylvia helped Loni by using the suffocation spell on the earth fairy that Loni was ineffectively distracting and then shoved the girl into the protective bubble with the other three witches. Loni fell on her hands and knees, definitely skinning her palms and knees on the rug. Guilt pounded down on Sylvia's shoulders, but she didn't have time for that.

A mahogany branch swiped past Sylvia's leg and scraped a shallow gash into her. She yelped and reached her hand down to feel it, but another branch knocked into her hand. The branches whipped and writhed in their small area of the entry way. They were growing longer. Something hit her torso and she fell.

Branches swarmed her. Sharp pain stung her arm, then her gut. The branches were burrowing into her.

Sylvia threw every spell she could in the direction of the plant fairy. Nothing connected. She dodged easily.

A branch slammed into one of the dressers, and a bowl smashed to the ground. Among the glass shards lay a ring of keys. Sylvia ripped her bloody arm from a branch and grabbed them. She launched the keys at the plant fairy and performed the flash spell.

The plant fairy blinked away confusion, and her mahogany branches stopped their torrential movement. She was motionless, they were motionless. The two branches digging into Sylvia receded just a tiny bit, a momentary reprieve. The branches didn't move if the plant fairy wasn't paying attention.

Hope and excitement got Sylvia to push herself up off the ground in a heave. She was exhausted but couldn't stop yet.

Sylvia heard screams as Ellie won her battle against two fairies. Chrysa was also finishing up with her opponent. She would soon win.

The plant fairy gained her bearings and started to dance again. The branches lashed, invigorated.

A branch hit her back, and Sylvia put her arm up. She conjured up a small tube of fire, lengthening it and wrapping it around the branches and then around the armoire itself. More branches tried to hold her and pummel her, but she avoided the worst of the assault. When her fire tubes were ready, she released the energy holding the magical tube together. The tree and armoire burst in rather large flames.

The plant fairy screamed in pain as the branches were licked raw by fire. Just like Sylvia had hoped for.

As if by silent cue, Chrysa threw her own fire ball at the fairy who tried to roll on the ground. Nothing the plant fairy tried was successful. She died, and the Glamour dissipated.

Three fairies left now? One fairy was

David's opponent. Another was Maria's. The last fairy was one Sylvia hadn't registered; he hadn't used any magic yet and she wondered what he was hiding. Was he just watching? Sizing them up? Perhaps he was working a slow type of magic. Perhaps they'd win the rest of the battles, but then this fairy would swoop in with his slow insidious spell and obliterate them all.

David's opponent fell. David shot Maria's exhausted opponent in the chest and then in the head from close-range because he was such a poor shot.

Then there was one fairy left — the one who had not yet done anything that she noticed. Sylvia's sky necklace charm glowed brightly.

She tried the suffocation spell and the flash spell, but he barely seemed interested. Sylvia couldn't accurately focus the spell. Her energy was gone. She swayed.

Chrysa's fire attacks blew past him, as did Maria's energy ball. David's bullets whipped around him. Ellie's fire curtain just dissipated before it had a chance to establish itself.

The fairy laughed.

He used wind magic, Sylvia realized. Wind was a tricky magic. It uniquely eluded attacks, but wasn't so powerful with perpetrating its own attacks. The fairy had to be felled with a sneak attack.

She let the others continue to attack and slinked back to Loni quietly.

After several minutes, Loni was able to knock the man out by selectively targeting his aorta so blood didn't get to his brain. He wasn't dead, and Sylvia was glad that it wasn't Loni who had to do such a thing.

Sylvia went to question him, weighing him down with the restraining spell. "Who knew about you coming here?" she asked sharply.

He shrugged. "It doesn't matter. Someone will find you." He wasn't laughing anymore.

That allayed Sylvia's fears, because she knew that now they had been found by chance. Fairies often did not share information because they were greedy creatures. "What can you tell me about the headquarters?"

"Headquarters?" the fairy asked in return. He looked at his fellow dead fairies and hardened his mouth.

"The fairy court in L.A.. What can you tell me about it?" Sylvia asked.

"Nothing you should know about," he said with an honest-to-god snarl. That was a hard expression to accurately manage, but this fairy did. It was so animalistic with viciously sharp teeth.

Suddenly Sylvia wondered why with all the Glamour that the fairies wielded didn't change their teeth. To fit in, they should make them flatter and more square. But all the fairies she'd seen thus far were particularly sharp-toothed. Perhaps they did not closely examine those they were copycatting, like an inattentive artist painting blue eyes instead of green in a portrait. Or maybe they liked their teeth ready and the Glamour prevented that. Of course, she hadn't seen fairies use their teeth, so she didn't know what purpose they served. Fairies were like humans; they might need incisors, but, for the most part, they caught and prepared their food. They didn't rip it apart. Perhaps they needed it evolutionarily at some point.

The fairy attempted to stand, but her restraining spell knocked his physical balance off.

They would kill him, Sylvia realized. They had no way to keep him. They had no way to safely contain him, unless they wanted a witch to waste her time watching him instead of getting immunity. And that certainly didn't make sense. Though maybe Patty could do it. She asked.

"I've decided to come with you all today," she answered. "I think I'm safer in the group. So unfortunately I won't be staying here."

Before anyone had a moment to speak, David stood over the fairy and fired his gun point-blank.

Sylvia twitched. She did not turn to see the others' reactions. She didn't know if she wanted to see. If they were glad or appalled or disgusted or scared. Any of those reactions would make her feel worse about what she had done, because if they felt it when he did it, they surely felt it when she did it. Sylvia felt scared and glad that the fairy was dead. His Glamour had faded to reveal a rather slight fairy body.

After waiting three seconds, she turned to face the group. She surveyed them for signs of injury. Everyone was whole. She wondered if this battle was too easy.

David looked worn. Beads of sweat glistened on his face, and he had cuts and scrapes all over exposed skin, primarily on his arms. Sylvia felt bad, like she hadn't done enough. But everyone was alive. They had battled seven fairies and lived to tell the tale.

She felt something warm drip down her arm.

"Sylvia!" Loni rushed forward.

"It's not a big deal," Sylvia said quickly, not wanting the attention on her.

"It's bleeding a lot." Loni tenderly wiped the blood away with her shirt.

Sylvia tried to pull her arm away, but the young girl was much stronger than she expected. Or perhaps Sylvia was weaker. This attack had sapped all her strength. "I'm fine. I've seen way worse on the playground." She had felled multiple living creatures. They knew. She wanted to hide.

"No one likes a martyr," David said, annoyance tinging his voice. "You help no one by suffering in silence. And you won't get any fucking points from me."

"Who wants points from you anyway?" Sylvia wanted to add the word asshole, but she refrained, remembering their company. David had no clue.

But she let Loni treat her. It was best not to cause a fuss. She calmed.

Everyone milled around. The air was full of the same apprehensive energy that existed in the morning after a sleepover. It was sad and on the tail end of adrenaline, which was always so weird. Like they didn't know what to do other than move their bodies. Penelope picked up splinters from the armoire and made the hem of her shirt into a container.

Maria started to cry. Her mom came over and wrapped an arm around her.

Even as she healed her arm, Loni's lip quivered. She was also ready to cry.

The sadness would catch on with the rest of the group quickly.

Sylvia made eye contact with Patty and raised her eyebrows. "I'm sorry about your armoire."

Patty nodded and sighed. "I guess it's not too much of a loss," she said, even though she was clearly lying. "I couldn't find the key for that armoire anyway." She stretched her mouth into a smile.

That statement seemed to snap everyone out of the silence but not the sadness.

"I didn't like that," Maria said to her mother. She was shaking.

Her mother put a comforting hand on her back and moved it slowly. "It's okay, honey. None of us did. If you're too scared next time, you can go with Patty in the bubble."

Maria hardened her mouth and didn't meet her mother's eyes.

Ellie, on the other hand, was stoic, standing apart from her family eyeing the ground. She quickly picked up the rest of the pieces of the shattered armoire and took them to the kitchen with her mom.

Shock made everything in the room spiky. Maria and Loni winced as they helped clean up. Staying in the house would not be good. They needed to leave.

"Why are you guys fucking cleaning?" David asked incredulously. "We need to leave!" David hemmed and hawed. He was wearing her nerves thin, like a student she had two years before who insisted that Sylvia write up her assignments on a printed out sheet, instead of him copying them down in his binder reminder. She liked her students to practice writing and being responsible. He didn't need an accommodation, but he got his mom involved. She had never met a sixth grader with such an entitled attitude. They eventually went to the principal, and Sylvia was made to print out a separate sheet for him. She had been beyond furious, and that was rare for her. David was precariously close to that same fury. And she agreed with him! She sealed her mouth.

"This does nothing," he continued. "This is just delaying the inevitable. The fairies are just getting stronger. We need to go. Like now."

Sylvia breathed in slowly and nodded her head.

Chapter 24 - Thom

When the Court received news that a hunting party employed by King Puck had not reported back to him, the whispers and wide eyes rolled through the room as if a drop of water had hit the still center of the fairies and waved out.

Mother gripped his hand tightly. "We better be careful," she said.

"Of what?" Thom asked, not wondering why a hunting party missing was alarming. They probably got lost, he thought.

"The implication—" Mother said with clipped words "— is that witches killed them."

"It makes sense though," Thom said. "I would fight back if people were out to hurt me." He didn't get why everyone was aghast.

Mother huffed like she was annoyed.

Grandmother walked over in an unusual outfit of fuzzy white in a long dress. She tended to do whatever she wanted, not sticking to the main Court fashions of the day. It was easy with Glamour. Thom hoped to master Glamour and magic like that one day — without the eccentric outfits. "Thomas," she said with a smile that told him she intended to make a point to him.

Pin prickles of discomfort creeped up his back to his neck.

"Surely, you realize now why we must hunt the witches," she said.

He frowned. Grandmother was worse than Mother and Father. She just hid it better. "No, I do not," he said with a forced formality. He didn't want to talk to her anymore.

"They kill us," she said. "Six or seven of ours are lost to those witches. Thomas, it is important to not blind ourselves to the greater good when we squirm with discomfort about a few... insignificant details."

He felt trapped. What could he say? There's was no way to convince her when she viewed the witches as insignificant details. "You are right, Grandmother," Thom said without any enthusiasm. Maybe she would leave him alone now.

Her smile was benevolent and beaming, as if she were doing the greatest good.

Thom didn't feel good.

Grandmother turned her attention to Mother and began speaking of security. She switched so easily, as if talking about killing was not a problem, as if it was no more tense than wondering what was for the feast that day.

He scrunched up his face, tears suddenly threatening to fall from his eyes. His opinions didn't matter. They treated him like he was five years old, but he was eleven! He was much more grown-up now. He understood that sometimes there is a cost to getting what one wants. He knew that. But some costs were too high. Did they not see that?

The day swirled in a mass of greens, oranges, yellows, purples, reds and browns. The mounting excitement of the end of the Hunt drawing near made the laughter louder and the smiles whiter. It was a mockery of how Thom felt though. Frivolous festivities covered the truth of why they were there, to celebrate the killing of the witches, to gloat in their power.

When they got home, Thom came up to his mother, hoping his new tactic would help.

"You are going home soon," she said with a rare warmth in her tone.

"I'll be happy to climb trees again," he said, anxious to get to his point. The den was dark, like their home in the caves in Tirt. Dark did not scare him usually, but this darkness felt somber and ominous.

"When we come back, they will treat us with more respect," she said with a smile and distant eyes.

Thom saw his opportunity then. "Respect is important. I wonder if we get any respect for sending Father's employees to hunt for us."

"What do you mean? Of course we do. We have a lot of magic. Your father has chosen his hunters well."

"It looks weak to have others do for us what he can't," Thom said. His chest was tight.

"Thomas, everyone has hunters. It is beneath nobility to work," Mother said, shaking her head. Her warmth was gone.

"King Puck did it himself, and he is king now," Thom said, feeling a surge of pride from making the connection.

Mother tilted her head like she always did when she reconciled ideas. She spoke slowly when she did. "He does not have much respect."

"But what is more important: respect or power? He is king," Thom said quickly. He beamed. The room seem brighter suddenly.

"Perhaps you are right." Her eyes stared through him, past him. No doubt, she was imagining having the power. No one would roll their eyes at her. Smile and tease her and say mean things when she was gone.

Thom could hear these thoughts in her head just by watching her now. Mother would certainly be easier than Father to convince.

When Father got home from Court, Mother approached him first and more enthusiastically, explaining Thom's idea.

"But no one likes him," Father said. He squinted his hazel eyes and shook his head.

"But he is king," Thom said. It was something his parents understood, royalty was the highest to achieve. It was almost surprising how simple it was, more astonishing that he'd never thought to do this before.

"He is," Father said. "But you will be king as well."

"But you won't be," Thom said, risking the sting that he knew his father would feel. "You need the respect and power. They need to know you aren't afraid of anything. You are strong. You will be a strong regent. King Puck showed us that he's willing to do anything. No one has yet spoken against him."

Father nodded. It was like trees falling in the forest, bringing down other trees.

Thom's heart calmed, and he held Mother's hand, squeezing it tightly as she always did.

They then discussed how Father would go to Court the next day and announce he would finish the Hunt, giving his employees the day off. He was strong and kind.

Chapter 25 - Sylvia

They piled into two cars. David beeped his car open, and the sound was uncharacteristically high-pitched. It didn't match his personality. Sylvia pursed her lips to keep from outwardly laughing. That grouch had this mosquito of a car. Penelope also volunteered to drive. Sylvia suspected that she wanted to be useful and have something to distract her from their impending danger.

Sylvia sat up front in David's car. Chrysa and Patty sat in the back. She could hardly think. Staring straight forward and pretending not to exist was a good solution.

As they pulled onto the highway, Sylvia asked to no one in particular, "Are we doing the right thing?"

"Saving our lives? Yes," Chrysa answered promptly. Chrysa always played it blunt with her.

"But to involve Penelope's girls," Sylvia said. Her voice wavered on the word "girls," because that's what they really were. Girls, girls who hadn't even graduated high school. Girls who loved their mom and dad dearly. Girls who didn't know the bad of the world yet.

"We need them. They need them. There is no other way," Chrysa said. "You saw them, right? Ellie took on two fairies herself and held her own. Maria took on one. Loni protected her mother. They're not children."

"But you saw how Maria was afterwards. She looked so guilty, and she hadn't even killed any of them," Sylvia said.

"You were feeling guilty too," Patty said, her first words since hopping in the car.

"But I knew full well what I was doing," Sylvia said. She examined the lines and wrinkles on her hands, occupying her mind momentarily. Submitting these girls to this was not letting them live a regular childhood. They wouldn't grow old in the normal way. They'd grow old way too fast.

Chrysa snorted. "You don't give them enough credit. Those girls understand more than you think." She and Sylvia exchanged faces. "When I was a kid, girls their age were getting married and having babies. You had to grow up fast. I know I did."

Patty turned suddenly to face Chrysa, and her face was sympathetic. "Are you saying you got married and had children?"

Chrysa nodded. "Yep. They're all dead now, because I had a son."

"Oh, I'm sorry," Patty said, reaching across the empty space to put a hand on Chrysa's forearm.

"It's been a while," Chrysa said toughly. Sylvia knew that when push came to shove, her friend always downplayed pain like that. Probably because she wanted to save face.

Sylvia had never married or had children and maybe she thought she should be grateful for that decision, the pain of loss was great. She had had no interest. At least in marrying. She loved children and had a few times wondered if she might marry just to have children, but that'd be unethical to her. And contrary to the popular belief when she was young, she thought marriage ought to be between two people who loved each other. She'd known so many unhappy people as a kid; she thought that, at least, people should marry someone who didn't make them sad or angry. Maybe a reasonable level of flatness. Of course, there were the ones who liked each other, and everything about their lives seemed better for it. Sylvia liked the turn in popular opinion in the last 30 years. People were choosing love or bust. And while that might not be 100% effective even still, she saw lots of young folks fairly happy. Love was an odd thing. It didn't mean people had chemistry or compatibility. It meant intense feelings of desire and comfort, ignoring flaws. Sylvia always noticed flaws, maybe that was why she had never been in love, though she did love so many people. It was just never as irrational and uncontrollable as people made romantic love sound. That loss of control was something Sylvia didn't do.

She refocused on the conversation to Patty whimpering. "It was the only time I ever got pregnant," she said through wet sniffles.

Chrysa reached across the car and touched her in a comforting way.

"I bought so many things to prepare for her. And then she didn't make it," Patty said the words through constricted lungs.

As Patty talked through sobs, Sylvia caught up to the conversation and realized that the purses in the bureau in the room that Sylvia stayed were for Patty's miscarried daughter. It made Sylvia's nose burn — that feeling right before tears.

Being a witch was a lonely life without a daughter or a sister or — in Sylvia's case — a friend. The way Penelope talked, she thought her daughters were the best gift she could have ever received. They meant the world to her. Patty had no one like that. Sylvia was glad she could at least be her friend.

It was amazing that all these witches had found each other, when the witch population was so miniscule in comparison to humans.

Suddenly,, they drove past the Pavilion — she hadn't even noticed they'd gotten to Downtown. Sylvia said, "Shit! Do the hide in plain sight spell!" She hurriedly did it, and felt the others do it too. It wasn't the best protection, but it was better than nothing.

No one on the street looked at them, but

Sylvia saw several fairies. On a bench across from the Pavilion near the park, there sat an older fairy who let the Glamourized version of herself look older, which was probably unheard of for a fairy, but Sylvia was positive she was a fairy. The energy she gave off was undeniably hazy and uncomfortable. She had silvery hair, full lips, brown-that-glowed-orange-in-the-sunlight eyes, and long, delicate fingers clasped primly in her lap. She wore a yellow sundress and didn't seem one bit bothered by how cold it was outside. She didn't seem to be on watch, though. It was rather like she was just enjoying herself.

Two other male fairies stood near her. They were much sharper looking than the woman on the bench. Both had this sharp look in their respectively blue and brown eyes. The first sported dull brown hair and athletic wear, though he clearly had no intention of running around. The other was dressed as a tourist in an overly-flowery Hawaiian shirt. It almost seemed silly. He seemed like a secret service man — a really bad undercover agent who clearly has no idea what "blend" meant.

Six other fairies dotted the streets — each in an incongruous outfit from the next one. They all seemed to have an eye on the silver-haired fairy, and Sylvia wondered if she was important.

They parked a few blocks away in the same parking structure as last time. They all stood together between their cars and discussed their best options.

"When we went last time, we had no problem with anything," Sylvia said. "It was fairly empty. So I don't know why there are so many this time."

"But there are," Chrysa said with a sigh. "Didn't you say there might be another way in from underground?"

"The spiral staircases from the service tunnel? Maybe, but I don't know where they lead," Sylvia said.

No one really knew what to do. It was a roadblock. They didn't want to go in from the ground level, but they also didn't know what else to do. It wasn't like they could get helicopters and repel down, as David quietly suggested, because that was way too obvious.

"What about the Los Angeles tunnels?" Ellie asked.

"The Los Angeles Tunnels?" Sylvia asked. She didn't know what the Los Angeles tunnels were.

But Ellie seemed confident. "I read about them on the internet once. They are a series of tunnels under Downtown L.A.," she said. "They are super cool, I thought. But they were supposedly for drug running and the prohibition era when that was still happening."

"And you think they connect to the service tunnel?" Chrysa said.

"It's definitely an idea," she said with absolute confidence. But she didn't know. She didn't have a map. No one did apparently. That was the beauty and curse of the tunnels, Ellie explained. One might know one section, but not another. It was incongruous and not well-planned. It wasn't planned at all, it turned out. There was a well-known tunnel in the Hall of Records in Downtown. But it was a ways from the Opera house, and they didn't know what might be in the area.

Maria brought up a map on her smartphone, and they started looking things up. It was really quite amazing, Sylvia thought, phones these days. It was cool they could instantly compile data from so many sources. There were mostly other entertainment buildings and some government buildings. The Los Angeles Department of Water and Power was right behind the Pavilion. Ellie pointed out that one. Her index finger pushed on the little screen, and she just kept pointing. Sylvia guessed this was her premonition skill coming to its best use.

Sylvia took that as her cue to get the whole group walking. They didn't know what to look for. They didn't know what to do. When they got there, they'd be flying by the seat of their pants and hoping some fairies didn't pass them by. But they had a direction, and Sylvia was so thankful for that.

David walked awkwardly at the rear. He clearly wanted to go another way. He always wanted to go in guns blazing. Sylvia knew him well enough at this point to know that about him. He was impulsive and had very little regard for anyone but himself. Though she had not really seen him interact with humans, she suspected his human interactions were devoid of sunshine and daisies as well.

Sylvia pulled up in the group to walk beside Chrysa.

They walked in silence for a minute before Chrysa asked, "Do you think this will work? Some secret underground tunnel? That may or may not exist?"

"I don't know," Sylvia said. One minute she thought their group was invincible, the next she thought they were all going to die, because what could they do? But Penelope's girls could do a lot. Chrysa was an extraordinarily gifted witch. Patty was a good person. David had a gun. And Sylvia had her wits. They could do this. They could. Ellie was so quick-thinking that she thought of prohibition tunnels. Sylvia wouldn't have thought of that. She was proud of the girl. She was amazing. She was meant for great things. She could do so much with her time. She would be someone one day. Sylvia could feel it. So what she said to Chrysa was: "I believe the tunnels are real, and I think we could be onto something. We're amazing, and we're gonna kick ass."

"I think you're being a little too optimistic. You sound like you've joined a positivity cult," Chrysa said. "We're in an actually dangerous situation. This is not a classroom. Or some hippie farm in Idaho."

She felt like she was being scolded, and she didn't like it. She was friends with Chrysa. Chrysa was not her mom, and that tone was frankly really annoying. She didn't say anything, though she was sure her face showed her anger. Her training as a teacher said that she should never confront someone while emotional. But god, if there was ever a time emotional responses were allowed, she wished it was now.

Group morale was important. There shouldn't be in-fighting, though it was so tempting right then. They walked, and Sylvia said nothing.

It was stupid, so stupid to have to keep quiet, she thought. When she was angry, she ought to be able to say something about it. Silence was dumb. But she knew she wasn't thinking all that clearly.

They wound up in front of the Department of Water and Power. It was an odd building. It looked like a stack of cards. It was obviously a design from the time when people thought all concrete buildings were cool, but the glass windows made it much more modern. Sylvia was alive when they did that, the concrete buildings. No one ever thought they were pretty.

"I like the way this building looks," Ellie said to no one in particular.

Sylvia did a double-take at her and pursed her lips. It was actually quite funny that they were both thinking of the aesthetics of the building and drew two whole different conclusions about it.

"It's an interesting building," Penelope commented to her daughter. Clearly she was of the same mind as Sylvia, but she would never tell her daughter that.

"I think it should be in an architecture magazine," Ellie continued. She didn't seem to want to listen to anyone else's opinion, but she clearly liked to have her own on the matter. Sylvia had noticed that about her on multiple occasions. No one had the energy to say their opinion, so Ellie was able to talk freely about the building. She mentioned how much she liked that kind of stacking.

Sylvia tuned out until they walked into the building. She asked them not to speak when they walked in. She talked to the attendant by the front door, asking for the history of the building.

The attendant shrugged and apologized. "Sorry," she said. "I don't think there is any 'history' on this building. It's not that old."

"Is there a basement?" Sylvia asked.

"Of course," she said. "The bill adjustments office is down there." She pointed at a nearby elevator. "Take the elevator and just press B."

"Thanks," Sylvia said.

"What's the big group for?" the attendant asked.

Sylvia turned around and put her lips together tightly. "What group?" she said. The

266

witches and David took the cue very quickly and all started milling around, pretending to be ghost-like.

"You don't see them?" the attendant asked with her eyes bulging. "They came with you?"

"I don't know what you mean," Sylvia said. "I came to get my bill adjusted."

"There are a bunch of people that walked in the door after you," she said.

Sylvia shrugged and started walking towards the elevator. "I drove myself. I don't believe in ghosts, ma'am."

"Lord almighty." The attendant blinked. "Ghosts. I knew they were real."

She hit the button for the down elevator, and the witches and David came over to wait with her. No one said anything.

The attendant stared and scratched her head. She blinked and rubbed her eyes.

The elevator came and she got on and it was creaky. Everyone piled in after her.

Sylvia's serious face cracked when the elevator doors shut. She couldn't believe such an outlandish routine had worked. She laughed, feeling just on the edge of hysteria, but she reigned it in.

The elevator took three decades to go to the lowest basement floor, which was actually B3, not B. Sylvia said with a nervous laugh, "That elevator ride took so long that the Hunt might actually be over by now."

No one laughed, but Penelope sighed wistfully. "Wouldn't that be a dream?"

No one responded. They hopped out at B3. It looked like storage rooms and maybe a few forgotten and unused offices. The air was musty, and it was clear very few people came down here. Sylvia kind of liked that abandoned quality.

She looked around, not sure where to start.

"I'm going to do a draft spell," Chrysa said.

"What's a draft spell?" Ellie asked.

Chrysa took in a slow breath, not sure if she wanted to take the energy to explain.

Sylvia hopped in for the explanation to let Chrysa take care of the spell. "It colors the air and different winds so that they are visible."

"They have a spell for that?" Ellie asked, clearly not understanding the purpose.

"Witches in the past needed wind sometimes," Sylvia started. "You're doing runes, and you need a North wind? Witches didn't want to lick a finger and hope they got it right." Sylvia hardened her mouth.

"Hardly no one does runes," Ellie said.

"And why do you think that is?" Sylvia asked with raised brows.

"I don't know," Ellie shrugged. "They're hard and not really strong."

"Runes have a place in a witch's magical repertoire," she said. "There is always a place for every type of spell." She thought about the decline of rune use. She hadn't been alive at the time, but she read about it in a witch history book. "They are hard to do. So not many witches know how to do it. And they are meant for very specific types of charms. A long-lasting, subtle magic. They might've actually come in handy for fighting the fairies, since they are virtually undetectable unless you know what to look for. Or you actually see the rune symbols." Sylvia's charms were actually an evolution of runes. She was good at runes too.

Ellie stopped paying attention, but Sylvia could see the wheels turning in her head. She was glad that the young woman was so receptive to ideas and so inquisitive. She didn't know what she'd do without a tough young woman like her in the Hunt.

The air suddenly became full of dark colors. A dark, deep purple color drafted in the hall from the left. Dark red and dark green drafts came respectively from vents nearby. Their colors swirled and mixed with the dominant purple color. In the distance to the right, a dark blue draft curled in the corner.

Chrysa moved her shoulders around. "I think we should investigate the purple and then if that's no good, the blue."

"Not the green or red?" Loni asked.

Penelope quietly explained to her daughter why the vent drafts weren't really the first option to investigate.

Chrysa led the way, keeping up the draft spell. They rounded a corner to the right.

Sylvia noticed that there were so many doors down here. They reminded her of school doors, with their glass windows reinforced by metal. She wondered why government building always had that. Maybe to prevent breakage. She didn't know.

Chrysa stopped in front of a door at the end of the long hallway. The draft was coming out of the room. It was kind of odd. Sylvia tried to think what it might be other than a tunnel to some outside area. She had no clue, but she was hopeful.

Chrysa tried the door knob. Nothing. She tried more roughly. It didn't budge, then she was about to blast it with an energy ball spell, gathering the magic in her hands.

Patty stepped forward. "I know lock spells," she said quietly.

Chrysa stepped away and said, "Go ahead." She didn't seem pleased. Sylvia knew that Chrysa liked to show off. And she was able to show off so much because she was just that good of a witch.

Patty tested the knob, looking for the best spell in her mind to use. "Ah," she said. She whispered something. A sharp blast of air went in the keyhole. The draft spell was working and the blast of air looked dark pink. The key mechanism turned automatically at the same time. Patty turned the handle and pushed the door open. "A regular door lock," she said with a smile as she turned back to the group.

"Where'd you learn that?" Ellie asked in

awe.

Patty put her lips together and smiled. "My husband didn't make his money from the stocks, like everyone thinks."

That made Sylvia widen her eyes. Patty had a smug little smile. "Seriously?" She was suddenly as inquisitive as Ellie.

"He's on the up-and-up now," Patty explained with a loving chirpiness. She looked up and away like she was remembering something. Then she frowned. "I told him to leave town until the end of the week," she added somberly. "I'm glad he was able to leave."

Sylvia got somber too.

Chrysa just walked into the room, maintaining the draft spell. The air was warm, very warm.

Sylvia flipped on an old-fashioned light switch to the right of the door.

The room was a furnace room, and it was a little disappointing to Sylvia. She was hoping that it was somehow a magical tunnel or something. That would've been nice. And simple and easy. But nothing had been easy thus far. Why was nothing easy? She guessed that staying alive when people were out to get you was much harder than she had known. No one had ever been out to get her, at least to her knowledge. She just hoped that the secret tunnel out of the building was on B3. She didn't want to waste all their energy searching instead of actually getting into the fairy court.

Chrysa continued the draft spell until she confirmed that the heating up of the furnace was indeed causing the air in the room to rise, and as it cooled, it pushed other air away. So this was definitely not the color of their tunnel wind.

"Alright," Sylvia said. "On to check the blue."

The walk back to the elevator took longer than she felt it should've. Sylvia was beginning to feel pain in her back. Probably from the stress.

Patty told everyone about how her husband used to steal art for pay, back in the 1980s. She even went on a few jobs with him. He knew she was a witch and they were very successful at it because of her talents and his honed skills. They stopped, though, when security systems got more complex.

"I never would've expected that from you," Sylvia said. She was impressed, but also kind of saddened that the woman had pretended to be inept when they were preparing. She wondered why that was.

"At the end, we were almost caught several times," Patty said. "And I was shot at. Then I was done. No art or money is worth that."

Sylvia wondered if that was why. She knew what it was like to be hunted.

Chrysa led the way again. The blue draft was much weaker and much harder to see. Chrysa had to concentrate more to make sure it stayed visible.

They ended up in front of a door on the right side of the hallway.

"Patty?" Chrysa said after trying the doorknob.

Patty got it unlocked, and this time she went into the room first.

Chrysa turned on the light. It seemed to just be a storage room. There was nothing special about it. Racks with dusty cleaning equipment lined the walls.

Sylvia touched some of it, wondering if anyone had used this room at all.

Chrysa followed the slightly stronger blue draft now. It was coming from behind one of the racks. Sylvia helped to remove things from the shelf.

"Hello," Chrysa said with a smile. The wall was exposed brick here for some reason, instead of the concrete that the rest of the building had. "This is interesting."

"Let's move this," Sylvia said to everyone, gesturing to the shelf.

David made quick work of the chemicals, and he and Penelope lifted it away, with the help of her daughters.

"That shelf thing was much lighter than I thought," Penelope said. She looked at her hands and smiled, as if pleased that she was strong.

Chrysa touched the bricks and strengthened her draft spell so that the blue was actually glowing in the dark room. "Does anyone have a spell for brick and mortar removal?" she asked.

No one volunteered. None of the witches had ever really dealt with that sort of thing. Sylvia liked domestic spells and charms. Chrysa liked entertaining spells or things she learned in her youth. Patty had a bigger repertoire than they thought, but she didn't volunteer. None of Penelope's daughters were studying anything like it. They looked at each other with blank faces.

Sylvia hardened her mouth. She certainly didn't want to stop now after getting so far.

"Are you all so inept?" came David's annoyed voice. "We just smash it."

"Okay," Chrysa snapped back. "You do it then. Go ahead." She stepped out of his way and gestured for him to go for it.

David raised his shoulders and let them drop tensely. He looked around the room for something to hit it with. He found an old crowbar and began bashing the bricks.

It certainly wasn't as easy as he had thought it would be, but chips came off. None of the witches offered to help him, so he labored away. His face was strained and angry.

The witches were not pleased either. No one liked him. But they saw his need, Sylvia thought. He would do things that none of them were willing to. That counted for something. She watched him closely, wondering what spell she should use to disarm him quickly without causing long-lasting damage. She knew in her gut he'd do something rash at some point.

He finally made a hole in the bricks that he could stick his hand through, and there was clearly nothing behind the bricks.

"You've gotta finish, bucko," Chrysa said, so unamused when David turned back smugly triumphant. "None of us can fit through that tiny hole you so valiantly made for us." Her words dripped with malcontent, but Sylvia was glad that she hated him too.

Hating people was not Sylvia's normal state of affairs. She consistently wanted to give folks the benefit of the doubt. But she couldn't with David. Everything about him rubbed her the wrong way. Everything.

He continued bashing the bricks.

Penelope checked out the hallway, just in case anyone was coming to check on the noise. No one was. They figured that anyone who heard it wouldn't think to check the bottom level of the basement first. And sound traveled through solid material different than air, and it made it hard to pinpoint where it was coming from.

All of the witches watched him for twenty minutes. Loni seemed to get antsy and asked her mother if she should help David, quietly. Her mother whispered back that she didn't think that was the best idea. Loni asked why. Penelope said that sometimes people have to do somethings on their own. Loni didn't say anything further.

But David made a hole big enough for them

to get through. And this time he turned back with an exhilarated face. The exercise had done him good. He was happy for doing this thing. Some people were like that. Work made them feel better.

Sylvia was probably similar.

David crawled through the hole first and realized that climbing through a waist-high hole was bound to contribute to a fall.

He disappeared from view, downward. They heard him move around in there and curse.

"Everything alright?" Sylvia asked.

"Of course," David said back and swore again. He came back up and his face had a cut on it. He raised his eyebrows. "Are you coming?" His triumphant mood was clearly gone.

Sylvia went through next, but she didn't fall. She helped everyone else through, David did not.

Chrysa and Maria did a lighting spell. What they were in was cave-like. It had the classic rough rocky walls and that musty smell. The air was significantly colder in here than in the storage room, and definitely colder than the hallway.

"Who knew there was stuff like this in L.A.," Patty said. Her mouth was open as she stared.

Sylvia silently agreed. It was cool. Way cooler than anything she'd ever done. The Hunt was good for something after all, even though it was nothing close to bittersweet. She didn't know why she kept on trying to see the bright side of this situation. It was crappy. It was worse than crappy. But she was an optimist. She didn't like to be down.

The cave led to an actual tunnel. It was clearly an old tunnel, carved by manual tools. The cave outlet to the Department of Water and Power must have been a coincidence that just happened, though the builders of the building had clearly not originally walled it up. Sylvia couldn't see why. If she was building a building and the plans called for a wall, she'd build it. Not do it, then brick it up later. She had no real reason, except maybe that they thought it was cool. And it certainly was cool. That was for sure. L.A. wasn't known for its mystery or history. It was known for bright lights, hungry actors, beaches and that chill attitude. She'd heard people say Angelenos were rude and mean, but in her travels, she liked the way Angelenos were best. Always willing to help, but they wouldn't be friendly if someone was just walking past. People in Texas were friendlier. In passing, lots of folks said "hello" to strangers. Apparently that was supposedly super friendly — the epitome of good — but Sylvia didn't think much of it; it just seemed superficial.

"I can't focus at all," Sylvia said, slightly panicked. She wasn't thinking about the problem at hand. What did Texas have to do with anything?

"It's okay," Penelope said, putting a hand on her shoulder. Her voice was calm. It made Sylvia feel embarrassed and immature. Penelope was truly the best mother those girls could ask for.

The tunnel led in two directions, solidifying

the idea that the cave to the Department of Water and Power building connection was purely on accident, or perhaps secretly dug out. Sylvia asked for Maria to get out her smartphone again and GPS for them, but she wasn't getting service.

"Is there a spell for that?" Maria asked. "To boost my phone's signal?"

"We might be better off just using a compass spell," Chrysa said with a little laugh. The generational difference was apparent. Chrysa took a bobby pin out of her hair and laid it flat on her palm. She whispered a spell to the metal and it began to float. The rounded part pointed straight forward. "I think the Pavilion is in the southeast direction," she said. "We go right."

No one else had any suggestions, so they went that way. Sylvia crossed her fingers, hoping that they wouldn't end up going in the complete opposite direction. Luckily they had time, and it was unlikely that the fairies would find them down there. With so much ground and earth, it was unlikely that they'd even sense Chrysa or Maria, much less Sylvia. She wondered if they should just stay in the tunnels for the next three days. It might've been worth it, but she didn't suggest it. There was no guarantee that a fairy wouldn't come across them, and if they were battling this close to the fairy court, someone was bound to notice.

They walked for a few minutes, no one said anything. Sylvia welcomed the silence. She usually liked talking and listening to people, but her thoughts were so loud now that other people's voices were too much. It was silly, she knew, but that was how she handled stress, she supposed. She felt so lost, like a little guppy in a gigantic lake. She had to reassure herself that guppies managed to survive all the time. She could too. She'd never experienced anything like this.

The tunnel made a sharp right, and that felt good to Sylvia, a step in the right direction. She hoped. Hope was great and terrible at the same time. It kept her going, but it let her be so disappointed when things didn't go right. Though if she really analyzed the situation, their group had been doing pretty well. They were all alive. All relatively unscathed. That was a miracle in and of itself. But that led her to wondering if their luck was up. Something was bound to happen, wasn't it? She hoped and hoped not, but it was likely. Or maybe each encounter was separate and distinct and they had the same amount of luck per instance. And it just so happened that they succeeded the first few times. And this next time they'd succeed again.

That was something to hope for, that they'd somehow manage to walk into the fairy court, ask for immunity and get it. Could it happen like that? She didn't know. She was doubting that they'd just give immunity because she asked, unless it was some long-held tradition or something. Maybe it was, but rumors were wild. She knew that. Her sixth graders sometimes thought the most ridiculous things. She once heard an exchange between two kids in the sandbox area. One said, "Don't dig too deep."

The other said, "Why not?"

The first one said, "I heard that if you go down far enough, you hit water. And if you touch that water, your hands will never be dry again."

The second one stopped digging immediately, as if wet hands were a terrible curse. And as if that were even possible. Sylvia knew curses, at least a few, and wet hands was the silliest supposed one she'd ever heard of. Most witches didn't use curses, because they tended to be the weapon of the vindictive. And witches lived so long that vindictiveness wasn't really productive at all. Curses, like runes, went out of style. Curses were similarly hard, subtle magic and hard to remove. Might as well spell someone temporarily, get a laugh and then be done.

Their group was mostly silent, so when a voice fluttered down to them, Sylvia gave a little jump. She didn't know what to do, so once she calmed herself, she put her finger to her lips. Everyone was easily compliant. They knew what was up. They knew, she didn't even know why she bothered. They were much more competent than she was giving them credit for. Sometimes she treated people like she treated her sixth graders, and that was clearly a mistake. She spent so much time with those kids that it was silly how much she got stuck in that mode.

She strained to hear what was being said, but it sounded like it had been said in passing, because they heard nothing else. She went forward and looked around the cave, doing her own light spell. She looked up, but she saw nothing, so she rounded the next corner and there were the staircases, or least what she hoped was the same staircase she saw in the service tunnels at the Pavilion. She almost jumped for joy. She peered her head back around the corner and motioned for everyone to come over. She was happy. This was actually working. It was.

She tried to climb up the steps as quietly as possible, but they were not quiet. Not one little bit. She took her foot off the first step and looked at the group. "Any ideas?"

"For what?" Ellie whispered back. Her whisper wasn't exactly quiet, but Sylvia was pretty sure that no one was in the service tunnel at that moment.

"To quiet the stairs," Sylvia said.

Patty's eyes lit up. "Me," she whispered with a smile. "I have a spell." Sylvia beamed with pride. She hadn't realized how useful Patty would be when she was back at her house. She felt bad for underestimating her. This woman was definitely someone to be reckoned with, or not. Probably not. No reckoning. Though Sylvia did know that Patty didn't have a vicious bone in her body.

Patty whispered a spell that she clearly didn't want anyone to know. "Proprietary stuff," she whispered to them with a gleeful smile. She was coming alive. It was nice to see.

She then put a test foot on the stairs, and no sound came out of them. Not even the usual sound of a shoe on a surface.

Patty went up first, sneaking from a hunched position. Sylvia watched her with awe. There was a cat-like grace to her that Sylvia had never noticed, but it certainly shined now. Sylvia tried to do the same thing but failed miserably. She stopped behind Patty, who had stopped at the gate at the top of the stairs. This was definitely the service tunnel under the Pavilion. That made her giddy and excited. She had sort of made it. The service tunnel didn't have anyone in it, so Patty did another unlocking spell and she swung open the gate. She ventured out. Sylvia followed her but motioned for everyone else to wait.

Patty had this serious, appraising look in her eyes. Sylvia appreciated it. After about getting twenty feet from the spiral staircase, she hurriedly sprinted back like a gazelle in the quiet of morning to Sylvia and pushed her down the stairs, without letting her fall. "Someone's coming," she said, barely audible.

Patty pushed Sylvia further down the stairs so she could crouch, hidden, but still able to see what was going on. Sylvia couldn't, but she could hear fairly well. She suddenly wondered if a spell similar to the vision enhancement one that Penelope had taught would work if used on the ears. She altered the words slightly and tried it out. The sound of beating hearts was the first shocking thing that assaulted her ears. And the breathing, the low but oh-so-loud breathing. It was annoying, but she attempted to direct it up to the service tunnel and moved her neck so she might be able to hear better. She heard two faster-than-human heartbeats, fluttering at relatively high speed in comparison to the hearts in her group, even though they were all nervous and up on adrenaline.

"I hate her," one voice said.

"She's... her," the other one said with resignation.

"I don't know why she gets to act like she's so important," said the first.

"Connections. We're but lowly fairies," said the second.

"Is she even doing anything productive here?" said the first.

"Well, she's definitely not going to hunt, if that's what you mean," said the second. "She's too lofty for that. I mean, we're not even hunting. It's mostly for the free-range fairies and the hired help."

"I think they're having more fun," said the first.

"Some have died already. It's surprising, actually. I thought in past Hunts, our people didn't really get hurt," said the second.

"I don't know. Even the fall family's King

has gone hunting this time," said the first. "Though everyone knows he's a little crazy. Maybe I should be so crazy." The first one sighed wistfully.

The two fairies faded down the hall, though Sylvia could still hear them, it didn't sound too important. Apparently these fairies liked court gossip.

Patty turned to look at Sylvia. "What do you think?"

"What do you mean?" Sylvia asked.

"This lady fairy they were talking about. I wonder who she is," Patty said. "She might come in handy."

"I bet she's that silver haired woman we saw outside. She looked a bit too important," Sylvia said.

Both of them went back down the stairs. The group waited with raised brows. "What's going on?" David asked.

"Well, it's definitely the right place," Patty said.

"And what are we going to do?" Chrysa asked.

"Sneak?" Sylvia said with not much confidence. She hadn't thought this far. She didn't know what would be a good idea at this point. There were too many variables. Should they all go up? Go in guns blazing, a la David? Or sneak in two by two to get to the Court room and hope that they didn't get ambushed while they were separated?

"We all go together and fight whoever we see," Ellie said suddenly, confidently.

Her mother nodded solemnly.

"I don't know if that's the best idea," Patty said. "When Roger and I used to –"

"This is war, not a bank robbery," Penelope said sharply.

Sylvia was surprised by how sharp she was. Penelope was generally very gentle. The stress was probably getting to her.

Patty put her hands up. "Okay, if you feel strongly about it."

"We stand a better chance of winning that way," Ellie said as way of explanation. Sylvia wondered if that was her precognition or just strategy. She hoped a little of both.

They guessed it was decided. No one but Patty had even bothered to offer an alternative. And David seemed pretty happy with that option.

"We should probably decide the order to go in and have people watching the rear, so we don't get snuck up on," Sylvia said.

And so the order was decided. Chrysa and David were at the front. Next came Ellie and Sylvia. Sylvia didn't think she was strategically the best choice for being right behind the people in front, but she figured it was because they trusted her and her pseudo-leadership. In the third row came Penelope and Loni. Picking up the rear were the backwards-walking Patty and Maria.

Off they went, or up they went. It was slow

going, because they still didn't want to go and once they were up there, there was really no turning back if someone saw them. Sylvia suddenly didn't like the idea of being in a concrete tunnel underground. There were legitimately only two ways for escape. Backwards or forwards, but they had no clue which would be ultimately better. It was so up in the air but actually down under the ground.

Chrysa probably didn't like being in front. She was wild, but she didn't like the responsibility. David— Sylvia was sure— loved it.

They walked quietly for a minute before suddenly they heard some noises. Noises definitely weren't good.

It seemed the noises were coming out of two doors ahead of them. But they were committed now. There was no way they could make it back to the cave tunnels now.

They froze. Maybe, hopefully, whoever was coming out of those doors wouldn't see their group until they made it a little ways down the hallway.

As luck would have it, the two fairies that exited didn't even look in their direction. They walked down the hallway farther away from the group. They silently sighed relief. They didn't want to fight now.

They'd have to soon, there was no doubt. Sylvia was not looking forward to it. There was nothing nice about this. Her whole body ached. Her shoulders were particularly tense. That was not nice. Her heart caught in her throat the next time the door opened, because they would not be so lucky again.

And she was right. These fairies were coming straight at them. They were looking at each other and talking animatedly, so they didn't notice the witches' group right away.

Sylvia focused herself and performed the suffocation spell on the one on the right.

Both fairies stopped, as one gestured to their throat. The one suffocating caught a glimpse of the witches before falling down. The other one was soon after hit by a relatively quiet ball of fire from Chrysa. Fire in small form, like a candle, was very quiet, but the bigger it got, the more sound it made. Sylvia wasn't sure why. But the fire was not loud enough to cause anyone from the court room to come check. The fire consumed the fairy, and afterward, there remained a charred green body. The group came up on the bodies. Both were ugly and disgusting. The one that Sylvia had suffocated had purple lips and bulging eyes that weren't closed. She thought that she ought to close them, but she didn't want to touch the body. She had acted so quickly, she was kind of disgusted with herself, but she surely didn't want the fairies shouting for assistance.

Battling in the hallway was a better option for them, she realized. They could come across the fairies in a smaller setting where the numbers were matched and that would help them fare better.

They stepped past the bodies and made it to the door. It looked like a regular human made door, but Chrysa stopped Sylvia from touching it.

"What?" Sylvia said, barely audible.

"There's no turning back after this, you know that right?" Chrysa said.

Sylvia nodded. She looked at the rest of the group and raised her eyebrows.

Everyone gave their own little affirmative action in response.

"We rush in quickly and demand immunity then," Chrysa said.

"In one..." Sylvia said looking at her groupmates. "Two..." No one looked ready for this. But running in and asking for immunity might just work. "Three..."

Patty and Chrysa yanked open the doors. They clearly did not want to be the first ones.

Sylvia barreled into the room and shouted, "I demand immunity!"

She was about thirty feet into the room when she finally stopped. She hadn't noticed but everyone was with her.

The room was huge. It looked grand like the inside of a cathedral. Beautiful carved archways and candles everywhere. Rich red and purple tapestries hung from the very tall ceiling. It was magnificent.

Then she saw the myriad fairy faces looking at her with what? Shock, awe, disgust? She couldn't tell.

"There is no immunity from the Hunt," said the silver-haired fairy. She was sitting at the head table, which was elevated from the rest of the room.

And that's when, yet again, David fired his gun and started a fight. But this time he didn't miss, and hit the silver-haired fairy squarely between the eyes. It was gruesome. Shock registered on the old fairy's face for a moment, and a bit of blood leaked out.

But Sylvia didn't have time to be disgusted.

The whole room broke out into chaos, and Sylvia could only focus on what was before her.

A fairy to her right was working on a fire spell, so Sylvia tried to do a water spell, but it was clear to her very quickly that she didn't have enough magic left for such a power-intensive spell. Instead, she lunged past that fairy and hoped another of the witches would take care of him. She focused on a sneakier style of fighting which consisted of her hiding and attacking when they were busy with something else. She kept using the suffocation spell, because it was silent and no one could see where it was coming from.

She downed three fairies when she noticed that Maria was struggling — double-teamed by two rather bulky looking male fairies. Sylvia left her "hiding" place and stumbled across the floor and pushed Maria down to the floor before a string of lightning hit her.

Maria shook and said breathlessly, "Thank

you." They both pulled each other into a standing position at the same time and faced the two bulky fairies. They were working on a joint spell, so Sylvia looked around the room for something metal and saw an old-fashioned goblet on the ground just rolling. She scooped it up, did the flash spell and launched it grenade-style at the bigger of the two fairies.

It flashed brightly and then hit her target on the forehead. He stumbled backwards but didn't fall. He looked angrier, though.

Maria still hadn't done any spell since Sylvia got there. There were no things that she could do in a pinch, Sylvia realized. Maria wasn't good under pressure, so Sylvia shouted, "Go to Patty!" Maria didn't move, but Sylvia put a strong hand on her shoulder and steered her behind her.

Sylvia stared at the two fairies in front of her and realized she'd need to face them head on. She also had to conserve her magic. It would not do her well to run out of magic very early in the fight, and it wouldn't be short.

There was something off about these two and she hoped that if she figured it out she'd be able to beat them without using up everything she had.

They launched more lightning, and, this time, it was a two-pronged bolt that came from both directions. She froze for a quick second before leaping forward, out of the way of the lightning. She barely made it and felt the hem of her shirt was slightly charred. She was lucky that the material wasn't conductive. She was now significantly closer to them, and she stared at them through narrowed eyes. They looked surprisingly similar. Not exactly similar, but she quickly realized that was because of the Glamour. Their bone structures and the way their eyes looked, dull and empty, were startlingly similar, like brothers or maybe twins. With the twin idea, there had to be something there. Maybe it was linked to the way they did magic. All of their spells had been joint. She wondered if that was necessary or just a way to increase their power. She hoped it was the former. But she had to test her theory. She realized she certainly couldn't outrun such young, obviously fit men, but they didn't look too sharp and she'd use that to her advantage. She looked around for something to help her. She didn't see much. There was very little in the room that might help. There was an expensive, painstakingly-made drape hanging near the elevated table.

She sprinted for a few seconds to rip one of the drapes down, which was not easy at her age. Her joints creaked on her first few strides. The drape was much heavier than she had anticipated, so it wasn't easy to pull with her, but she managed and got it back to the bulky fairies as quickly as she could. They were working on their next spell, completely engrossed—boy was she lucky! She wondered why it took so long for them to make a spell, but she was grateful regardless; it gave her time to think, and she really needed it.

She'd need to get close to them to try it.

She dodged their next spell, which was much harder than she thought, because this time they included some element of tracking in it. A tracking lightning spell was hard to do, and she only avoided it by being lucky enough to not have a strong magical presence to track. She threw one of the fairy element charms onto the ground from her neck and the lightning attacked it. She might not be that lucky the next time. It was now or never.

She drew the drape into her hands and threw it — with the life-saving help of her magic — over the bigger of the fairies and completely covered him, like putting a tablecloth on a table. He stood very still. He was certainly a little dull, but his counterpart seemed equally confused. He stood still; Sylvia guessed that he might be trying to do a spell.

She took her chance and did the suffocation spell, downing the free twin as he removed the drape from his brother. The remaining twin looked at his fallen brother, and Sylvia wasted no time. She couldn't take the risk. They had been blissfully slow. She was really lucky, so, so lucky.

Both bulky fairies were on the ground when she looked up to survey the room again. She noticed some fairies were fighting other fairies, and she couldn't have been more thankful. It was the best stroke of luck that fairies were taking this opportunity to in-fight, because that only helped the witches. She checked on her group. Patty had Penelope and Maria in her bubble. The women were fighting as a cohesive unit. Patty told them all what to do and they did it because they had the time and safety to do it in her protection bubble. Some people needed to be told what to do. Leaders were for those people.

She didn't need to help them, so she looked to Chrysa and Ellie who were clearly the powerhouses of the group. They were magnificent. They fought like they'd done this all their lives, and they clearly had not. Well, Ellie for sure. Sylvia didn't know enough about Chrysa's whole past to know with absolute certainty. Two hundred years was a long history. Comparable to the length of the United States. She thought it was amazing nonetheless.

They were holding their own, so she thought it was best not to throw the wrench of her involvement into the mix. She might not actually be a help to them.

So that left Loni and David. She didn't see Loni at first, but when she did, she saw that the young witch was dutifully handling a fairy on her own. The girl was using a laceration spell that she must've learned from Ellie. It was not a pretty sight. The girl didn't seem to be disgusted by the blood, though she clearly wasn't happy about the pain she was causing. A true healing witch.

Sylvia wasn't sure if she should intervene, but she figured that if the girl was willing to fight, as young as she was, she deserved the respect of not interfering in her fight. Sylvia dealt with children a lot because of her job. That girl was not a kid anymore.

She turned her focus to David, who was among the loudest in the room. He was shooting at anything that moved, but luckily he was faced away from the rest of their group. It was something that Sylvia didn't want to be involved in. And at that moment, burning fiery hot consumed her left arm and she screamed.

She wasn't watching for herself when she checked on everyone else. Stupid oversight, she told herself.

She whirled around and faced her attacker. It was an older-looking fairy.

"You're not going to be able to keep that arm," the fairy said with a pleased and vicious smile. There was elegant terror that emanated off him.

Sylvia couldn't manage any words against him. She'd never been quick with comebacks. She just focused on the pain in her arm. It wasn't on fire, which surprised her, but a viscous purple liquid dripped down her elbow. All the flesh looked charred. The pain was unimaginable. She couldn't even think enough to face the fairy or assess him — just the fiery burn of the purple liquid.

"Fire is my element, if you're wondering," he said with a shrug. "Most folks aren't really sure.

Always did like chemistry, so I combined my elements. It's effective and powerful. Only folks it doesn't work on are other fire element folks. Like your red-haired witch."

Sylvia didn't know why he felt the need to tell her his whole life story, but she was glad she had a few moments to think. Her brain blocked the extreme reaches of the pain from being registered. Adrenaline and the body were amazing.

Her opponent was a tall, thin fairy dressed in exceptionally classic fairy garb, nothing Mundane about him. She suspected he thought himself above the hunt. But she was glad. He was clearly a cut above the fairies participating in the hunt; she didn't want him out there victimizing other witches. He carried a satchel that was draped over his shoulder. His hand had remnants of the purple stuff, but his skin looked fine. So the magical component of the liquid wasn't added until he threw it.

She definitely knew she couldn't be hit by it again. She couldn't withstand that pain, and she was sure that he was correct in his assessment that she'd lose it, though she clung to the hope that maybe Loni could do something.

When he finished his waxing comments, he scooped up some more purple stuff and flung it at Sylvia. She just barely dodged. A tiny bit touched her upper right arm. It seared through the fabric of her shirt and burned her skin. She wasn't quick enough to dodge this fairy for long. She looked around for something, there was nothing that wouldn't burn, except maybe some metal tableware, but that wouldn't really protect her, it'd burn her once it got hot enough.

His penchant for talking was probably her only chance.

She had to get him talking. "What family are you from?" she sputtered out.

He raised his eyebrows. "I'm a free agent, but the Lodes family currently pays my bills."

"What does that mean?" Sylvia asked, not curious in the least.

He smiled, reveling in the opportunity to talk. "Well, it means I do odd jobs for them. Mostly intimidation. Sometimes more. Sometimes I gather information. It varies on their needs. And I'm not picky."

Sylvia took this opportunity to do the suffocation spell, but her magic was easily pushed off.

He gave her an unimpressed look. "Did I pick the weakest witch in the bunch? I saw you pick off so many fairies so efficiently that I thought you might be pretty powerful... But I guess that lack of aura I see in you is not a trick?" he said.

"I'm the weakest," Sylvia admitted. "Most of those women are much, much more powerful than me."

"It's still interesting that you've been able to hold your own among them though," he said with a fairness about him. "It's commendable. But I still have to kill you, you know."

"It'll be funny when you get taken down by the two least magical in the group," came David's never-before-so-welcomed voice. Sylvia turned to see David standing with his gun aimed at the fire fairy.

He shot and hit the fire fairy in the shoulder.

The fairy wasn't going to talk anymore, but Sylvia was thankful she had back up — though she felt a pang of guilt that she hadn't wanted to backup David just minutes before. The fairy catapulted a big glob of purple stuff at David.

David stepped back so it didn't hit his chest or torso, but the bulk of it hit him just above the knee. David dropped his gun, though he didn't scream. Sylvia didn't have the time to think, but she would've been impressed with his control.

Sylvia looked back at the fairy. Her chance was now, she hoped that maybe the bullet in his shoulder weakened him enough that he wouldn't pay her spell mind until she had her hold.

She performed the suffocation spell for the second time on him. This time it actually took hold. His eyes panicked and his fingers clawed at his throat. She could feel him pushing back against her spell. He was so much more powerful than her, it was embarrassing. She could feel her hold over him melting like it had the first time.

Then a resounding bang rang through her ears and blossomed in the fairy's chest. David shot him. That was one way to take care of it, she supposed. She looked at David who was lying on the ground with his gun lowered by his side. His leg was worse than her arm, so bad that there was basically nothing holding his thigh to his calf. The purple liquid had hit there after all. Sylvia didn't know what to do, so she dragged him with her good arm out of the center of the room and helped him prop himself up so he could still participate. But he whimpered and said, "My leg, my leg." Sylvia didn't know if her arm was going to make it, much less his leg. And the pain was so bad, she didn't know how she was continuing, but she was. She had to make sure they all survived. She'd led them here, it was her responsibility.

She watched her back this time and made her way to Patty, but a tiny fairy blocked her way.

He was white-blond and looked so innocent in comparison to everything. Sylvia then remembered that she knew him. It was Thom.

"You've got to leave," the boy said. He sounded sad.

"We're trying to survive, Thom," Sylvia said. Her teacher's voice was more present than it had been in the past week.

"No one will notice if you leave now. My grandmother is dead and so is another King. Everyone is fighting," Thom said.

Captain obvious. "We're trying," Sylvia said, gripping her hands. She needed to move. She pushed past the boy into Patty's bubble.

"Your arm," Patty said with a horrified look. It must have looked real bad. She didn't even want to look. She then stared at Thom who stood outside the bubble, watching with large eyes.

"What else is there to do?" Sylvia asked Patty.

Patty let her eyes linger on Sylvia's arm for just a second before going back to watching the fairies all around them. "I say we get out of here. There is no immunity, and there's no point in staying here."

It was easier to think inside Patty's protection.

There were people with dogs and snakes fighting people with plants. Lightning fighting swords. It was something to witness. She'd never actually see the Court squabbles of the fairies, because witches mostly didn't involve themselves with such things. Their treaty — that Sylvia was seriously starting to doubt — had been sufficient. But this was another level of Court squabble.

Ellie was still fighting, so was Chrysa, but everyone else was just watching.

She went — with Thom in tow — to see if either witch needed her help, but they didn't need it. They were at the tail end of their fights. Sylvia wanted to laugh. This wasn't the best scenario, but it was far better than she could've imagined. Except for her damned arm. She didn't know what she might be able to do with it. It hurt so bad, and there was nothing that was moving when she thought it was moving. She hoped there was a solution for it.

When Chrysa and Ellie disabled their opponents, the group went under the protection bubble of Patty and they walked back out the door. Thom was their shadow.

Then Sylvia remembered David. He had saved her life, she very well couldn't leave him there. He was witchblood, he would be killed.

"We have to go back," Sylvia said.

"What?" Penelope said, tightness in her voice

"I left David in there, he can't walk. His leg is like my arm," Sylvia said. But she didn't want to go back. "Chrysa, could you help me lift him?"

Chrysa sighed but nodded. They left the protection of the bubble and fast-walked back into the big room.

"I'll help too," Loni said and left the bubble with them.

"No!" Penelope shouted loudly and reached to grab her, but Loni was already out of the bubble.

She turned back to her mom and gave a questioning glance. But her mom didn't have time to say anything. She threw herself outside the bubble and pushed her daughter away just as a bolt of lightning struck where she had been. And instead of Loni, it got Penelope. Loni screamed.

Chrysa and Sylvia were astonished to see Penelope wide-eyed and lifeless on the floor, but necessity got them back to work. The two best friends haphazardly tugged at David and dragged him back. They pushed Loni into the bubble too before another bolt could hit them.

The little boy Thom seemed not to attract any of the lightning. "Get out of here," he said imploringly.

They all stared in shock at Penelope.

Thom stood between them and Penelope, blocking them from seeing her.

Maria and Loni were already sobbing. No one knew what to do.

"Go!" Thom said, putting his hands out to the bubble. It seared his hands and he yelped.

Ellie said quietly, "She wanted us to live, so we better get out of here." She put her hands on her sisters and pushed them out towards the service tunnel.

The whole group moved as fast as they could. They left Penelope behind. They could help David hop, but there was no way to take Penelope with them.

They made it back to the cave tunnel, and Maria screamed with sobs. "We can't leave her!" She stood still, no one could move her. Sylvia guessed she was using magic to plant herself in place.

Ellie said quietly, "Wait here for me." And ran back to the fairy court before anyone had time to process what she was doing.

No one wanted to follow the young woman. Sylvia realized she'd have to — as the de facto leader. She made it halfway to the fairy court, when she saw Penelope floating horizontally towards her. For a half-second, she thought it was Penelope's ghost, until she saw a sweating Ellie behind her.

Ellie was using tremendous energy on a levitation spell to bring her lifeless mom back. "That boy was sitting with her," she said. "He said sorry."

"He wants us to live," Sylvia said, not sure what to make of it.

She and Sylvia came back to the group solemnly, and Patty re-locked the black gate to the spiral staircase.

They moved and moved until they were back at the Department of Water and Power storage room on level B3.

"You knew," Loni accused her sister. "You knew!"

Ellie nodded and gently released her mom's body from the spell. She almost looked like she was sleeping.

"Why didn't you tell us?! We could've changed that! We can always change it when you tell us about your visions," Loni said through tears.

Ellie shook her head. "I told mom about it. Every time I made a different decision, one of us would die, and mom said that wasn't an option. She made me promise." Ellie tried to hug her sister, but she was pushed away. "She said goodbye in the car."

"I didn't know it was a real goodbye!" she said. "I didn't know that it wasn't just an 'in-case' goodbye." Loni looked at her other sister. "You let me kill her!"

"If it wasn't you, it would have been me or Maria or anyone else. She made her decision," Ellie said. She was so matter-of-fact about it. It must have been because she'd known all along about her mom's eminent death that the pain had lessened. And she had had a proper goodbye, unlike her sisters.

Sylvia wasn't sure if she should intervene.

"I can't believe she's gone," Maria said blankly. "Just one moment there and one moment not."

Ellie didn't explain herself further to her sisters. Instead she went into a corner of the store room and cried silently, rocking back and forth subtly.

Sylvia looked at her best friend. "Do you have any ideas for my arm?" she asked. She was surprising herself with how much composure she had, considering the pain she was in was incredible.

Chrysa took a long look at it and shook her head. "It looks obliterated, honestly. What happened?"

"A fairy threw burning purple liquid on me... and David too," Sylvia said. She was being selfish, but she wanted to be looked at first. Her arm was "better" than his, and she might have

303

something to salvage. She was positive that he didn't. His leg barely looked attached at this point.

Chrysa continued shaking her head. "Loni might be able to do something, but not me. This requires a real healer."

"Why isn't she a ghost?" Patty asked. "Was it too sudden? Did they take her soul?"

As if on cue, Penelope glowed for a moment. And then Sylvia saw her friend's spirit separate from her body, like a sticker being painstakingly pulled from the wood bed post of a Lisa-Frank-obsessed daughter of a Martha Stewart disciple mother.

She looked around the room. "Girls," she said. Only Ellie looked up to see her mom. "Loni... Maria..."

Loni burst into tears. Maria's face contorted into such a sorrowful shape.

"I love you, girls. And your father. I need you to stay strong for me. Be the best you can be. Save the world again. And look out for each other. And fall in love."

"Aren't you going to stay with us?" Maria asked. "Ghosts can stay!" Hope glimmered in her eyes.

"It's not right," Penelope said. "And you know that. You girls need to live your own lives. Not haunted by your mom's ghost." She said it with finality, like she had already thought it through.

And then Penelope's ghost form

disappeared.

All three daughters cried, Ellie separate from the other two.

The ache in Sylvia's arm reminded her that she had to do something. She looked at Loni, the small crying girl, and wondered if she should bite her tongue, but she couldn't. She needed help. And working might even help the girl, she tried to justify in her mind. "Loni, I know you're upset right now. I am too. I want to cry and wail, but some things still need to be done. Would you be able to do anything for my arm?" Sylvia asked as gently as she could.

Through sniffles, Loni looked up and over at her arm. "Maybe," she managed to get out with a sandpaper-like quality. She stepped over and looked at Sylvia's arm from all angles. After a long moment, she tenderly put firm hands directly on the red and black remains of her arm.

Sylvia did everything she could do to not scream. She did ask if they could sit down. Together they sat on the ground, and Sylvia watched as the magic poured out of Loni's hands. It was sharp, searing pain for Sylvia. She watched, though. She thought if she saw it, the pain would seem more sensible, but it didn't. Still hurt like hell. She chewed her top lip. She didn't want her arm to be gone. Loni regrew the skin starting from the top. It was a slow process. And it was odd to watch. The skin grew on her like interlacing snakes. It was beautiful and gross. She could just watch.

At just below the elbow, Loni stopped.

"What's wrong?" Sylvia said.

"I'm not a necromancer, and the rest is completely dead," she said.

Sylvia looked at it all. Tears welled up in her eyes. If not even Loni could do anything, there was nothing left. She had lost her forearm and hand. She didn't want to cry while the girls were mourning their mom. She was mourning her too, but the solidity of the loss of her hand was too real, the straw that broke the camel's back.

She bawled, letting the charred flesh dangle below her elbow.

Loni moved onto David, not crying anymore. She saved less of David's leg than of Sylvia's arm. And she didn't do anything about the dead remains. They were still somewhat attached, but either Loni didn't have the skill or the will to finish her healing. She went to hug Maria.

Patty crouched down beside David, asking him questions and keeping him conscious.

Chapter 26 - Thom

Grandmother was dead. Father was dead. King Puck was dead. The room was full of green bodies, lifeless and empty. The fighting had gone on past when the witches left.

Mother held him, breathing raggedly into his hair. She had no words.

The cavernous room echoed with the crying of various fairies.

His uncle's voice cut through the papery quiet. "I am king," he said. At first, it seemed to be a declaration to himself, but he repeated it louder. "I am King of the Lodes family."

Mother looked up at him. Her face held the meanest snarl Thom had ever seen there. "No, my son is king. I am his regent. You are a murderer."

His uncle drew back, shaking his head.

Mother had left Thom to help Father establish peace during the fight. For all his parents' warmongering and aggressiveness, they instinctively knew that a Court with no one in it meant no power for them.

Thom didn't feel anything. Although he

hated Grandmother and Father sometimes, he didn't want them dead. He slumped out of his mother's arms onto the ground. The cold of the stone seeped through his jeans, but he didn't care. Tears did not come to his eyes, as he had expected.

Mother stayed standing. She swayed like tall grass on a breezy day. It gave Thom the impression that hurricanes might bend her to the ground but she'd be intact, growing at an impossible angle.

Tears squeezed out of his eyes finally, and he was broken. He could not be strong like Mother.

"To me," Mother said. "Lodes family, to me." Her voice sounded above everything and roused the fairies.

The two remaining monarchs called their families to them as well. Fairies who had just been tearing each other apart with vines or leaping with their wolf at the throat of their cousin nodded together, as if nothing had happened.

"Our strength," Mother began, speaking to the remaining Lodes family members who had gathered. "... is our resiliency. Our ability to realize that when the dust clears, we are fairies. We must stick together against those that would have us fall." She pulled Thom up.

He tried to wiggle his way out of her hand holding the top of his arm. He did not want to stand. He didn't want them to look at him.

"I pronounce Thomas our King of Lodes,

may magic be always with him," she said.

"May magic be always with him," echoed the Lodes people, both nobility and common. Their eyes held him.

His skin prickled with the attention and expectation. His stomach floated. He needed to do well by the fairies, his fairies. And the witches. He was so glad some of them got away. But they had killed his grandmother. He cleared his throat and told himself what he had to do and who he would be. He was good and strong and kind.

Chapter 27 - Sylvia

They went to the hospital with their remaining limbs. They filled out an accident report stating that the two had gotten in a fire. The nurse didn't believe that they didn't call the ambulance when she saw their injuries. Chrysa drove David's car, and Patty drove Penelope's car. They put Penelope in the back of their car to take her home.

The vibe of the group was somber. They seemed not to care about anything. They were no longer worried about fairies. Was there something to worry about? They had caused chaos in the fairy court. Surely there were fairies still out and about, but Sylvia was sure that there were fewer fairies out and hunting now. And they probably wouldn't think to come to the hospital, such a public place.

Sylvia questioned every decision she'd made. If she had left David, if she hadn't gone back for him, if she had done any other number of things differently, those girls would still have a mother. She felt responsible. That responsibility felt the worst for her than the guilt of all the lives she'd taken. They had clearly been enemies. But

Penelope, she was supposed to protect her.

Sylvia and David were taken for emergency surgeries. Both amputations, Loni's assessment had been correct.

Sylvia didn't dream in surgery, and she woke having forgotten momentarily what had happened. She moved around and enjoyed the feeling of not thinking for a few very long moments. Not having to do anything was heavenly. She rarely allowed herself that.

Eventually the witches came to visit her. They told her that they'd be watching for fairies and that it seemed they wouldn't be hunted down any more. They'd gotten their immunity, though not through means they expected... chaos. The fairy court was disheveled.

"Thanks for keeping us alive," Loni said sadly.

"Thank you for saving my arm," Sylvia managed.

"I couldn't save it all," Loni said hurriedly, as if Sylvia had forgotten. "They had to take some away."

"Still thank you," Sylvia said. "The doctor says I'm lucky it was below the elbow. Means that prosthetics are easier." The word prosthetics cut at her throat.

They left her to visit David, who hadn't been so lucky.

Sylvia cried silently to herself. The stub of her arm was wrapped tightly, but there was clearly a large portion missing. She wouldn't get that back. She didn't know how to feel. She was happy to be alive, but this was much worse than what she had hoped for. She was selfish, she didn't like it. But she sobbed to mourn her arm, more than her guilt about killing, more than her guilt about not saving Penelope. She couldn't even imagine living. It was gone. Her body felt like it was weighed down, and there would never be any release. It felt hopeless. She had her life, but at what cost? The loss of an arm was a terrible deficiency. She wondered how she would teach, how she would do her charms. It was too sad. She was ashamed at how much it was hurting. Those girls lost their mother, Penelope lost her life. And here she mourned part of her arm. It was silly, maybe. But it was miserable. She didn't even feel like pretending that she was okay. She didn't feel like doing anything. She just wanted to lie down and wish it away. Or, rather, wish it back.

But that wasn't going to happen. She spent another day in the hospital, and she asked Chrysa to look up if there was a spell for arm regrowth. She surprisingly didn't have information for that. Would even magic fail her?

No fairies came to attack them, though the whole group stayed at the hospital to keep her and David safe. It was an amazingly sweet gesture, considering that they were so exposed in the hospital.

Everyone figured that the fairies' in-fighting

was causing a problem, and there was no extra attention given to the Hunt. Sylvia was sure there were still fairies out there hunting, though the majority were probably participating in the fairy power upheaval. Court struggles. Sylvia had to laugh that that was what was saving them. Not some battle between witches and fairies, but the fairies themselves, all gathered for a vicious tradition.

The Thin sisters went to the hospital's chapel and mourned in the quiet. Sylvia made it out of her hospital bed one day to join them, the last day of the Hunt. She felt unstable walking because the doctors had her really drugged up so she didn't feel any pain. The missing weight on her left made her lean funny. She was certainly an odd-looking 62-year-old woman. Her arm felt the sensation of air moving past it, but there was no skin to feel it. She wasn't sure why no one was bringing up her arm. It was like they didn't want to mention it, since they still had both their arms and she didn't. She still hoped someone would bring it up. The only person who mentioned it was Ellie.

When Sylvia entered the small multi-colored chapel, Ellie surveyed her and said quietly, "I'm surprised you're up. Your arm is looking good."

"That is a lie and you know it," Sylvia said, a little bitterness dangling on her tongue. "There's nothing to look good."

Ellie smiled at Sylvia. "Had to make a joke. I

know there is nothing there. Was it not funny?"

"I didn't know you were making a joke," Sylvia admitted. She looked at the young woman, and she couldn't help but feel sorry for her, not angry about the arm joke. And if she was in a better mood, the arm joke would've been funny, even to her. Ellie just had to work on her delivery. "How are you holding up?"

Ellie shrugged and moved her eyes to her sisters. "They are angry at me, but my mom wanted this. She didn't want either of them to try to stop her from saving them. And she knew I would keep quiet."

"Why did you decide to keep quiet?" Sylvia asked.

"Because I love her, and she chose it. So there is nothing I could do," Ellie said. "She wanted to do it. I am not one to deny a gift as great as that... as terrible as it is."

Sylvia comforted Ellie for a bit. Her decisions were understandable, but odd. When she moved on to the two sisters, their eyes hovered on her lack of arm for a few semi-moments before looking at her eyes.

"How are you two?" Sylvia asked.

"Alright, I guess," Maria said. She couldn't manage a smile like Ellie. "Just thinking about my mom, I guess."

"She was a great woman," Sylvia said. "She loved you three so much. She beamed with pride when you were learning new spells. She liked to know you were all such competent, kind girls."

"Thank you," Maria said.

Loni didn't say anything. She was the angriest of all of them, probably because her mom died saving her. Sylvia couldn't imagine living like that. Of course, what was there to do, except keep on living like her mom wanted her too.

Sylvia thought about everything for a moment. "I lost my arm," she said plainly.

That sparked something in Loni. "I'm sorry I couldn't save it," she said.

"It was gone before you had a chance to look at it, it seems," Sylvia said. "I'm grateful that you saved as much as you did." She didn't know where she was going with this. But then she said, "It was worth it." She wasn't sure if that was a lie or not. She wasn't sure at all. If the fire fairy had fought anyone else, they might've died, but she and David were able to stop him. And almost everyone had lived.

"You think it was worth it?" Loni said. She didn't seem to believe that.

Sylvia thought about it some more before answering. Was it all worth it? Would they have been able to hide out at Patty's mansion for another few days? There was no way to know. No guarantees. Ellie and her mother had thought this was the best option. They had been supporters of going to the fairy court and they knew most of the different outcomes. She surmised this was the best one, though she wished she had known to protect

315

her arm. There was probably a reason that Ellie didn't tell her. She hoped it was that and not an oversight. She had to remember that Ellie was dealing with a lot and she was the only one with precognitive abilities, so if she chose it, it had to be the best option. Ellie might be an odd girl, but she had the best of intentions. "I don't know what the other outcomes could've been," she said slowly at first until she figured out what she was going to say. "But you girls are alive and as beautiful and talented as ever. Patty is alive and well. Chrysa is fine just like she always is. Me and David are injured--" that hurt her to say "-- but we'll live. And your mother, she kept you alive. She's a hero. I know she always wanted to do everything for you three."

Loni's mouth softened. "Thank you," she said.

Sylvia sat in the chapel with them in silence for a good half hour. She examined the plastic version of stained glass with interest. It was lit up from behind. And the pictures on the plastic were varied, including images from lots of religions that Sylvia didn't know about. They brought her comfort. There was a lot of light and salvation imagery.

She personally wasn't religious in a human sense, but humans certainly understood inner peace and how to find oneself through solitude. She didn't look at her arm, but she thought about it. She still so desperately wanted any solution over it just being gone. It was a terrible fate, and something she had never anticipated. But she'd have to get through it somehow. There was clearly no other option. The Thin sisters would get over the loss of their vivacious and kind mom, and they would grow into these beautiful, similarly vivacious and kind women. She knew it. Otherwise, what was the point of all this? Survival at all costs wasn't admirable. Survival obviously had a cost, but it just shouldn't be everything. At least, Sylvia thought so.

She looked around after a bit and realized the girls had left. They were probably in the hospital cafeteria or something. She wasn't worried about them. They had proved themselves, not that they needed to. But Sylvia could relax some of her desire to always control everything, because she clearly couldn't, though she was able to alter events more than she ever knew. They'd survived against odds.

When she went to see David laid up in his hospital bed, she raised her eyebrows. "At least you can't complain about the scars on your leg anymore." Being soft with David was never going to happen.

"I can complain all I want," David said with a little laugh. "I still got one leg and it's covered in the boiling scars."

Sylvia rolled her eyes. "Don't you at least hate fairies more now?"

"I hate everyone equally."

"I don't. I just hate you," Sylvia said. She snorted and couldn't help but smile.

"That's the glue of our relationship, neighbor."

Epilogue - Sylvia

Everyone got together for Thanksgiving. Except David, he didn't want to participate in the hoo-ha-we-won-let's-be-thankful crap, as he so delicately put it.

Sylvia didn't blame him. She lost her arm, she was in a similar boat. She had already looked up so much about amputee witches. Admittedly there weren't many, because witches usually could stop damage to their body before amputation was necessary. But accidents happened. She still had hope that she'd find something about re-growing it.

In the meantime, she had all the information about witches using a magical limb. Some witches, albeit those with a large magical supply, could recreate an arm and basically feed it magic consistently to keep it going. It was a very forceful approach to the amputation solution. It used power in a massive way. The witch, Zara, she'd connected with over the internet said it was exhausting to keep up, and her power level was much higher than Sylvia's to begin with. Sylvia knew that wasn't really an option for her. Zara said that other witches chose more elegant solutions. One was a combination of human technology and witch magic that perfectly melded the two. When her arm stub healed, she could go to a prosthetics specialist. They would fit her up with the most suitable prosthetic, considering her needs and her current state. They had very complex prosthetics that had computers in them that responded to muscle movement in the remaining part of her arm. With magic, she could theoretically increase the range of motions. It would not be like having an arm again, though. She wouldn't be able to feel sensation; the prosthetics were not that advanced. Still, she had to love humans, they had solutions that weren't just for powerful people, even a weak witch like herself could benefit from technology. It equalized.

She couldn't really help with Thanksgiving dinner, but she sat around talking to Patty and her husband.

"So... favorite theft?" Sylvia asked.

He looked at Patty and raised his eyebrows. "I thought we weren't telling anyone?"

"I trust them with my life," Patty said. "And it just kinda happened, me telling them."

"She saved our butts with her skills," Sylvia assured him.

He smiled at his wife. "You're my hero." He looked back at Sylvia. "This woman said she'd divorce me if I didn't leave L.A. Otherwise, I would never have left."

There was something sweet about that, though Sylvia was sure that not everyone would agree. She was so thankful that she didn't have to tell anyone to leave. She selfishly wouldn't have wanted them to leave. Sylvia wasn't sure if she'd leave if someone she loved was in trouble. But it worked for them.

Sylvia saw Penelope's husband Mark cooking in the kitchen with his three daughters. He was surprisingly upbeat for the situation. Sylvia wasn't there when he was woken up and told that his wife was dead, and she had no clue how he had taken it. She didn't want to ask. People made their decisions. That's all there was. Decisions and consequences.

Patty and her husband told her about the time they robbed a private collection of art in a billionaire's compound. They had gotten chased by dogs. Patty got bit and had to get a rabies shot, but they successfully stole a figurine that was still sitting in some forgotten room of their house. It was hard to comprehend that they secretly hoarded all this art in their house and never really showed it to anyone. She wondered what the purpose of it was. They had sold some of it get their fortune, but a good portion of it was just sitting, gathering dust. Sylvia would've been apprehensive to talk to Patty before the Hunt, but now she just accepted her past. They were good friends, and that's all that mattered. Well, she hoped at least. They didn't steal anymore and that was good. It was a thrilling past, and she liked to watch TV shows about it on occasion, but real-life thieves were a different story.

Sylvia talked about her sixth graders, which she had dropped in to see on that past Monday. Some of the kids were scared of her without her arm, like she was a monster now. But others came up to her and asked when she was going to be back for real. The administration was not happy about her sudden and mostly unexplained absence, but when she explained her loss of an arm, they gave her leeway. And she had tenure, so she was lucky. She didn't have to worry about her job too much, though she would be missing for a while more. She didn't want to miss too much, but she wanted to get her arm under control and she was one who understood pacing.

Chrysa came over in the middle of Sylvia talking about her students.

"Are you still going on about your students?" Chrysa asked loudly. "She tells everyone about them. We get it, Sylvia, you're a saint with one arm. Get over yourself." She said it with a tone that didn't offend Sylvia.

"Can't I be happy that my students are doing well?" Sylvia asked with some incredulity. Her best friend did not have patience, preferring her own voice over others'.

Chrysa rolled her eyes and launched into some story from the 80s.

Sylvia went into the kitchen to see the Thin family. "Hi Mark," she said. "How's the food?"

Mark was a gentle man, just like his wife. He wiped his brow and said with a heavy tone, "It's coming along. Always had Penny to help me with it, and I'm kind of at a loss." Tears hovered at the edge of his eyes, but he blinked them away.

"You need my help?" Sylvia asked. She wasn't sure what help she would be, but she thought she'd offer.

"Do you know anything about sweet potatoes?" he asked, sticking the temperature sensor into the turkey.

Sylvia lifted her shoulders. "I'm sure I could figure it out," she said.

He just pointed to a bowl of mashed sweet potatoes.

Sylvia tasted them, and they tasted bland. She didn't know why. Her mother always told her to add salt and pepper to make anything taste better, but she could tell that had already been added. She whispered over the potatoes: "Taste good like you should." The magic fluttered down over the potatoes. She stirred them a bit and then tasted. Much, much better.

Thanksgiving was good, all things considered.

About the Author

Georgia Tell lives in a house full of animals: cats, dogs, lizards, rats and fish. When she's not writing books, she loves to knit, crochet, and create many elaborate financial spreadsheets.

If Georgia could have any wish granted, she'd wish to know what happens forever: the history of the universe -- past, present and future.

www.GeorgiaTell.com
Twitter & Instagram: @GeorgiaTell

www.ingramcontent.com/pod-product-compliance
Lightning Source LLC
Chambersburg PA
CBHW030415180626
46812CB00005B/2022